THE GARDEN OF SECRETS

A.J. RIVERS

The Garden of Secrets

PROLOGUE

Ten years ago

Run.

THE WORD KEPT REPEATING IN HER HEAD, DRUMMING INSIDE her skull and sliding down the back of her throat to form a painful knot behind her tongue.

Run.

It wasn't the first time the word had dominated every part of her thoughts and drove her forward. The last time hadn't been long enough ago for her to have forgotten the feeling. She knew the feeling of her heart battering her rib cage. Of her muscles aching. Of everything rushing past her so fast it blurred in her peripheral vision and she could barely see what was happening around her. Of the footsteps pounding into the ground behind her. Of the anticipation of hot breaths against the back of her neck.

Run.

He was so close behind her she could hear the branch under which she ducked hitting him in the chest as it snapped back. She had to move faster. But she didn't know where she was going. She didn't know where she was. She'd never been to this place before, and as the clouds rolled over the moon overhead, it seemed the trees were getting thicker and the woods stretching on forever.

His car was somewhere behind, parked on an old gravel patch that was missing most of the larger rocks and had bits of grass growing up through the dusty dirt. Maybe it used to be a driveway or a clearing in front of a garage. Now it was just forgotten. Like the rest of this forsaken expanse of forest.

She wasn't supposed to get out of the car by herself when he parked. She was supposed to wait so he could walk around and open the door for her. It wasn't chivalry. It was so he could unlatch her seat belt. He didn't think she would be able to do it with her hands bound behind her. But her hands weren't bound anymore. Weeks of fasting and losing her sensitivity to pain allowed her to twist her wrists within the bindings until her hands came loose.

There was a window of only seconds. She had to time it so that he was already stepping out of the car and had his back to her, but wasn't so far out that he could quickly react to realizing she'd freed herself and was running through the woods. He came after her like a shot. But those few seconds of a head start were enough to get her among the trees and put branches and roots between them.

Getting hit by the branch made him pause. She knew by the sound of his footsteps going backward and then falling silent rather than coming after her. She'd become very familiar with the sound of his footsteps and the direction they were going. She had to. It let her know which rooms to avoid and, unable to hide, when she was going to have to prepare herself.

Now it told her she had a brief respite from him being just inches behind. She used it to slip behind a massive tree and duck low into a dense pile of fallen branches. New vines used the debris as a skeleton, growing around it to form a creature in whose belly she crouched, hoping not to be seen. She could only give herself a few seconds there before she had to keep going.

The moon was almost completely blotted out now. There were only tiny slivers of light to let her see what was just feet ahead of her. *Night is darkest just before dawn.* Not long now. If she couldn't get out of the woods, she would just run and pray for that darkness.

But she wanted to get out. This wasn't a sprawling park or a nature preserve. They'd gone by driveways as he brought her here. She'd seen mailboxes. They were few and far between, but they were there. Before they left she heard him talking to someone, and he mentioned an address. She couldn't remember it. At the time it didn't occur to her to try to grasp and pin it somewhere in her brain for recollection. But that wasn't the point. He'd mentioned an address. It meant this place was documented. It was located among others. There had to be houses somewhere close, and if she could orient herself well enough to find them, she could ask for help.

No longer being able to hear his footsteps behind her didn't provide any reassurance. The silence was more terrifying. She knew he didn't give up. He wouldn't just walk away and let her disappear into the trees to find her way to someone who would listen. The words she would have to say to them weren't ones he would ever allow anyone to hear.

That meant he was somewhere. She couldn't hear him. She couldn't see him. But she knew he was there. It was more frightening not knowing which direction she shouldn't go, because she could be running right into his arms. Or how close he might be. Even with the exhaustion and weakness overtaking her, she kept forcing herself forward. She ran through the thick, tangled woods confused and disoriented. She could no longer tell whether she was moving forward or if she had turned herself around and was going back the way she came.

She kept going, waiting to hear the snap of a branch beneath his feet or his breath coming through the chilly night air toward her. Unable to detect him after a few minutes, she allowed herself to stop. She just needed to give her aching leg muscles a second to recover. She focused on her breath, trying to stop from gasping too loudly in and out of her strained lungs. She needed to be able to hear around her, and she didn't want him to hear her through the darkness and find her. She had come to a shaky truce with the dark. It concealed her. It kept her among the shadowy shapes of the trees so she wasn't so easily seen. But that also meant everything around her was just as hidden.

Those long seconds turned to minutes, then longer. He didn't come. She didn't hear him breathe. He wasn't calling her name to him in the sickeningly calm voice that made her skin crawl just thinking about it. There had been many moments over the last several weeks when she would've chosen to never hear her name again rather than hear it come out of his mouth one more time. This was one of those moments. And it seemed like maybe she had actually gotten away. Maybe there was something else more pressing and he didn't have the time to chase her around the woods anymore. Maybe she just wasn't as amusing as she had been.

And maybe he was just trusting the dark and the cold to do his bidding for him and would come back the next morning to find what was left. Right then that didn't even matter to her. If that was his plan, so be it. As long as he had walked away, she had a chance. She could keep going and find her way out of the woods.

Just as the thought went through her head, a piece of shadow beneath a nearby tree broke off and rushed toward her. In her spinning, confused, and terrified mind, it took several seconds for her to even process that it was him. As he came down on her, she tried to turn and run, but there was nothing she could do. A kudzu vine crawling across the forest floor in search of something to climb on took hold of her ankle, and she couldn't stay on her feet. He didn't need any second longer than that moment of vulnerability. A bright light suddenly flooded her eyes, blinding her.

She thought she heard another branch break, but quickly realized it was the bones of her forearm snapping beneath his foot. Her hand dropped away from the thick branch she'd been holding. She could have gotten him. If she'd been able to get it off the ground, that chunk of wood could have done enough damage to save her.

But she couldn't. Instead, she looked through a cold, white light, which he immediately took out as soon as he knew he had her. She watched his head tilt to the side. A smile that never reached his eyes formed on his lips, and she knew.

Her prayer had been answered.

The darkness had come.

Seeing smoke tendrils in the sky above a stretch of woods was never good at any time, but it felt particularly ominous in the early minutes of the morning. Jacob paused on the narrow makeshift path made by hunters' boots beating down the undergrowth for decades, and he watched the billow of smoke coming from the trees overhead. It was so early in the morning, and the light was so dim he thought for a moment his eyes were just playing tricks on him.

It was possible that a transient or a camper was making a fire for warmth and for their morning coffee, but Jacob doubted it. This wasn't a campground. The tree-covered area was right in the midst of expansive farmland and residential plots. But the nights were getting cold, and the thick growth could get disorienting for anyone who didn't know it. It was possible someone just lost their way and settled in for the dark hours. He decided to go toward the smoke to see if he could offer any kind of assistance.

If anything, he wanted to warn whoever it was that starting a fire out here was dangerous and that they were skirting a piece of personal property. He didn't want somebody to get hauled off to jail for trespassing and an unauthorized fire just because they wanted to stay warm.

As Jacob walked closer, the smoke got thicker. The smell was choking him, wafting past the scarf he had wrapped around the bottom half of his face and making his head a bit woozy. It didn't smell like a normal campfire. Soon he could see the flicker of the flames between the trees.

"Hey!" he called out. "Hey, are you okay?"

There was no answer, so he crept further. The still silence of the early morning out here was usually a comfort to him. It was his time to be by himself and think. Even when he didn't manage to go home with a deer or wild turkey to fill his freezer, the sense of peace and contentment it gave him felt worth it. This morning though, that peace wasn't there. The quiet was unnerving. If this fire belonged to a camper or a transient, he should have been able to hear the person walking around. He should have seen them. But there was nothing.

"Hello? Anybody around here? You really should be moving on. And you shouldn't leave a fire unattended. These woods could go up in a second if an ember jumps onto the wrong pile of leaves."

He still didn't get a response. Now he had reached a thinner area of the woods than he had ever been before. He finally saw the flames burning on what appeared to be a mound of brush, almost like someone was preparing to clear the space, but there were no other signs of a controlled burn or anyone there to monitor the fire. It was starting to get larger, creeping out over the edge of the mound. Jacob set down his gear and took the rubber inner bladder out of his hydration bag. Opening it, he poured the water down over the flames.

It didn't completely extinguish the fire, but it helped tone it down. Jacob extinguished it the rest of the way by smothering it with scoops of dirt from a nearby pile and stirring the wet mixture with a long stick. It disrupted the mound beneath, and as the embers died down, he could see something beneath the leaves and twigs. He pushed them aside and stumbled back, the stick falling to the ground.

Sticking up out of the mound was a burned human hand. Hanging around the wrist was a bracelet with a single dangling charm of a rose.

CHAPTER ONE

Now

THE STONE AT THE HEAD OF THE GRAVE SAYS ONLY "ROSE DOE" along with a date. The one of her death.

They didn't know what else to put on it when they ordered the marker. No one had ever been able to identify the brutally murdered body of a young woman found beneath the hastily built funeral pyre. She had no name, no identity. No one knew when she was born or where. They couldn't inform her family. After ten years, the pain and frustration of the meager information on that stone still bothers Sheridan Morris.

With the hood of her sweatshirt pulled up over her head to ward off the chill of the November morning, Sheridan walks through the rows of other graves heading to the back corner of the cemetery where Rose Doe was laid to rest. She carries flowers to give the girl. Roses, like always. But she likes to bring different colors to keep things interesting. This time in addition to a bouquet, she carries a small pot with her. When she gets to the grave, she crouches down and nestles it against the base of the stone.

Sheridan brushes some wayward bits of grass and leaves from the stone and tosses aside a small twig that has landed on the grave during last night's storm.

"I brought tea roses for you today. I thought you might like a bush rather than just cut flowers. These will stay alive even during the winter and bloom in the spring." She takes the bundle of bright orange blooms that she has tucked under her arm and rests them in the center of the grave. "Of course, I have these for you too. You have to keep looking your best."

Her lips press together in a tight smile, and she lets out a soft, bittersweet laugh. She stands and moves back a couple of steps to the small cement bench positioned off to the side of the grave. Looking down at the flowers on the grave, she feels her lungs tighten just a little, like they always do. She has chosen the orange roses because of Thanksgiving coming up soon. The color looks festive, yet warm and welcoming at the same time.

The official report of her death estimated her age to be no more than her early twenties when she was buried out on that overgrown farmland. At that age, she should be fussing over what outfit to wear and buying new jewelry and cute accessories for holiday gatherings with friends and family. She should be going Christmas shopping and maybe hoping for something sparkling from some special person in her life. But she can't do any of those. She's here, encased in dirt, cement, and wood. The roses Sheridan brings are the only way things change for her.

"I really can't believe it's almost Thanksgiving. I keep saying it like if I tell myself and other people enough, then it will start feeling more like the holidays. But it just really doesn't. I'm not sure what it is this year. Maybe because I was so busy all summer with work and trying to fix all the damage from that flood in the basement. I didn't really feel like I got a summer vacation. So maybe the seasons don't feel like they've changed enough. I don't know. Dealing with that flood, though, was awful. Remember how I told you I had that contractor come and give that estimate? Well, not only has it taken him a month and a half longer to fix everything than he said it would, but now he's trying to charge damn near three thousand more than the estimate was. He said there's damage in there he couldn't have anticipated. I don't understand how that could possibly be true. He knew he was coming in to fix a flood-damaged basement. Wouldn't that mean he would be able to anticipate water, mold, and cracks in the foundation? Aren't all of those things just kind of part and parcel of that kind of situation?

"Actually, now that I think about it, maybe that's why it doesn't feel like the holidays are here yet. When the basement flooded, it ruined most of my holiday decorations. Thankfully, the really special heirloom ornaments and the quilt my mother made me are kept up in the attic, so they're fine. But all the other little things, like the dishes I only used at Thanksgiving dinner and the wreath I made at that class last year, were destroyed. I should really look and see if the craft store is having that class again. It was really fun. I mean, I don't think I'm going to have some personal renaissance and start a second career as a professional holiday decorator or anything, but I think the wreath ended up cute."

Sheridan takes her phone out of the pocket at the front of her sweatshirt and opens the picture gallery. Sliding past a couple of images of Christmas gift ideas her sister sent her for her nephews, she pulls up a picture of her front door. The wreath hanging there is an assortment of bright orange, yellow, and red artificial leaves, brown plastic vines, and little plastic acorns. A large gold-and-beige bow with glitter along the edges takes up the upper center, and a fake bird perched at the bottom brings it all together.

She holds the phone out toward the grave like she's showing the girl buried there.

"See?" She turns the screen back toward herself and scans the image, scrutinizing every detail she'd added to the wreath. "Maybe the bird wasn't necessary. But it was the only one, and it was sitting there on the table looking like it really wanted to be part of a wreath, so I couldn't bear leaving it there and having them just toss it back out to the shop floor. What do you think?"

She turns the phone toward the grave again for a second, takes another look at it, then shrugs and tucks the phone away.

"I guess I'm going to have to go shopping for some new Thanksgiving decorations. I don't even know what I'm doing for the holiday this year. I guess the group will get together like we usually do, but we haven't made any solid plans yet.

"That's kind of strange too. Usually, by now, we would have already decided what house we were going to have dinner in or what the plan was after Black Friday shopping. We just haven't put them together this year. Something feels different. I know that sounds really morose. I feel like I'm in the opening scene of some women's network holiday movie. Like I've lost the spirit of the holiday season, and through a series of funny and completely illogical events, I'll discover the true meaning of Thanksgiving and the love of my life." She laughs. "What's really terrible about me describing it that way is I would probably watch that movie. Just between the two of us, I'm as obsessed with the whole terrible sappy Christmas movie thing as anybody else. Don't tell anyone.

"I guess as far as vices go, that's better than it could be. Maybe. Anyway, I have got to tell you about this new case that Andrea just dug up. It's so twisted and confusing. But she's completely wrapped up in it and has decided that's what she wants to do her whole talk on at the meeting this month. Anyway, so it's about this girl who was leading a totally normal life and then got convinced she could contact the dead. She got obsessed and decided she was going to become a famous medium."

As she recounts the details of the cold case to Rose Doe, Sheridan takes the small backpack off her back and reaches inside for the thermos of hot hazelnut coffee and the bagel with cream cheese she put inside before leaving the house this morning. This is like nearly every visit she makes to the grave. She chats with the unknown girl like they are old friends. In a way, they are. Sheridan and her group have been following the Rose Doe case since it first appeared on the news. They've researched her, tried to understand her case, and fought for her to be recognized and honored as a person rather than just some nameless victim left in the woods.

If it hadn't been for Sheridan's group, the girl would have ended up in a potter's field with nothing but a number on a plain marker, if even that. She might have just been buried without any kind of commemoration. Her case was the hottest thing on the news for several weeks a decade ago. There was something mysterious and morbidly exciting for people about following the story of a young woman found in a mound of dirt and brush, lit on fire in the earliest hours of an autumn morning.

She got her moniker from the charm bracelet she wore around one wrist. The delicate rose charm had somehow escaped from being completely destroyed by the flames that burned away so much of what might have been recognizable about her, including her face. It was coated in soot and had been slightly warped from the heat but was in good enough condition to be photographed and shown on all the news shows, hoping someone would see it and know whom it belonged to. No one ever did.

An alert from her phone stops Sheridan mid-sentence. She takes it out of her pocket and looks at the screen. It's a message in her chat with the group of true crime–obsessed friends she spends nearly all of her time with. She opens the chat and reads the message. Her eyes go wide and snap to Rose Doe's headstone.

CHAPTER TWO

Ten years ago

IT WASN'T SUPPOSED TO HAPPEN THIS WAY.

Everything was planned out so carefully. I knew exactly how I wanted to do every step. It would have been so beautiful. It would have been everything I'd been preparing for. But it all fell apart, and as I followed her through the woods, I couldn't help but be disappointed in how last night turned out.

It shouldn't have been this way. It should have been everything I had dreamed of. She never should have been able to get out. But even more than that, I was hurt that she would run away the way she did. I thought she understood. I thought she knew how important it was that everything happened the way I wanted it to. I explained it all to her. I told her everything. And she stayed. She stayed right there with me. Right up until this morning.

It was still so dark when she ran into the woods. If she'd just waited, she would have known exactly where to go. I would have happily shown her the way. I had it prepared for her already. I started getting ready for her weeks ago. She would have thought it was beautiful. I knew she would have.

She just never got the chance to see it.

I tried to stop her. I followed her through the woods and called her name. I tried to coax her back to me. But she was defiant. I stopped following her and stayed silent to calm her. It let me get close to her again, but she wouldn't stay calm. Everything I had planned was ruined.

I looked down at my feet where she lay. She was so beautiful once. I would never forget how it felt the first time I saw her. I knew in that instant that she was exactly what I had been looking for. I had always heard the same old adage everybody else did: that you find the perfect one when you stop looking. That if you search too hard, you'll miss something amazing. That almost happened to me. I almost missed her. But then there she was, right in front of me, and I knew immediately.

But it brought us here. I couldn't just walk away from her. It would have been easy. There would be no way for anybody to know what had happened. The trees didn't tell their secrets. But my heart wouldn't let me. I still needed the light I brought with me to help me through the trees, so I looped it around my neck before scooping her into my arms. I was still going to make the most of this. It was still our special night.

I didn't have to carry her far. She was only a few yards away from where I would have brought her if she had let me. The fact that she had found it on her own while running through the darkness just proved everything I thought about her. She was meant to be here. This place was crafted for her.

I set her down gently on the ground and moved the branches aside, which I placed over the trench I already dug. It didn't look deep enough now that I was seeing it again. Propping my light up against the base of a tree to help me see, I went to work, making the grave deeper. When it was ready, I built her bed of brushes and leaves.

When it was perfect enough for her, I picked her up and carried her one more time. Resting her on the bed, I took the box from my inner pocket and opened it, breathing in the fragrance that came from inside. Setting the ribbons and bundles on her chest, I leaned down to kiss her forehead before lighting the match.

I stood back to watch the flames move over her. They caught her clothes and traveled along the ribbons. They danced in her hair and covered her face. I knew they wouldn't last long without any kind of accelerant to help them. But they did everything they were meant to do.

As those flames died down, I took my time to cover her with the branches and dirt I had set aside. At least this part could be what it was meant to be. What she deserved.

The second fire started quickly and easily. It was just another sign. More proof that she was the one all along. At that moment, I wished I didn't have to be there alone. Others should have been able to have this kind of stirring experience. But at the same time, this was for us. We could share these moments just the two of us. And at that moment, I realized maybe that was why it turned out this way. Things changed so that I could appreciate these precious moments even more.

But it was all ruined.

The fire started to burn brightly, the light and warmth from it corresponding with the first hints of sunrise until it seemed they were burning away the darkness and ushering in the new day. Then I heard something in the distance. It was unmistakable. Footsteps. Someone else was here. Someone had come to my private land and was coming toward us.

I had no choice. I couldn't be standing there when whoever it was came into the grove. I had to go, and she couldn't come with me this time. I had to leave her behind, and it hurt me so deeply, but I couldn't take the risk.

I walked away feeling broken and knowing a new truth deep within me: everything would have to change now.

CHAPTER THREE

One year ago

"DEAR GOD, WHAT THE HELL IS THIS?"

Detective Devon Bowen walked past the uniformed officers standing at the perimeter of the clearing and up to the team taking pictures of the horrific scene they'd just uncovered. It was technically his day off, but he was next in line in the rotation to head up a homicide investigation, so when a couple of Girl Scouts hiked into this clearing and stumbled on a human leg bone that had been dug up out of the earth by an animal at some point, Bowen was the one to get the call.

He didn't get any more information than that, but now that he had gotten to the fairly obscure clearing in the woods, he knew it was far more than just a set of skeletal remains. The team that first responded to the frantic phone call from the mother of one of the girls immediately recognized another depression in the ground fairly close to where the leg bone protruded. He knew better than to disturb anything at the scene until every detail had been properly documented by the crime scene photographer before any real investigation could begin.

Instead, he took evidence markers out of his car and started marking out everything about the scene that stood out to him. By the time Bowen arrived, the clearing was littered with tiny hot-pink flags. The photographer was taking pictures of the bone coming out of the ground as well as the rest of the scene. They were in a beautiful area of the woods with distinctive blue and purple flowers growing nearby. A few other flowers were scattered around, and there were signs of more that had already gone past their bloom for the year. He didn't know much about flowers, but the detective did recognize that these ones weren't wild.

"Detective, you need to take a look at this," Officer Barrett Courier said, gesturing to Bowen from across the clearing where the hot-pink flags were at their most dense concentration.

"What is it?" the detective asked as he walked across the grass and stopped beside the officer.

Courier gestured at the flags. "If you look carefully, the ground is compressed in each of these locations. It isn't random. There are distinctive borders that seem to have been made with a lot of precision and time. I think there are more graves. And they weren't just haphazardly dug."

Bowen could see exactly what the officer was pointing out. He nodded and asked, "Has this area been documented?"

"Yes, sir," the photographer told him.

"Good. We need some shovels."

Usually, the detective would have arrived at a crime scene in a suit. It was part of what differentiated him from the uniformed officers, and it made sure anyone who needed to know could readily identify who was in charge. But that morning Bowen was frustrated to have been called away from his son's soccer game to come to the scene and had arrived in a pair of jeans and a T-shirt, his shield over his neck the only thing identifying him as a detective.

Now he was glad. His suit and dress shoes would have made it much more difficult for him to take up one of the shovels, which were being passed around the team, and start digging.

The leg bone sticking out of the ground turned out to be just the first of six graves. Just as the officer described. Each of the graves looked like it had been very carefully planned out and dug. They weren't just shallow holes carved into the ground to dump a body into. These graves were meticulously planned and made with a considerable amount of effort and attention to detail. Not only did that indicate forethought and planning, but it also hinted at the type of person who had created them.

"We are not just dealing with some run-of-the-mill killer here," Bowen said to Detective Ashley Carr when she arrived to assist him. "Whoever did this wasn't just plucking girls from wherever he could find them, killing them, and tossing them away. This isn't a dumping ground. It's a graveyard."

"What do you have so far?" Carr asked.

"Six graves. They were all made to almost exactly the same dimensions and specifications, but it doesn't look like they were dug at the same time. Each one of them has one set of remains. We're going to need a lot more information from the medical examiner to be absolutely sure, but it looks like they are all women, fairly young. From the condition of the bodies, it looks like they died several months to a few years apart. This wasn't a spree. Someone has been maintaining this area for a long time."

"We found another one, sir," another uniformed officer said, approaching the detectives. "Looks like a daisy."

"A daisy?" Detective Carr asked.

Bowen led her over to the graves. Blue tarps had been stretched out across the ground next to each of the now-open vaults in the ground. A body rested on each, the cloth used to wrap them before placing them in the ground still beneath them.

"Each one of the women was wearing a charm bracelet with a flower on it when they were buried. They each have different flowers."

"They were burned," Carr said, looking down at the remains.

Bowen nodded. "Each one of them has evidence of being burned before being put in the grave. There are also pieces of wood, likely branches, inside the graves that were also burned. What's left of the clothing on some of them looks like they were dressed alike. The decomp on the oldest ones and the damage to all of them is making it hard to get all the details. There isn't any obvious cause of death yet, and for right now, none of the victims has been identified. There aren't any personal effects in the graves with them except for the clothes they are wearing and their bracelets.

"One of the graves seems fairly recent, maybe within the last few months. There's also some evidence that people have been coming to visit the area. The girls who found the bone from the first grave came here to work on a project for their Girl Scout troop. They say they haven't ever been to this particular area but have visited the woods around this several times before. It isn't like this is a completely isolated area, but at the same time, it doesn't look like it's used very often.

"Whoever did this is extremely familiar with the area and knew it wouldn't be detected. Or that if somebody did come by this place, they would see the flowers and might not think anything of it. But somebody is clearly coming here on a fairly regular basis. There are some cut flowers near some of the graves as well as a couple of pieces of melted wax that look like they were probably from candles. If I had to take a guess, I would say there are rituals being held here. This person didn't bury these victims to just hide them and forget about them. The spot was chosen specifically. At least some of the flowers were planted. They correspond with the flowers on the bracelets found with the remains."

Carr looked around at the graves and the flowers growing around the clearing. "This isn't just a graveyard. It's a garden."

The rest of the day was spent with the crime scene investigation team scouring the entire area trying to find any little bit of evidence that could indicate who was responsible for these murders. The remains were carefully removed, loaded into individual trucks, and brought to the medical examiner while Detective Bowen went to work trying to identify any of the six women found buried among the flowers.

It was very obvious that he had been called away from his day off to handle a serial killer, but that was all he knew. They didn't have any leads or even the beginning of an idea of who might be responsible for the killings. As he sat at his desk going over missing persons reports, he never once thought of the girl found on fire in the Virginia woods nine years before. Or the rose charm that had been dangling from the bracelet around her wrist.

CHAPTER FOUR

One year ago

WATCHING THE NEWS THAT NIGHT MADE MY BLOOD BOIL and my heart ache. For nearly ten years, everything had worked out. After the devastation of having to leave my cherished girl behind, I had to change everything. My entire life shifted, but I didn't let go. I held on to the dream that I had been carrying, and this time, I made it come true.

Nine years of happiness. Nine years of cultivation and beauty. And now they had destroyed it all. The news showed footage of officers tromping recklessly around my garden. There was no reverence, no honor. They didn't even know what they were doing.

It disgusted me to hear them talk about "recovering bodies." As if that was all they were. As if that was the only thing that mattered about that sacred piece of ground. It took me so long to find the right place.

But then I finally did. And now I would never be able to return to it. That was my garden, and they ruined it. They desecrated every inch of it and took away my precious flowers. I had been taking care of it for so long, giving so much of myself to it, and now it had been exposed.

They violated my space. They defiled my garden. I would never be able to go back there, to spend time there again. I could never speak with them and close my eyes to hear them speak to me. I would have to move on again. Just the thought of it made my stomach twist. I hated the idea of having to walk away, of having to try again.

They didn't know what they had done. They didn't understand how important the garden was and why they never should have touched it.

CHAPTER FIVE

Now

SHERIDAN CARRIES THE MASSIVE MUG OF COFFEE INTO HER LIVing room and sits down in her favorite corner of the couch, tucking her legs under her and tugging a throw blanket over her lap. The rest of the furniture in the room, as well as some of the floor, is taken up by the rest of the members of her group—and the sometimes overwhelming documentation and notes they've collected over the years.

"There's no way this is a coincidence. No one can tell me that these graves don't have anything to do with Rose Doe," Grant says, gesturing to a printout of a newspaper article. "There are just too many similarities."

Sheridan had been at the cemetery visiting Rose Doe's grave for the anniversary of the day she was found when she got notification from Grant that something new had come up. She was shocked just by the idea that there was new evidence, something to wake the case back up after several years of frustrating, seemingly endless slumber. But that shock was nothing compared to how she'd felt when she actually heard what he had uncovered.

A message from Barrett Courier, a police officer in Cabot, South Carolina, suddenly changed what they thought they knew about the case, and now they are gathered together to sort through the chaos.

"I don't understand how we never heard about this. How was uncovering six graves not big national news?" Cara Barker asks. "I feel like this would be something that they would be talking about all over. It would be on every network. It would have shown up in every internet search. How did we not know about this with all our research for an entire year?"

"And how did we never link it to Rose Doe?" Sheridan asks.

"Exactly," Grant says. "These deaths should have been cross-referenced. It should have been easily obvious they have something to do with each other."

"But we don't know for sure that they do," Emily Goshen says, reaching for a cookie from the plate in the middle of the sea of papers on the coffee table beside her on the floor.

"Are you serious right now?" Grant asks. "Did you not read about the case? Were you not paying any attention?"

"Look, I get that there are similarities. I see how it looks, but you can't just fly off the handle and automatically assume that this has anything to do with Rose. It's entirely possible the reason we never came on this case when researching hers is, they simply aren't related."

"I don't think the 'entirely' is applicable there," Sheridan mutters.

Emily cuts her eyes over at Sheridan before looking back at Grant. "Right now all we have is that there are some shared elements of each crime scene. How can we be sure that whoever killed these six women didn't just read about Rose the way we did and decide to take inspiration for his own crime spree?"

"They were found nine years apart," Wyatt Pearson points out. "And in different states."

"By definition, serial killers kill in different locations with a cooling-off period between them," Mercy Johanson says.

Sheridan holds up her hand to stop the burst of fury she can see threatening to come up out of Grant. "I'm pretty sure we're all familiar with the definition of a serial killer, Mercy."

She looks over her shoulder in response to her doorbell ringing. She starts to sit up and put her coffee down, but Grant is already on his feet.

"There he is."

Grant rushes to the door and opens it. Sheridan can hear him greeting someone and a murmured response before the door closes, and Grant comes back in with a thin, dark-haired man with eyes that say he's been staring at headlights and rain pelting a windshield for several hours.

"Everybody, this is Barrett Courier," Grant says, gesturing at the man.

Sheridan gets up and walks over, reaching out toward him. "I'll take your coat."

"Thanks," Barrett says, shrugging out of the long, heavy trench coat he's wearing and handing it to her.

It's damp from the rain, so instead of putting it directly into the coat closet, Sheridan brings it to the downstairs bathroom and puts it on one of the hangers she keeps on the shower curtain rod just for this purpose. Grant has already ushered Barrett into the living room, and Mercy is in the kitchen fussing over the coffeemaker when she gets back.

"About five hours," Barrett says, looking at Wyatt. "It's not too bad except for the rain."

"You really didn't have to come all this way," Sheridan tells him. "We could have just done a video call."

He shakes his head and accepts the coffee Mercy hands out to him as she comes back into the room. "Thank you." He takes a sip. "No. I needed to come here. This is really important to me, and I needed to know someone was going to take it seriously."

"We take it seriously," Grant assures him. "We've been following Rose Doe's case since the day she was discovered."

"What can you tell us?" Emily asks.

"Wait. Give him a second to breathe. He just drove all that way. He might need a break before we all jump all over him. Can I get you something to eat?" Sheridan asks.

"Umm…" Barrett says. He has the look of a man who is hungry but doesn't want anyone to slow down for him.

"I'm hungry," Cara offers. "I was so swamped at work today I didn't even stop for lunch, and then I came right here when I got off."

"I'm starved," Wyatt says.

"Then let's order some food," Sheridan declares.

She has a feeling this is not going to be a short conversation. Fortunately, it's Friday, and none of them have work in the morning, so the drawn-out night she knows is ahead of them isn't going to cause any disruptions in that way. She eyes the new, if temporary, member of their group as she walks around him and heads into the kitchen to fish a handful of takeout menus out of the kitchen junk drawer. She wonders how he found Grant and why he chose him to send the message imploring him to look into the Garden of Bodies murders from a year ago. She's extremely intrigued by the possibility of him offering more insight into Rose Doe and a possible link to other murders, but she's also wary. After so many years, her protectiveness of Rose makes it hard for her to trust anyone venturing too close.

"Barrett was one of the officers that responded to the initial call about the Garden of Bodies," Grant says. "He was there from the very beginning."

"We didn't know it was going to be that big when we first responded," Barrett tells him. "The call was for one possible human bone. The rest unfolded after that."

Sheridan tosses the menus onto the table and gestures at them. "Take your pick."

Usually, it's a whole production to get the entire group to agree on the food they want to order, and more often than not, they end up with several different deliveries arriving at the door. Tonight, however, they are all so focused on wringing every drop of information they can out of Barrett Courier that they come to a consensus in record time.

With pizza on the way and fresh cups of coffee and hot tea all around, the group settles in to hear what the officer has to say.

"The bone was found by two Girl Scouts working on one of their higher awards. They went into the woods to document human impact on what is intended to be an undeveloped area of land, and one of them noticed the bone sticking up out of the ground. They went back to the adults, who were camping on one of the established hiking paths, and they called us," he says.

"The bodies were found somewhere public?" Emily asks. "That doesn't jive with Rose Doe at all."

"She was found on private property," Sheridan says.

"The land where the bodies were found isn't exactly public," Barrett clarifies. "It is adjacent to a very small campground, but it's just a wooded area. Apparently, the girls had gone further than their mothers thought they were planning on going. They got wrapped up in the excitement of their project and ended up more than half a mile away. The area where the garden was found is uninhabited, undeveloped. If it wasn't for them, it probably never would have been found."

"No hunters there?" Mercy asks.

"No. Hunting is prohibited in those woods."

The group exchanges glances. That detail may seem small to other people looking at the case, but they understand its significance.

"Rose Doe's body was discovered by a hunter," Sheridan says. "He thought he was still on his usual hunting track but had ended up crossing over to an old private farmland that had grown into woods after not being used for decades."

"Grant mentioned that," Barrett says. "Look, the reason I'm here is because I haven't been able to stop thinking about this case since I responded to it a year ago. I was the one who noticed the other graves. The initial search was just for that one bone, but I noticed the depressions in the dirt that looked like the ground had been disturbed and could be further graves. I became very attached to the case, and it's disturbing to me just how little progress has been made on it over the last year. Essentially nothing has come of it, and I think it's completely ridiculous that no more effort and energy has been put into trying to solve the murders of six women.

"So I started looking into it myself. I wanted to see what I could find out and if maybe there was a way to push the investigation forward. I'm not a detective, but I have been involved in other murder investigations, and I'm driven to see this one resolved. While I was researching the characteristic features of the murders, trying to trace them to any other killer, I found your website. I had never even heard of the Rose Doe case, but as soon as I started reading about her and all the research you've done, I could see the similarities. I had to reach out. That's how I got in touch with Grant."

The explanation answers Sheridan's questions about the officer's involvement, and she can see just how much this case has actually affected him. It's the same kind of impassioned need to understand that motivated her group to essentially adopt the woman called Rose Doe as their own so she wouldn't be without a family and would never be without people advocating for her.

Heavily featuring her story on the website the group maintains is just one part of that. They keep up the site as a way to chronicle the cases they research and connect with others who may have information about them. It isn't as sophisticated as many of the forums and blogs floating around the internet to entice armchair detectives and true crime fanatics, but it ensures those cases aren't forgotten. Particularly Rose Doe's.

Grant has always been the communications manager of the site, checking the emails that come in and responding to them. Very rarely are the messages anything significant, and this is the first time one has actually altered their understanding of a case as fundamentally as this one.

"So you know that we have thought from the beginning that Rose Doe was a single killing," Sheridan says.

"Yes. And that's completely understandable. There was nothing in her case to indicate that there were any other victims. And from the information that we were able to gather from the six women in the Garden of Bodies, their deaths came well after hers. If I'm right and they are connected, she wasn't the only one. She was just the first.

"I need you to understand, this is still considered an open investigation, even if there hasn't been any movement on it. I went back and forth a lot about actually coming here and talking to you about it. I'm concerned because I don't want to get in any trouble or lose my job over talking about the case or trying to investigate it, but I also feel like it's my responsibility to try to find out what happened to these girls and if they had anything to do with Rose Doe. I can't explain it. I don't know why I feel that way about them. But I can't just let it go.

"Rose was found in a different state and under somewhat different circumstances, but there are so many similarities between her death and the deaths of those six women. I can't fathom why these investigators aren't willing to look into them as being connected. I mentioned Rose Doe to the lead detective, Devon Bowen, and he completely dismissed it. He said that even though that case had never been solved, it also had never been considered the work of a serial killer. He doesn't want to complicate the investigation by bringing in other victims, other departments. He's just going to pretend there's no link. I am happy to help you in any way I possibly can. I can tell you as much as I'm able to. But like I said, I'm not a detective. I can't take on this investigation as a whole," Barrett says.

Sheridan thinks for a moment then says, "I know someone who might be able to help."

CHAPTER SIX

I'VE SPENT MORE TIME IN GEORGIA IN THE PAST SIX MONTHS THAN I have in the decade and a half since I left it. When I drove away from Magnolia Glen, I never thought I would see it again, but it keeps dragging me back. Brielle keeps pulling me back.

As soon as I finished the case of the Hallow's Eve killer, I was immersed again in Brielle's death and the disappearance of her teenage son, Owen. Technically, I'm working for her husband, Alexander Bardot. He has hired me to track down his son and find out what has happened to his wife. There are rumors swirling around about Owen's involvement in the brutal murder of his mother, but he didn't have any part of it. I know that. Alexander agrees, but what started as simple discomfort at confronting Brielle's life after me by meeting her husband has deteriorated into suspicion.

Their daughter, Colleen—younger than Owen and still in a state of wide-eyed sweetness that keeps her from understanding the true impact of the things she says—told me about Brielle frequently leaving the house when Alexander wasn't around and bringing files of papers with her. Delving deeper into their relationship and his career has started to reveal cracks and dark, ugly corners of what so many described as a perfect marriage.

Alexander is paying me to track Owen, and that's what he thinks I'm doing. He knows I've looked into his son's movements and interviewed the friends he's been known to spend the most time with. He knows I've watched every bit of surveillance footage I could possibly get my hands on that may show his movements in the days leading up to and following his mother's murder.

He doesn't see my shadow. While I report to him what I've learned about Owen, I'm also digging deeper into Alexander and his relationship with Brielle. I'm trying to understand the son who may have encountered something so horrible—or so liberating—that he walked away from his life.

In the only contact I've had with him, Owen told me to stop looking for him. I won't. And I won't stop fighting for Brielle. After years of not hearing her voice, she called me in her last twenty-four hours on earth and begged for me to come help her, saying I was the only one who would understand, the only one who would be able to help. I didn't get there in time. But I won't stop until I've fulfilled my promise to her.

And that search has led me to a tiny bank almost an hour's drive from her wealthy neighborhood in Magnolia Glen. It is an unassuming brick building in the midst of a hunkering, decidedly lower-middle-class area. Here Brielle kept a safety deposit box with just one instruction related to authorized access. Alongside her maiden name, Brielle Adair, my name is listed as the only other person allowed access to the box no matter what the circumstances are. Even in the circumstance of her death.

The clerk I have spoken to at the bank didn't give any indication that anyone else has come to try to claim the safety deposit box, so I don't think Alexander knows she took it out. Putting my name on it though, and giving the very clear condition that no one else had access—that even after her death it wasn't to be turned over to anyone but me—means Brielle had concerns about it being found. Maybe she thought Alexander knew what she was doing. Maybe she worried her parents were tracking her. Whatever her reasoning, the box has remained untouched and is now sitting in front of me on a stark table in the back room of the bank.

It's a strange feeling, listening to the security door close behind the clerk. I'm familiar with the sound of jail cell doors closing, of hidden locks dropping into place. There's a chill that settles into the core of your bones when you hear it, an innate sense of defensiveness that immediately makes you feel far more alone than just not having anyone around you.

But I don't think about the sound of the locks or the uncomfortable heaviness in the air of the small room. Around me, the walls are covered with the little metal doors protecting deposit boxes locked away for others. One stands open, the vault empty, the box in front of me ready to be opened.

I open the box and look inside. The stack of papers inside is both a surprise and exactly what I expected. Since Colleen told me that her mother had a habit of leaving the house with accordion folders like the ones Alexander brought when meeting with his clients, I have had the feeling that Brielle was hiding copies of important documents. It seems to me she was questioning something her husband was doing, and possibly her marriage, and was carefully preserving evidence of everything she thought was important. The fact that these papers exist and are kept in a safety deposit box at a bank Alexander would never have any reason to visit isn't a surprise to me. The fact that my name is on the box, clearly set up well before she made the phone call to me, is.

I wish Xavier were here to look over the papers with me. The specification on the box is so stringent I cannot even bring him into the room with me when opening the box. He is at the hotel having a video chat with Nicole as she takes care of his starters. This is quite the development, considering her refusal to have anything to do with the sourdough babies the first few times she came to be with Xavier when I wasn't home or at the house when we both left.

Now she has gotten used to the somewhat overwhelming task of feeding and watching over a continuously growing menagerie of sourdough starters. When I left the hotel this morning, Xavier was reminding her that today is the day both Flour Power and Yeast Meets Zest should be dehydrated for long storage. Each time this happens, it's an emotional process for him. I think it's the closest thing he has to sending children off to school for the first time.

I take all the papers out of the box and spread them across the table to look over. There are hundreds of documents, most being dense and complex business contracts and agreements. A few are financial records and even some personal correspondence. I'm not sure what it all means. There's far too much here for me to sift through it all and understand the reasoning behind Brielle wanting me to see them while I'm standing here in the bank. I'll need to go through them more carefully to decipher their purpose and determine why she left them for me.

Piling all the documents back up, I tuck them into a folder and press the button to let the clerk know I'm ready to come out of the room. She left me here so I could have privacy when opening the box. I have a feeling people store all kinds of secrets and sensitive items in these secure containers, and it can be a decidedly uncomfortable experience for both the clerk and the person opening the box for them to be around when those are exposed. And yet, there's curiosity burning in her eyes when she comes back to the door. Even with the possibility of embarrassment, it must still be tempting to try to find out what has been stowed away within each of the little metal cubby holes.

She looks disappointed when she sees the box is empty and I'm carrying only a folder. I thank her and let her know the box won't be needed anymore. She nods as she lets me out of the room. I watch as she puts the empty box back into place on the wall, peering into it for just a moment to check and make sure there isn't anything lingering.

I put the folder on the passenger seat and sit for a moment looking at it. According to the bank records, the last time Brielle came and accessed the box was just a couple of days before her death. There's no way of knowing what she might have put in there. However, I can't help but think that the timing has significance.

The sun is shining brightly, and the temperature is still quite warm here in Georgia, making it seem even less like Thanksgiving is coming up soon and then we'll be on the slide toward Christmas. It's on my mind as I drive back toward the hotel. Our holiday plans are what they always are: Thanksgiving week at my cousin Emma and her husband Sam's house with our friends Bellamy and Eric and their baby, Bebe. Sometimes Emma's father, my Uncle Ian, comes as well, but that's always up in the air. His work isn't exactly conducive to long-term plans. When he does come, it's in the form of a surprise arrival, and we're never sure how long he's going to stay.

Whether he's there or not, the traditions follow the same schedule. Dinner takes up several hours of Thanksgiving Day along with the televised parade and a couple of obligatory football games. But as soon as the food has been put away and the meal is over, Xavier officially makes the transition to Christmas. His festive pajamas go on, he fills a glass of eggnog, and it's to the living room to decorate the tree that has been standing vigil waiting for that moment. Gingerbread men end up in the oven at some point during all this, and the next day we're in full-on Yuletide splendor.

I'm looking forward to the fun and the time with the family like I always do, but there's a knot in the pit of my stomach, a feeling that it isn't going to be as easy this year. Emma has been tangled in one difficult case after another while grappling with her recovery from a coma she slipped into this summer, and last I heard, Eric hasn't been feeling well. There's still a couple of weeks to go before the holiday, so I'm sending good thoughts that everything will work out. I only hope enough the holidays don't pass by without answers for Brielle and with Owen still missing.

CHAPTER SEVEN

THE VIDEO CALL IS OVER BY THE TIME I GET BACK TO THE HOTEL room, and Xavier is propped up in one of the beds eating a pile of pistachios. His laptop is still beside him, and I hear voices coming out of it, but the screen is dark.

"What are you doing?" I ask.

"Listening to a podcast," he says. "I wonder if anybody has caught on to the fact that this isn't new. It's just a radio show."

"I think most people have caught on to that, Xavier," I say, kicking off my shoes into the small closet.

"Video killed the radio star, and radio came back in a computer mask for revenge," he says.

"Something like that."

I bring the folder over to a round table standing near the window. I leave it there and go over to the coffee maker to brew a cup. I haven't been sleeping well recently, and even though I have yet to develop quite the taste for coffee my cousin has, I've become dependent on regular doses of the stuff to get me through. At least not being a devoted fan of it means I can even gulp down hotel room sludge if it's augmented with enough tiny creamer cups and packets of sugar and not see much of a difference.

I make a face as I gulp down the coffee and toss the cup.

"Liquefied cardboard and bitter memories," Xavier says, cracking open another nut and tipping it from his palm into his mouth. "Doesn't matter if you're staying in the nicest hotel, the coffee is still not good."

"Yeah, I don't understand that. I've had this brand before. And it did not taste like that. How is it that one of the most basic amenities in a hotel can go so terribly wrong every single time without fail?"

"Cheap hotels don't want to invest financially in better equipment and higher-quality coffee that might give at least a moderately improved experience because they don't have motivation, considering that their client base is loyal simply for the small price tag and not lavish amenities. Higher-level chains provide coffee because of expectations but aren't interested in making it exceptionally good because then they would lose revenue on room service and in-house coffee shop sales," Xavier says, eating another nut. "And bulk paper cups don't help."

"What about the hotels that don't have coffee shops in them and only basic drip coffee for room service?" I ask.

"Rampant conspiracy to funnel all caffeine purchases to the corporate overlords who then send buzzed people out into the workforce with improved productivity but lower social capacity so they make more money for their employers, which in turn trickles back to the hotels in the form of additional corporate bookings," he says.

I nod. "As long as there is a simple explanation."

He notices the papers on the table and lifts his chin slightly, like he's trying to read them from a distance. Sometimes when he does things like that or reaches for things that are clearly too far away for him to get without moving, I think there may be a small part of him that believes if he keeps trying, he'll eventually be able to crack into the unused portions of his brain and manifest superpowers. And other times I think it's more likely he's training me and the other people around him.

"What did you find in the safety deposit box?" he finally asks as I look down at the cup I just put in the otherwise empty trash can and wonder if I should fish it back out to make another cup of coffee.

"A lot actually. I'm just not sure what any of it means." I duck down and pluck the cup back out, stuff it into place in the machine, and get another cup going. "I didn't really go into too much examination of it while I was at the bank, but from what I saw, it looks like contracts, agreements, and some other business documents and correspondence about Alexander. Obviously, he was doing something Brielle thought needed to be recorded and that I would eventually need to see."

I pour the last of the creamer tubs and sugar packets into my coffee and bring it over to the table. Xavier's podcast has ended, so he closes his computer and comes over to join me at the table. As I'm going through the papers, I start to wonder if there could be something in them that may help me track where Owen could be. Brielle's behavior in the days and weeks leading up to her death and the way Owen and his friends have gotten wrapped up in the whole situation has been bothering me.

The way Brielle was described casting Owen's friends away and banning him from ever seeing them is so far out of character for her I can't actually imagine her doing it. Especially not in front of the neighbors the way it was portrayed. The interaction feels like it was designed to cover something up, whether the boys knew it or not. I'm not deaf to the rumors swirling around Magnolia Glen. Owen's disappearance at the same time as his mother's horrific murder is so obvious, people say. He's either the one who killed her or he knew something about it before it happened.

But I don't believe those rumors. I want to see it differently. I want there to be another reason. And maybe that reason, or at least something that can help me to find it, is somewhere in these papers. It's all I have to go with right now. I haven't had any luck talking to any of his friends, including the one of the supposed burglary ring who has been arrested and put in jail. I couldn't get any more information out of his sister. Even crawling my way through the wilds of teenage social media hasn't produced anything valuable.

All of Owen's profiles have gone completely dark, which is unusual for a boy his age, particularly one of his means. While he isn't being raised with the same level of privilege and luxury as his mother was, he is certainly not familiar with any kind of struggle. The Bardot family is very firmly ensconced within the upper class, and it seems to only be moving upward. That would usually mean a teenager fully devoted to splashing his social media with as many pictures of gaudy indulgences as possible. That is an unspoken, unwritten line of differentiation between the wealthy and the ultra-wealthy, the new money and the old.

The truly established, powerful families don't show off their money that way. That's the territory of what they see as people of a lower class, even if their bank accounts rank them close to the old money families. It's only those who aren't confident in their status and need validation that put their money on display in such frivolous, ostentatious ways.

I didn't grow up in the time of opening up a phone and documenting every second of life with pictures, captions, videos, and check-ins, and the idea of giving everyone and anyone that kind of access to your life is still decidedly unsettling to me. The only benefit I've found in using it is when I'm going through a period of dark spells, when my memory slips and I lose chunks of time ranging from a handful of seconds to whole days. Since a particularly horrific experience—wondering for the second time in my life if I've been responsible for a brutal murder I couldn't remember—I've learned to document tiny bits of my life on a private, secure profile. It's like leaving breadcrumbs for myself and hoping I don't need to collect them.

But what's as obvious to me, as it is to anyone else who's a part of society today, is that teenagers seem to see their social media as their absolute lifeline. And that's what's so strange about Owen's profiles. They're not only dark, but wiped.

He has removed nearly every post from the last year and many from years before. His father was able to gain access to the profiles through the company, but there's nothing to be found. Only a few brief interactions with his mother and sister are still there. All other conversations have been deleted.

It's definitely strange, but not if he's purposely trying to hide. I've definitely seen kids his age get busted after committing crimes due to their continued social media use while on the run. But I don't see Owen falling into that. From everything I've learned about him, Owen is a smart, very aware kid who isn't known for causing trouble. Not using his social media accounts would be the perfect way to continue to conceal his location and actions.

Xavier and I settle in for a long afternoon of reading through the papers, and it isn't long before we start noticing strange patterns and details in the contracts and agreements.

"The wording of these contracts is really odd," Xavier says, holding one in either hand and looking back and forth between them. "It sounds like they were written up by someone who was purposely trying to make them confusing and misleading. It's legal language, but there are a lot of phrases and terminology that are rarely used, and some of them actually contradict each other. I don't even know for sure what some of them mean, but they don't sound like they should. These should be standard agreements, and they are definitely not."

"Alexander apparently works with a lot of very specific clients. Maybe they required that the contracts be customized to suit their specific needs," I say.

"I mean, yes, that is certainly a possibility. But the question is, what are those specific needs?"

The further we go into the papers, comparing contracts and correspondence, the more I realize Alexander's career is far from what the people around him think. Some of the activities outlined in these papers range from shady and unethical to very possibly illegal. I am not a lawyer and can't say for absolute certain that my understanding of the papers is accurate, but considering Xavier's past working for the Order of Prometheus and his extensive knowledge of business practices and the delicate legal game businesses often play, I trust the way his eyebrows knit together when he reads the contracts and his muttering about the strange wording.

I set aside the most recent contract I've been reading and find papers that aren't like the others. Picking them up, I scan over them quickly, then show them to Xavier.

"Look at this," I say. "It's loan papers and a deed. Have you seen anything else like this in here?"

"No. What are they for?"

"I don't know. They don't fit in with anything else. They list the property as a business. Magnolia Enterprises."

"That's generic," Xavier says.

"That's certainly a word for it. There's nothing in here about what the business actually does or how the property is used. Just a general business description. Alexander's name is on the loan papers. He must have bought the property and set up the business but didn't want to link it to his other businesses."

I get my computer and run a quick search for Magnolia Enterprises.

"There really isn't much of a trail here. There are a couple of skeletal websites, but they don't look like they are actually used for anything. They just say things like 'providing turnkey assistance for your individual business needs' and 'boutique services designed to elevate your business to the next level of success.' That could be anything. The information looks legitimate on the surface, there's even a Contact page, but no names, testimonials, or pictures of real people."

"Money laundering?" Xavier asks.

"That's a real possibility." Picking up my phone, I dial the number listed on the Contact page. "Let's give them a call and find out."

It rings several times before an equally generic voice mail message picks up. I consider leaving a message just to see if anyone will get back to me, but I stop myself. If Alexander really is purposely hiding this business from everyone, knowing I have found it could make him angry. Considering there is still a missing child involved in this situation, I want to tread lightly. At least for now.

Instead, I run a search for the address of the property listed on the papers: Thirteen Liberty Manor. It is located in Revel, Maryland, but the search doesn't come up with anything concrete. There's no picture of the outside of a storefront, no map pinpointing an office building. As a last-ditch effort to get more information, I reach out to the real estate company that managed the transaction and leave my information, asking that they get back in touch with me as soon as possible. Something about this is strange. More than just the possibility of money laundering. Brielle included these papers for a reason. She wanted me to find them. I just need to find out why.

CHAPTER EIGHT

When my phone rings early the next morning, I'm expecting it to be the real estate company calling me back. Instead, I'm surprised to see Sheridan Morris's name on my phone screen. I met Sheridan a few years back while investigating a case, and we've stayed in touch since. It's been a while since we've spoken, but I can still detect the anxiety in her voice when I answer.

"Hey, Sheridan," I say. "Good to hear from you."

"Dean, I know you're probably busy, but I need your help," she says.

I take a handful of creamer tubs out of the bag the front desk sent up, after my third call asking for replenishments, and dump a few of them into my coffee.

"What's going on?" I ask. "Are you all right?"

"I'm fine," she tells me. "But something potentially really serious has come up, and you are the only one I can think of who could handle it."

"All right. Tell me."

"You know about Rose Doe," she says.

It's an introductory statement more than a genuine inquiry to make sure I'm on the same page as her with the conversation. She doesn't want to have to do a recap, and she doesn't have to. I'm very familiar with her obsession with the long-cold murder case of a girl only known as Rose Doe. She told me about it when we first met, detailing the devotion her group had developed toward the unfortunate victim. I've never met any of the friends that make up the group of crime enthusiasts who spend all their spare time researching cases and getting together to discuss them.

She hates it when I refer to them that way—"crime enthusiasts." She doesn't think they are the same as the internet lurkers who inject themselves into investigations and frequently create problems for the real investigators. She wants to think they are far more like a book club. Just instead of getting together to chat about the newest pseudo-literature to hit the market, they pick crimes and discuss those.

It was far more casual before the death of Rose Doe. That case captured all of them and has become a part of their identities. Despite that, I've never been drawn into it like they have. Sheridan gave me a brief overview of it when we first met and told me about the website her group maintains where I could read more about the case, but I've never looked into it.

It isn't that I didn't care about her fate or that her case was never solved; it has just never particularly intrigued me. There are thousands of cold cases. I stay away from them until I'm hired to investigate them. The reality is the vast majority of cases that go cold will never be solved. Spending too much time looking into them distracts attention and energy from the ones that can be.

"Of course," I tell her.

"There's been a development in the case," she says, her voice sounding urgent. "Something huge."

"A development in her case? Do they have a new suspect?" I ask.

"No. New bodies."

That's enough to catch my attention. I listen as she tells me about the six women found arranged like a garden with many of the same characteristics of Rose Doe's death.

"I'm not even in Virginia right now," I tell her when she asks if I can come meet with the group to hear the full details of the case. "I'm in Georgia on another case."

"I know you're busy," she says.

"I am. I just finished a major case..."

"I know. I was following it. You did a really incredible job unraveling those murders. And I know you could do the same for this. I know you're busy. I know there are other people that need you. But so does she. She's been waiting ten years. If this could have anything to do with her death…"

Hearing Sheridan talk about the victim with so much emotion and humanity gets to me. She never even met this girl, but she's able to talk about her as though they were dear friends. It isn't for show. It isn't theatrics. Her attachment is real, and so is her desperation to grasp any chance that they may be able to make progress in her case. And so is the victim. She deserves someone to tell her story.

"All right. Tell me everything you know," I tell her.

She makes a slight gasping sound, and I feel compelled to temper her optimism.

"I can't promise you anything right now. This case is changing by the second, and I don't know where I'm going to be or what I'm going to be doing. I'll listen and tell you if anything stands out to me and what I think you should do next."

I want to calm Sheridan down. The edge of anxiety in her voice when she first started speaking has increased until she sounds like she's spiraling. She clearly thinks this is a major situation that needs to be handled immediately. I'm willing to hear her out and see if I can guide her in any way.

"The bodies were found a year about near Cabot, South Carolina. Six women were found in individual graves deep in the woods. They were not all killed at the same time. The medical examiner estimates that the oldest body was between five and six years old, and the most recent body had been there for only a few months. Even though it was found in an undeveloped and unused area of the woods, the entire garden area was pristine. It was very clearly being maintained by somebody.

"The women were all buried with obvious ritual elements. Their hair was braided identically. What clothing could be salvaged was the same. There was evidence of similar makeup, as well as the presence of herbs and other materials that suggest skin treatments and burial rituals, such as burning sage. Each of the bodies showed signs of being burned before being placed in the graves. There were beds of brush and leaves in the graves and evidence that more had been placed on top of the bodies and then burned again. Each of the women was wearing a bracelet with a charm of a different flower on it. Those flowers were present in the area.

"Now, going back nine years from that, Rose Doe was found on a bed of brush, on fire. The ground beneath her had been dug away to be turned into a grave. She was wearing a bracelet with a rose charm on it. That's how she got her name. The medical examiner also noted the presence of sage at her burial, she appeared to be wearing similar clothing, and she was buried in the woods. There are definitely differences, I'll admit that. There weren't any roses anywhere around her. They couldn't prove she was wearing any makeup because the fire had damaged her face so much. But they are too much alike. I don't see how anyone reasonable could say otherwise, but…"

I frown. "The investigators aren't looking into them as possibly being related to the same killer?" I ask.

"No. Much of the information we got came from an officer who was involved in the initial investigation of the Garden of Bodies one year ago. He was looking into the case himself and found our site about Rose Doe. He brought the information to the lead detective, who completely rejected him. They won't even consider looking into it because they say it would muddy the investigation and make it more complicated."

I'm surprised by the revelation. Even just the overview Sheridan has given me is enough to at least run a secondary investigation into the possibility that Rose Doe was not a one-off killing but the first for a serial killer. Unfortunately, as absurd as I think it is, I can't say I'm completely shocked. This wouldn't be the first time I have encountered cases that seemed clearly linked but were kept separated simply because they were in different locations and the departments didn't want to cooperate—or the cases had gone cold and it was more challenging to piece them together.

This situation has taken on new meaning. It isn't just a cold case she is chasing after. There is definitely something here.

"All right. I'll look deeper into it," I tell her. "Again, I don't know how much capacity I'll have for it right away. But I'll do some digging."

"That's amazing. Thank you, Dean. I'm going to introduce you to Barrett Courier. He's the officer who brought us into the investigation," Sheridan says. "Barrett, I want you to talk to Dean Steele. He's the best private investigator in the business. He's going to help us."

There are muffled sounds on the other end of the line, and a man's voice comes over. He greets me and introduces himself again. I return the favor, and we exchange a few words before he tells me he'll send me all the information he can send me so I can go over it. I thank him and hang up, letting out a sigh and looking over at the papers still sitting on the table by the window.

Brielle's murder happened only a couple of months ago, and I'm trying not to let it slip through my fingers and leave her in the same chill as Rose Doe. I can't imagine never knowing what really happened to her. I have to try.

CHAPTER NINE

Rose Doe

Eleven years ago

There were no seats in the back of the van. Heavily tinted windows prevented anybody on the outside from noticing. They couldn't see that the carpeting had also been ripped out, leaving only the cold metal shell of the floor. If anybody saw the inside of the van when no one else was in it, they would immediately think it was being used to haul cargo. They didn't know it was hauling people.

She was on her side, her cheek pressed to the metal. She could taste blood from when the van lurched and her face smashed into the metal latch coming up from the floor of the van. It was put in place there by the manufacturers to secure a car seat, making babies safer. They could never have imagined the damage it would do when it rammed lips into teeth. At least this time, she wasn't chained to it. There were many times before when she had been. She hadn't been able to move at all, her wrists and ankles chained together and then attached to the metal piece with a strong, securely locked hook.

On those rides, it felt like her arms were being ripped out of their sockets. The skin of her wrists would bruise and break. Countless times her head would smash into the wall of the van behind her. She learned to press her feet hard into the floor and her back against the wall to try to stabilize herself so she didn't move as much with the sway of the van. Many times it felt like sudden turns and sharp shifts in speed were done purposely just to torment her.

It wouldn't have surprised her. The injuries along her body were a testament to a twisted sense of humor mangled with vicious, obsessive control.

And it was those same things that made her not want to know why the carpeting was gone from the back of the van. She knew it had been there once. She saw it. A rich shade just darker than royal blue that looked soft and plush the first time she laid eyes on it. By the time it was gone, she no longer asked questions.

She didn't even care that night. All that mattered was not being chained to the latch coming out of the floor. She could move her legs. Her hands were down by her sides. They believed they'd broken her. And just beneath the surface of her skin, she believed it too. But deeper, buried beneath the scar tissue and tapestry of unseen cuts and bruises that only made her stronger, she knew they were wrong.

They hadn't broken her. And she wouldn't let them. That night they trusted her. They shouldn't have.

She'd learned to differentiate the different paths they took around town by the sway of the van. A dark cloth barrier was put in place between the front seats and the empty back months ago, so she could no longer look through the windshield to tell where they were. Instead, she had to detect the turns and count the seconds as they were going straight. It wasn't perfect, but it was enough for her to make guesses about where they were headed.

This time, she knew when they stopped that they were at the gas station. It didn't give her much hope. If she was right and they were where the map in her mind placed them, they were far away from the suburban neighborhoods or busy city streets she had hoped. But that couldn't matter. This was her chance, and she had to take it like it was the only one she was ever going to get—because it probably was.

She was terrified, but she told herself she wasn't. The van pulled to a stop, and the engine went quiet. She listened for the keys to come out of the ignition and the door to open. If she heard a conversation, it meant someone was in the passenger seat. If it stayed quiet, it meant she was being left alone.

The keys jangled. The door opened. A second later, it closed. Silence. Her body ached, and her heart was cold, pumping the chill of fear through her veins, but she had to quiet it. It didn't take long to go into the store and pay for gas. Even with a scan of the shelves for a snack or a stop into the restroom, she only had a matter of moments before the door would open again and her chance would be behind her.

She pulled herself up from the floor and paused for only a second longer before grabbing the cloth and ripping it down. The back doors would have the child locks activated, so there would be no way for her to get out of them. Her only choice was to scramble up over the front seat and go out that way. Pushing the fabric behind her, she climbed over the front seat and pulled the handle of the passenger door. It wouldn't budge. She clawed at the lock, forcing it off, then tumbled out of the open door. She didn't bother to shut it.

The door to the gas station opened as her body hit the cement. A shout ripped through the air as she got up to run. She didn't look back. Using every bit of energy she still had in her and letting the adrenaline and fear take away her pain, she ran across the parking lot toward the road. The cold was biting on her bare feet and almost-naked body. Taking away her clothes was meant to be a deterrent for things like this. It was supposed to keep her right where they put her so no one else could see her.

Right then she wanted everyone to see her. Behind her, she could hear shouting. It sounded like more than one voice, like people were arguing, but she didn't stop to pay attention to what they were saying. She ran out of the parking lot and stopped in the bright beam of headlights in the middle of the road.

CHAPTER TEN

Now

EMMA'S ATTENTION IMMEDIATELY GOES TO THE NOTEPAD I'M scribbling on when I answer her video call. We are very different investigators, but one of the things we do share is our propensity for writing things down. Rather than just keeping notes on a computer or making audio recordings, we prefer having paper and pen near us and being able to actually write down our thoughts and questions.

For me, the actual process of physically writing down what I'm thinking during an investigation gives me an added opportunity to process and think through those thoughts in more depth. I find it easier to remember things I've written down, and sometimes as I write, a connection to something I have previously jotted down appears where I may not have noticed it otherwise.

"Did something come up in Brielle's case?" Emma asks.

"Yes and no. Yes, something did come up. But that's not what I'm working on."

I tell her about the safety deposit box and the business papers inside. I still haven't heard back from the real estate company. No further digging around has given me any other information about the business apparently operating out of the piece of real estate Alexander bought a couple of years ago in Maryland. My next plan is to find the property records, but I will have to wait until Monday to do that.

"And no other word from Owen?"

"No. I talked to a couple of his friends again. I got Alexander to let me sit down with Colleen. But they weren't able to tell me anything. I don't think they're hiding anything either. I honestly don't think anybody knows where he is. Somehow that is both more frustrating and yet reassuring. If he was in some sort of conspiracy with these other guys, if they did have something to do with Brielle's murder, they would know something. And teenagers are not exactly revered for their ability to cover up lies and not give away what they are actually thinking. I'd be able to tell if they weren't being honest with me," I say. "It makes me feel better that I'm still not finding anything that suggests for a second Owen or his friends were involved and that I'm not the only one other than his father who doesn't know where he is. But it's also so frustrating that there's nothing to go on. He's just a kid and yet somehow he was able to just completely wander off the grid, living his life without detection."

Emma looks like she is about to say something but swallows down the words. I tilt my head at her, raising my eyebrows pointedly. Without even having to hear the question aloud, she knows what I'm thinking and shakes her head.

"Nothing," she says.

"What were you going to say?" I ask.

For a second she stays quiet, like she is still trying to hold the words back, but she knows I'm not going to let it go.

"I was going to say, you hope he's off living his life without detection."

The words hit me harder than they probably should have, and I take a second.

"What's that supposed to mean?" I ask.

"I stopped myself, Dean. I didn't say it because I didn't want you to think I was trying to imply anything terrible has happened to Owen. But the reality is, you've only spoken to him once since he disappeared, and no one else has had any contact with him. That's just one phone call. You weren't able to trace to a device, much less a location. You don't know where he is, whom he's with, or what he's gone through. Like you said, he's just a kid. A smart, put-together teenager who I'm sure can hold his own in many situations, but still not an adult who's equipped to handle a lot of things life can throw at him. Particularly in a situation like this where he's suddenly on his own without anyone to help him or any resources.

"That's something you have to think about. If he really is out there just trying to stay hidden, how is he surviving? Alexander is tracking his bank account. There hasn't been any activity on his debit card. No cash was taken out of his account right before he disappeared. He isn't using his cell phone. He has his car, but it hasn't been seen. You really have to wonder, how is he doing this?"

"I did it," I say. "And I had a whole lot less going for me than Owen Bardot."

"You had my father looking out for you. You had people there to help you. Maybe not the whole time, but there wasn't any point where there wouldn't have been a trail to you," Emma says.

"I'm not going to let myself think something has happened to him," I tell her firmly. "I can't sit here and let myself think that he might have been taken by the same people who killed his mother and they are holding him captive. That they forced him to call me so it sounded like he was gone of his own volition. We're not going to do that. If I do that, I'm giving up on him and I'm giving up on Brielle. I won't do either."

"Neither did Alexander."

Her eyes open a little wider, emphasizing the words and giving me space to find the meaning she has left in them. I realize she's right. Alexander has gone through many of the motions of trying to find a missing child. He has gained access to Owen's social media. He's been asking the bank to provide any activity updates on Owen's account. He has provided information about the car Owen would have been driving so that if any officer notices the license plate, they can pull him over.

He is doing all these things and talking about his son like he wants to know where he is, but at no point has he expressed any concern that the people who hurt his wife could have also taken his son. Even in those first moments, when we were standing on his front lawn and Brielle's body was still in the house, he only referred to Owen as being missing. He didn't ask if any of his blood was found in the house. He didn't question that his car wasn't there. At no point has he expressed any worry that Owen doesn't have what he needs to be navigating the world by himself.

"Alexander knows where he is," I say. "Or he has very good reason to not be worried about him."

"Maybe something to think about," Emma says. "With all those papers, seems like Alexander already has quite a bit of explaining to do. This could just be one more thing to add to the list. And speaking of lists, what are you working on if it doesn't have to do with Brielle and Owen? Did you already get hired for another case? I thought you were going to take some time after Halloween."

"That was definitely the plan, and I guess technically that's still what I'm doing. I haven't really been hired to do anything. I'm just looking into a case for a friend," I tell her.

"What friend?" she asks.

"Sheridan Morris," I admit, already knowing the reaction I'm going to get from Emma.

She doesn't leave me hanging. As soon as the name comes out of my mouth, my cousin's face contorts into a look of distaste. It only lasts a second. She's not great at holding back all her reactions when she's just talking to one of us instead of working, but she is very good at noticing when she has done it and backpedaling.

Sheridan and her friends are what Emma would refer to as "citizen detectives," and they are not among her favorite people. She had a case years ago when a woman from an online crime blog worked her way into Emma's life and the lives of those around her. That woman's connection to the second disappearance—and the eventual horrific murder of—her former boyfriend is something she can't shake.

"I've told you before, Emma, Sheridan and her group aren't like that. They're really more like a book club," I say, echoing Sheridan's sentiments to me.

"Except that instead of reading books and talking about them, they try to solve crimes," Emma says.

"They don't generally try to *solve* the crimes. They just find ones that fascinate them and talk about them."

"Oh, like that's so much better."

"I mean, is it not what we do in our spare time too?" I jab. "Anyway, this just happens to be a special circumstance. There is one particular case they have been following for ten years, and it's starting to heat up. They got some insider information from a police officer involved in the investigation of a serial murder case that seems connected."

I give Emma a quick rundown of Rose Doe and the Garden of Bodies. She agrees it seems very unlikely the two cases aren't linked in some way.

"Did they identify the six women?" she asks.

"Yes. That is one of the things that differentiates the two cases. Rose Doe went cold without anyone ever knowing who she was. The six women in the garden were all identified fairly quickly after the discovery of their bodies. But even with knowing who they are, there really isn't a lot to go on in terms of investigating their deaths."

"What do you mean?"

"They have investigated all six women extensively but weren't able to find any connections among them. Nothing. They don't look alike. They are all within the same basic age range, but that's where the similarities end. I was able to read some of the interviews of the friends and family members the investigators spoke with, but none of them had any idea what could have happened to the victims. All of them said essentially the same thing. They just suddenly disappeared.

"They really do seem completely random. When you look at each of the victims individually, some factors seem to give at least some context to their disappearances. One of the women, Shelby Connors, had only recently gotten out of an extremely abusive marriage when she disappeared. Her ex-husband was known to stalk her, and even after she got protective orders against him, he would break into her house and move things around to mess with her head, follow her around town, show up at her work, call her endlessly. Police interviewed her best friend, who said Shelby believed she was never going to escape him. It didn't matter what the police did, what the courts said, any of it. He was never going to leave her alone.

"As soon as Shelby disappeared, they immediately started looking into her ex-husband to see if he could have been responsible, but he was cleared. Another, Courtney Rogers, had a history of prescription drug problems but had started talking to her family about trying to get help and wanting to clean up her life. When they realized she was missing, they at first thought she might have gone into rehab or ended up in the hospital after one last binge. They weren't ever able to find her and came to the conclusion she had likely gone off to find something to take the edge off, died, and was just disposed of somewhere.

"The victim who has been there the longest, Bonnie Franco, was an artist who considered herself voluntarily transient."

"So she was homeless on purpose," Emma says.

"Essentially. She didn't like the idea of being tied down to the expectations and requirements of standard society, according to her parents. She started out by pitching a tent in their backyard when she was a teenager, then she left home and spent the next few years just wandering around. She slept where she could, found food where she could. She did her art. They were adamant she never sold her body or did hard drugs. Those were two things she was very outspoken about being against. She just believed that as human beings we could peacefully coexist and create a cooperative society that didn't require things like marriage, permanent housing, or ongoing employment," I tell her.

"Oh, one of those utopian types?" Emma asks. "I've definitely heard of those belief systems. They're… interesting."

I chuckle. "One way of putting it. And according to her parents, Bonnie was very happy with her lifestyle. She contacted them frequently, and she sent them pictures of her adventures. She seemed to always be able to find the right people to 'help her along her existence', as she put it. There was no reason for them to believe she was in any kind of danger or that she was unhappy.

"They always told her if she changed her mind or if she found herself in a tight spot, all she had to do was get in touch with them and they would make sure she could get home and get her feet under her again. She never pushed back against that. But then she just stopped contacting them. For a while they just figured she was enmeshed in another life experience and when she was done with that, she would move on and get in touch with them. But she never did. I think their interviews were the most difficult to read because they were never worried about her.

"All the other people had reason for their friends and family members to be concerned. They knew they were in danger and were just waiting to find out what happened. As horrible as it was for them to get the final news that their loved ones were dead, it also came as almost a relief. They finally had those answers and the closure they were waiting for, if closure is actually something you can ever get when you lose someone like that.

"But Bonnie's parents weren't afraid. They didn't have that worry or the innate sense that something was wrong. They were upset that they hadn't heard from her. They missed her and admitted their feelings were hurt that she just hadn't gotten in touch with them. But they both said they knew their daughter, and they believed she had just flitted off into her next adventure and didn't realize how disconnected and distanced she had become. Right until they found out she was killed, they believed she would pop back up again brimming with stories about the people she met and the art she created.

"Instead, the next time they heard about their daughter, it was finding out she had been murdered. There was no relief for them. That was when the agony began, and they had to add to it the feeling that they had never even suspected it. Both of them said they should have known.

They should have just realized their daughter was no longer on this earth. It should never have been such a shock to them."

"They can't blame themselves for that," Emma says. "I know there are always parents who say they were able to feel it the second their child died, but I would absolutely argue there are far more who hold on to the belief and the hope that their children are still living right up until the second they get absolute evidence otherwise. It doesn't make either one more or less."

"And that's exactly what I'll say to them if I have the chance to speak with them about the murders. They don't deserve to carry that for the rest of their lives. The way I see it, they were amazing parents. They knew their child and who she was to the very core of her being. They allowed her to be that without trying to change her or hold her back. That takes a kind of love and understanding some people just don't have no matter how much they try," I say.

"What about the other three victims?" Emma asks.

"One, Vi Taylor, didn't really have much of a story. She lived a pretty solitary life from what the reports said. She lived alone. Never married. Didn't have any children. She went to work every day and had the exact same routine of running errands once a week. That was it. Then one day she didn't show up for her weekly hair appointment, and the butcher she went to every week said she didn't come by. She was never seen again. The other two weren't ever formally reported missing."

The fact that the women weren't reported missing could seem strange on the surface, but it's an unfortunate reality that a large percentage of people who disappear never have a report filed and are never the focus of a formal investigation. They simply drop out of existence and are never seen or heard from again. The variation in the victims is also not unheard of for serial killers. Sometimes the preference of victim type is very obvious, and sometimes what the killer is looking for only has meaning to that particular killer. And sometimes it's just a matter of finding victims of opportunity rather than there being a specific target.

"What about the other victim?" Emma asks.

"Rose Doe?" I ask. "Nothing. No potential leads on her at all. There was nothing on or with her body to identify her. She didn't match up with any missing persons reports. They were able to take fingerprints, but it didn't do any good. There were such extensive burns and injuries to her fingertips, the prints would have been unidentifiable even if there was a match in the system. So there's really no way to determine if she shared any of the same kinds of life elements as the others. But since there was nothing to indicate any kind of overlap for the other six, it's likely safe to assume there wouldn't have been anything of note that connected her to the others either. Except that the same person probably killed them."

"You said there was a police officer involved in all this," Emma says.

"Yes. Barrett Courier, from Cabot, South Carolina. He was a responding officer the day the bodies were found and the one who detected the possible presence of additional graves. He knows he went out on a limb to get in touch with Sheridan and her group considering the case is still open and he's just a uniformed officer and not a detective. But he says his department isn't investigating the cases as connected. That's why Sheridan contacted me. Barrett can be actively involved in this investigation, and Sheridan and the group don't know how to investigate. She wants me to take the information they already have and work the case like it is one serial killer chase rather than two separate situations," I tell her.

"And you're going to do it," she says.

"I wasn't going to at first. I have so much going on with Brielle and Owen, and the case over Halloween was rough. But once I heard everything and realized something so big is being overlooked… I just can't ignore it. It's a blessing those six women have their names and their families were able to bury them. Rose Doe hasn't yet had that privilege. They've taken care of her, but it's not the same thing. And people connected to all of the victims are still suffering because they don't know who killed these women or why. If I can help, I need to," I say.

"Not a surprise," Emma says with a hint of a smirk. "It does lead me to a question though. What does all this mean for Thanksgiving?"

I let out a gust of breath. "I don't know. With this case and still dealing with Brielle and Owen, I'm worried some of the traditions might get interrupted."

"I'm worried about that too. The case I'm working on seems to just keep getting more complicated rather than easier, and I don't know if we're all going to be able to be in the same place at the same time like we always have been. That and Bellamy just told me Eric has the flu. Which means they're all going to get sick. I doubt they're going to be healthy by Thanksgiving."

"Hopefully, none of it will be a problem," I say. "Hopefully, everything will still work out, and we will all have the holidays just like always."

"Not like you to be an optimist."

"I'm trying new things lately."

Xavier comes out of the bathroom fresh from his bubble bath. That's his preferred way of isolating himself when he wants to think. It seems he has attempted to go full sensory deprivation in this bath because his hair is wrapped up in a towel on top of his head.

"What about Thanksgiving?" he asks.

Emma and I meet eyes on the screen. We know we're not just hoping for our usual holiday for ourselves. If things have to change, Xavier is not going to be happy about the upheaval. And with that will come a whole host of Xavier's attempts to gain restitution for the lost traditions. I'm not sure I'm ready for that.

CHAPTER ELEVEN

I WAS ALREADY PLANNING TO LEAVE GEORGIA FOR VIRGINIA THE next morning, but rather than staying in Harlan, we stop for one night and then get back on the road to Sheridan's house. She lives less than two hours from where Emma and Sam live in Sherwood, in a town nestled right between rural farmland and a bustling college town. She told me before it lets her live in a neighborhood without feeling like she has all the trappings of a suburb, and also live in the country without feeling like she's in the middle of nowhere.

Considering Harlan is essentially just a suburb of Middle of Nowhere, I can understand her sentiment.

Sheridan is waiting for us on her wide wraparound front porch when I pull into the driveway. She comes down to meet us, and I look at her over the open trunk.

"We really can get a hotel," I tell her.

"Absolutely not. You're staying here with me. I have way too much space, and I'm constantly rattling around in there by myself. It'll be good to have you around for a little while. And besides, no, you can't. There's one hotel within twenty miles of here, and it is always perplexingly and somewhat concerningly at capacity." She walks around to the trunk and reaches in to grab one of our bags. "Come on."

"We can get our own bags, Sheridan," I say.

"I know you can. But if I take one from you, you can't try to leave and find a hotel."

Xavier meets my eyes with a flat expression. "Do I need to call for help? Because I'm feeling like one of those TV shows that makes us yell at the screen. Don't go down into the basement when you hear suspicious sounds. Don't run upstairs when you're being chased by an armed intruder. Don't leave your car doors unlocked while you're sitting in a dark parking lot. And don't follow a stranger into her house after she has clearly outlined her intentions to keep you captive."

"First, Sheridan isn't a stranger. I've known her for years. Second, she isn't going to keep you captive," I say, taking the rest of the bags out of the trunk and handing one over to Xavier.

"Of course she's not," he says. He holds up the luggage he has in each hand. "She stole *your* suitcase."

I shake my head and close the trunk before heading to the porch. Xavier follows along behind me, but I notice him pressing his fingertip to the handrail and doorframe as we walk up the steps and into the house. Xavier's fingerprints are most definitely in the system.

The evening air has gone from crisp to decidedly cold, and I'm glad for the warmth inside the house when Sheridan shuts the door behind us. It smells like home-cooked food, and the voices coming from further inside overlap and blend together in the kind of familiar chaos that only happens among people who have known each other extremely well for a long time.

I have a strong feeling that Sheridan doesn't rattle around in this house by herself nearly as much as she tries to say she does.

She shows us to the rooms we will be staying in, giving us just enough time to put down our luggage before ushering us back downstairs and into the living room.

A group of six people are relaxing on various pieces of furniture and the rug covering a portion of the hardwood floor. They look up when we come in.

"Everybody, this is Dean and Xavier. Guys, these are Emily, Cara, Mercy, Wyatt, and Grant, and that is Officer Barrett Courier," Sheridan says.

Barrett stands and comes over to me with an extended hand. "Hi. We spoke on the phone."

I nod, shaking his hand. "Good to meet you. I didn't expect you to still be here."

"I took a couple of days of vacation time. I've never taken any before, so I have a bit built up," Barrett says. "I plan on being here another few days, then I'm headed for a fishing spot I heard about so I can take some pictures and let them think that's where I've been spending my break."

"Now that the guys are here, if anybody's hungry, there's lasagna, salad, garlic bread. It's all in the kitchen. Go help yourselves and then we'll talk," Sheridan says.

As everybody jumps up to go toward the food, she takes a step closer to me. "Dean, can I have a quick word with you?"

"Sure," I say.

Xavier has already joined the wave headed for the lasagna, so I step off to the side with Sheridan.

"I hope you don't mind that Barrett decided to stay for a little while. I don't want it to feel like he's stepping on your toes," she says.

"Stepping on my toes? Sheridan, I'm a private investigator. He is a police officer who is actually involved in this case. If anything, I would be stepping on his toes. It's good that he's here. He can provide really valuable insight."

Her eyes drift over in the direction of the kitchen, and I get the feeling his deciding to linger for a bit isn't solely based on wanting to see how this investigation plays out.

"I really appreciate you coming out here. And it's good just to see you," she says.

"You too," I tell her.

She pulls me into a hug. I'm surprised at the softness I'm seeing in her. Sheridan has always been a kind and welcoming person, but she is usually sharp and sassy. This situation must really be weighing on her. We step back from the embrace, and I nod toward the kitchen, suggesting we go get ourselves some food before everybody eats it all.

Once everybody's plates are full and we are gathered around the long table in her dining room, the conversation finally shifts over to the real reason I've come.

"Are you just here to talk about the case?" Grant asks. "Sheridan told us you said you would just look into it and let us know what you thought."

"That was my plan initially, but now that I've found out more about all the cases, I'm ready to be more involved," I say.

"So you will start an official investigation?" Mercy asks.

"Yes. But I just want to make sure you all understand. It isn't the same as the police department investigating. I don't know how much experience any of you other than Sheridan has with private investigators, but the approach is different, and there's some information I won't be able to access."

I'm not trying to discourage them, but I do want to temper their expectations somewhat. They are all clearly counting on this finally being the end of the long, difficult path they've all taken to advocate for Rose Doe. I want them to understand that even though the path looks clearer now, there's no guarantee we'll get any farther than we are right now.

"We understand," Wyatt says. "From what we've heard about your work, your approach may be even better."

I'm not going to argue with that. The reality is, I'm able to go into cases and investigate details in ways detectives can't. They are bound by protocols and rules I don't have to worry about. Sometimes it leaves me walking a fine line, and I'm not afraid to wade through a gray area to do what needs to be done. And there are times when I have stepped over that fine line and dipped my toes beyond the gray right into the black. Like I said, I'll do what needs to be done.

"Where are you going to start?" Barrett asks.

"I haven't decided that yet. I went over all the information you provided me and plan on doing some of my own research as well. Since the case is already a year old, a lot of the basic groundwork has been done, but since there hasn't been much progress, there's obviously more to do. And since we are operating under the belief that the two cases are linked, all the evidence from both investigations will need to be filtered through that perspective," I say. "It makes a considerable difference to how things must be evaluated if a murder is a one-off versus part of a serial case."

"We believe identifying Rose Doe and finding out what happened to her is going to be key in solving the other cases," Sheridan says. "It's clear she died years before Bonnie Franco. If she was the start of this killer's career, maybe something in her identity or what was happening in her life leading up to her death will be the detail we've been missing that will make all the rest of the cases click."

I nod. "I agree. She's the one who started it all. Maybe the killer didn't even intend to kill anyone else. He might not have even intended to kill her to begin with. But then it happened, and he got a taste of the experience. He tried to control it, but years later the urge took over. One thing virtually all serial killers who have been open and honest about the crimes they've committed have described is the intense urge to kill that comes over them after their cooling-off period.

"You hear all the time they say they couldn't stop themselves or they couldn't help it because of that urge. It's possible Rose Doe's murder stirred that urge in the killer and the six women who came after were just his way of trying to feed it. If we can find out how she got into the path of the killer and what triggered her death, it can help us unravel the stories of the rest of the victims."

"But where do you start?" Emily asks. "You don't know her name or where she came from."

"That's why we became so attached to her," Sheridan says. "All those efforts to identify her early on and nothing ever came of them, so it's like the investigators just gave up. She would have been left with nothing. It made us deeply sad that there was no one to be there for her, advocate for her, mourn her. So we took the responsibility for doing those for her."

"We became her family," Cara adds. "And that's how we still feel about her."

"We've spent the last ten years taking care of her," Emily says. "We started out by talking about her every time we were together. We told other people about her. We started memorializing her and making sure people knew her story. Even with the story of her murder being on the news so frequently, there were a ton of people who had never even heard of her."

"It was awful," Sheridan says. "And we knew if she ended up buried in some indigent graveyard, she would be completely forgotten. So we banded together and got her a grave and a tombstone. We didn't have any information to put on it other than the date the medical examiner believed she died and the name Rose Doe. We've visited it regularly ever since."

I nod. "I want you all to know I'm taking this very seriously. I can't guarantee anything, but I know how much this means to all of you. As for where I start, well… I guess I'd like to go see the grave, if you'll bring me."

"Absolutely. We can go in the morning."

Early the next morning, Sheridan and I drive out to a small cemetery behind a tiny white country church not far from where she lives. We stop on the way to get flowers, and she instructs me to choose roses for her. Rose obviously loved the blooms since the charm on her bracelet was one of them, and it has become a tradition. I select a bouquet of yellow roses to place alongside the purple ones Sheridan has selected.

Xavier is back at Sheridan's house. He does not like cemeteries. When I asked what bothered him the most about them, he once told me that for a man who is a deep believer in the afterlife, senses energies, and has a strong compulsion to appear to fit in with society by following social protocols and chatting with the people around him when necessary, cemeteries can be a bit tricky.

To this day, I don't know if he was being serious. As with most things pertaining to Xavier, I figure it's better to err on the side of caution and not force him into a cemetery if he doesn't absolutely have to be there. Today is not one of those days, so he has stayed at Sheridan's house to make French toast.

Sheridan leads me toward the back of the cemetery.

"When we bought the plot for her grave, we asked for something in the back so she could have her privacy. We didn't want people to easily be able to find where she was and treat her like a tourist destination. I've seen stories about people who find graves of murder victims or killers and go to them to take pictures. I just can't bear the thought of her being treated like that. Those of us who care about her know she's here and come to visit her often."

We get to the grave and place the flowers on it. Now that I know about the flowers around the graves of the other victims, the gesture feels a little uncomfortable, but I'm not going to question it. Sheridan has brought me here to help me connect to Rose Doe, and I will follow her lead.

"I started following her case because it fascinated me. But then I realized she was more than just an unidentified murder victim, and she deserved to not only be treated like that, but to have people there to make sure others recognized it too. She needed a voice and people to care about her.

"I've been coming here for so long and have put so much energy and love into trying to take care of her it's hard for me sometimes to remember that I don't actually know her. I don't know her name. I don't know how old she was or what she actually looked like. I don't know what she liked to eat or her favorite pastimes. All those little things you know about the people around you and take completely for granted. If we can find out who she really is, maybe I can finally learn those things," she says.

"I promise I'm going to do everything I can to find out who she is and what happened to her," I tell her. "I just need to start from the very beginning."

"Then there's somewhere else you need to see."

"Where?" I ask.

"The spot where her body was found."

CHAPTER TWELVE

Rose Doe was found on a piece of old, unused farmland not far from where Sheridan lives. We stop back by her house after the cemetery and pick Xavier up so he can come with us. Even before we get there, I know this will be the type of place that speaks to him. I also like having him with me when going to places like this because Xavier notices things no one else does. He finds significance in tiny details that pass right over other people and can offer new meaning to something that's been looked at a thousand times before.

The drive is serene, meandering along curving roads with sprawling fields and old, picturesque houses on either side. At one point we pass slowly by a large farmhouse with a winding driveway. At the end of the driveway, a blue canopy protects a folding table set up to display pumpkins, sunflowers, and jars of honey. A green metal box sits on the back corner of the table, a "Thank You" sign visible from the road.

It's like driving into a postcard from another time.

The road gets narrower, and Sheridan tells me the land is right up ahead. On one side of the road is an old church with a tiny graveyard behind it and a tent set up in front for a fall revival. On the other is a nondescript brick building painted white and devoid of any detail or decoration. The simple sign in the grassy front yard marks it as a Masonic lodge. It looks empty and abandoned, yet fresh tire tracks in front show it is still very much in use.

The mouth of the driveway is nearly hidden among trees and tall growth next to the road. An ancient mailbox with the numbers peeling off and one fractured reflector are the only things that let me know she isn't just turning into the middle of the woods when the car starts to veer off the road.

"We've talked about doing some improvements to this area, but at the same time, we don't want to call too much attention. It's the same as her grave. We don't want people finding their way out here just to walk around and gawk," Sheridan says.

"Does the group own the property?" I ask.

She shakes her head as we make our way up a driveway that was once gravel but is now deeply rutted from years of weather and use.

"No. We've just been given permission to come here. It does technically have owners, but it was abandoned shortly after Rose's body was found."

We get to the end of the driveway, and the close woods pressing in on either side suddenly open up to a large, cleared lot. Sheridan follows tire tracks worn into the grass to park off to the side, and we get out. There's an immediate sense of abandonment and neglect here. In front of us, set in the center of the lot, is a run-down old trailer. It's sagging into the ground, the sides rusted and starting to separate, the front window shattered. A yellowed curtain still hangs over the window in the front door, the little touch somehow both more humanizing and chilling.

Sheridan walks ahead of us, making a wide arc around a front yard defined by two massive black walnut trees and a stone statue of a dog sitting ominously in the middle of the grass.

"Generations ago, this was a working farm," she tells us. "If you look closely in the woods, you can still see the remnants of the old fields. There are fence posts and pieces of barbed wire. In a couple of places, there are collapsed barns and other buildings. Over here is the most recent attempt at actually using the land for something."

She gestures at several metal containers that appear to have once been used as raised planters. Now they are overgrown, weeds and vines spilling over the sides. As we make our way toward the back of the property, I stare into the woods that have taken over the former fields. Just a quick glance would show only trees and undergrowth. The deep autumn has turned most of them vibrant shades of red and gold, making it easier to see the hidden signs of what was once here. I can imagine in the summer, when everything is green and in full bloom, it would be much more difficult to see the abandoned farm equipment rusting into the ground, the old toys and other random objects tossed aside and being gradually reclaimed.

Behind the trailer is a discolored clothesline that still has rotting pins attached. A pile of debris off to one side looks like it may have been the result of someone trying to clean up the property at one point, but it also could simply be the accumulation of a hoarder that has finally overwhelmed their space and is now taking over the outside.

The atmosphere is creepy and foreboding—a heavy, unpleasant feeling pressing in around us as we explore the grounds. But even with the eeriness, even with the sense that we are intruding on something, there's also an undercurrent of something that feels close to hope. Like there's potential beneath all the horror.

"It's beautiful here," Xavier says.

I realize he is no longer walking along beside me, and I turn around to find him sitting on the ground. A gray cat is in his lap, an orange one by his side, and another is coming toward him from the trees.

"Xavier, where did you find cats?" I ask.

"They found me," he says.

As he does, several more cats begin to appear from wood piles, beneath the cast-off farm equipment, and even hopping down from the roof of the trailer where they have somehow gone unnoticed until now. Xavier looks nothing short of enraptured. Sheridan looks back and smiles.

"Oh yes. That's the colony. We don't know for sure exactly how many cats live on the land, but I've counted at least forty at any given time. As far as we can tell, they descended from the barn cats brought here about fifty years ago. They're protected in Virginia, so they've just been allowed to roam here. We bring them treats sometimes but they don't really go for them. We love seeing them here. I feel like it brings some much-needed light and joy to this place.

"When we first started coming, we noticed they weren't nearly as skittish as most feral cats and have never shown any aggression, so we're pretty sure the people who used to live here also interacted with them. We've made them shelters in the woods and brought them food when the weather has been challenging, but they are still wild. So it's the best of both worlds. Kind of like squirrels who will come eat peanuts out of your hand."

By now Xavier is completely surrounded by the cats. They are certainly not squirrels, but the delighted, peaceful expression on his face says he would happily just stay right there in that spot for as long as they would let him. He further confirms this by not getting up when we continue on, instead opening out his arms to try to touch as many of them as possible. My instinct says to tell him not to touch them, but that would make me a hypocrite. Not only have we been to the zoo and I didn't hesitate to touch everything that got anywhere near me, but I'm currently having some pangs of envy that none of them chose me.

Leaving Xavier to his new friends, Sheridan and I go deeper into the land, leaving the open space and walking into the woods. It only takes a few steps for the trees to close around us and obscure any view of the open space. A couple of minutes later, there's nothing but the woods around us.

"How big is this plot of land?" I ask.

"A bit less than thirty acres. Not tiny, but not a lot compared to some of the farms in this area. It was never intended to be commercial. This was just a family farm that produced food for a small number of people. Then they stopped working it, and it fell into complete disrepair. I can't help but think that contributed to this being where she was killed. It feels so desolate and cut off from everything else. Nobody ever comes here."

"Except for the man who found her," I say.

Sheridan nods solemnly and walks a few more feet before pausing in a small clearing. A wooden sign sticks up from the tall grass, painted with roses and marked with the date she was found.

"Right here," she says. "The man who found her hunted on the next property over and accidentally stumbled onto this land."

"What's over there?" I ask.

"It was an unused piece of land that used to be a part of a small private airfield. Years and years ago, more than a hundred acres to the back of the property were owned by a very wealthy man. He had a little plane he liked to fly around, and that was where he kept it. But that was decades ago. He had no family when he died, and so the local stories go, everyone who tried to live on the land ended up having bad things happen to them.

"One couple drowned in the pool with no explanation. There was a target shooting accident. A few fires. Just a bunch of strange things happened anytime someone bought the land and tried to live in it the way he did. Eventually, everything of his was completely removed from the land and it was just left. Hunters started coming and using the wooded parts of it, and the areas that used to have his house, pool, and other things on them became kind of an unofficial park for the area."

"It's odd to think of something with that much life being so close to this place," I say.

"There's at least fifty acres of woods between here and the used portion of that land, but it does feel like a completely different world. The hunter who found her said he was just out hunting that morning and must have accidentally crossed into the farmland without realizing it. There aren't any barriers or markers or anything. He noticed smoke and worried somebody might have started a campfire that could catch the trees and undergrowth. There are burn regulations around here because of how dangerous open fire can be for the farms, and he went over to it just to make sure everything was okay. When he got there, there wasn't anybody around, but there was a fire burning. He put it out, and that's when he found her body."

"If the fire was still burning like that, it must have just been started," I point out. "Her killer was probably still very close by."

"He probably watched everything," she nods glumly.

I look down at the ground at our feet. The grass is golden now, but I imagine it is lush and green during warmer weather. Sun coming through the branches overhead dapples the areas with little pools of light. It would be a perfect picnic spot, which just makes the reality of what happened here more sickening.

"I can understand why someone would choose this spot to bury a body," I say. "It really does feel completely isolated, like there's no chance anyone will ever come this way. But at the same time, you said people were living here when her body was found, right? That it was abandoned shortly after that?"

Sheridan nods, her eyes still on the memorial. "Benjamin and Mae Jackson. They lived in that trailer we walked past. He was known to be a cruel and aggressive man. We talked to the sheriff once, who couldn't give us any details but said they were called out here dozens of times. Benjamin was initially considered a person of interest in Rose Doe's murder. He lived on the property, he had access to the land, and he could easily get away from the area when he detected the hunter coming toward him. There were some rumors that some of the things that were found in her grave, the sage and some of the plants, were growing up near the trailer at the time, but I don't really know that for sure."

"What happened with that investigation?" I ask.

"The police looked at him, but he was cleared after not too long. Not many details came out about why the police were able to determine he wasn't involved, but they were adamant about it. A lot of people around here didn't believe it then, and likely don't believe it now."

"Was the scrutiny what drove them away from here?" I ask.

"No," she says.

"Then what happened? You said the land was abandoned soon after she was found dead."

"Less than six months after she was found, he was arrested for beating his wife to death."

CHAPTER THIRTEEN

As I stand looking at the spot where Rose Doe was found burning ten years ago, a thought suddenly occurs to me.

"When I was reading the file on the investigation, I saw a few notes about a total lack of DNA evidence found on her body," I say.

"That's right. The medical examiner did a really thorough examination, including a rape kit. Every bit of her clothing that could be salvaged was checked. They even checked through the grave and the surrounding area to find fiber evidence or anything that might have the killer's DNA, but they didn't find anything. Investigators largely attributed the lack of evidence to the fire, but it's obvious the killer was also just very careful not to leave anything behind," Sheridan says.

"There was no DNA evidence from the killer, but did the investigators collect her DNA to use to try to ID her?" I ask.

"Yes, but of course, it didn't come up with any matches."

"Which just means she had never been arrested for any major crimes or in any of the states with compulsory DNA collection at the time of any arrest," I say. "But that doesn't mean it can't still be helpful."

She looks at me with a curious tilt of her head. "If she wasn't in the DNA database, how could it be useful? We would need to have a known sample linked to her identity, and if we had that, then we would already know who she was."

"A known sample linked to her identity, or to a family member," I say.

"I don't understand."

"I think I have an idea. I'm sure you're familiar with the Golden State Killer," I say.

"Of course," she nods. "He was just caught only a couple of years ago."

"That's right. And he was caught because of a new investigative technique called genetic genealogy. He was the first killer to be identified and brought to trial based on evidence developed through that technique."

"Genetic genealogy," Sheridan says in a hushed voice that sounds more like she is saying it to herself than actually meaning to say it out loud. She's just processing the words through her head to try to assign meaning to them. "That sounds redundant."

"It does. But it's a really incredible technique. It essentially uses the same technique as private investigators who specialize in hunting down missing family members. People who were put up for adoption and want to find their birth parents, siblings who were split up when they were little. That kind of thing. It uses ancestry websites, DNA databases, all those types of resources to trace the family tree of an unknown contributor of a DNA profile. This then lets an investigator trace the family of victims or even perpetrators. They go through the trees, eliminating people who could not possibly be the person that you're trying to identify, and gradually narrow down the options to track the identity of the person," I explain.

"So we could run Rose Doe's DNA through these systems, find out who she's related to, and contact them to find out who of their relatives has been missing for a decade," Sheridan says.

"Exactly. I know there's a chance there aren't any of her family members who have submitted their DNA to ancestry sites, or there could be complications in the family relationships that still make it difficult for us to pinpoint who she is, but it's something," I say.

"It's something," she agrees.

"I'm going to need to get in touch with the medical examiner to find out what happened to her DNA samples and if any have survived," I say.

"Let's go," she says.

We walk back out of the woods and find Xavier just where we left him, now sprawled on his back staring up at the sky with an even larger group of cats lounging around him. He's speaking quietly to them, and I won't be surprised if I find out he has started naming them. Several of them scatter as soon as I'm within a couple of yards, and their movement makes Xavier sit up.

"Hey," he says. "Want to come look at cloud shapes with us? This place has a really good view of the sky."

His hair is ruffled, and a few pieces of grass stick up from it, but he's oblivious. He slowly strokes the gray cat who is still curled up in his lap.

"Some other time. We actually need to get going. I need to go talk to the medical examiner," I say. "Don't worry. I'm sure we'll come back."

Xavier looks at the cats around him. "Did you hear that? He says not to worry because we'll be back."

He wiggles around a little bit to get the cats to move off him and stands up. He looks around, taking in a long breath like he's filling himself with the space.

"Land never forgets," he says. "If you listen to it long enough, it'll tell you everything."

"What do you feel, Xavier?"

"This was a farm, but before that, it was something else. The trees grew back where they'd been cut down. The memories are still here. People in the woods. Voices. Rose Doe's spirit would be in good company. Whoever left her here didn't choose this place. It chose them." He looks over at me. "At least, that's what they believe."

"And you?"

"It's a beautiful setting for a garden."

Emma has worked with Keegan O'Hare several times, so I'm familiar with her, but this is the first time I've come to her for help with one of my cases. When she comes into her office, I extend my hand.

"Dean Steele," I say.

"Emma Griffin's cousin," she says. "I remember. It's good to see you again. Are you helping Emma with one of her cases?"

"No, actually. I'm here to ask you about a case I have just started investigating."

She looks vaguely confused. "As far as I know, I haven't had a murder victim come through here in the last few days."

"It's actually a cold case. A body from ten years ago. An unidentified murder victim found on farmland in Mineral. She is known as Rose Doe," I say.

A flicker of recognition crosses Keegan's face. I don't expect her to immediately remember the details of the case. She is responsible for hundreds of people each year, and in the time that has passed, it would be easy for her to set this one case to the back of her mind. But it seems the name at least sounds familiar.

"She was fairly young, wasn't she? Found in the woods, burning, if memory serves me."

"Yes."

"What can I do to help?" she asks.

"I believe finding her identity is a crucial step toward not just solving her murder but possibly stopping a serial killer. I've come to ask about her DNA samples."

She gives a knowing nod. "We took several samples to run through all the databases, but she wasn't anywhere we could find. No other DNA evidence was found on her, so there was nothing to link her to the possible culprit either."

"What about tracing her genealogy?"

Her eyebrows raise as though she's surprised by the suggestion. She sits back, tapping the end of a pen against the surface of her desk as she considers what I've said.

"Interesting. As far as I know, the investigators didn't try that. And even if they did, they obviously didn't get anything out of it."

"But it has been ten years, which means a lot more opportunity for members of her family to contribute their DNA," I point out. "If Rose Doe's profile is available, it can be run through all the different available programs and identify biological family members who might be able to direct us to her identity. And once we know who she is, we can find out what happened to her."

"Let me see what I can do," Keegan says. "I can't initiate the process myself, but I can connect you to the people who can."

CHAPTER FOURTEEN

The next morning the process of running genetic genealogy testing on Rose Doe's DNA is underway, and I'm left to wait for the results. There's no real way to tell how long it's going to take, but I'm hoping not long. While I continue to go through every shred of information I have about all seven victims, I get a phone call from a number I don't recognize.

"Deen Steele," I say as I pick up.

"Mr. Steele, this is Kimberly Burgess from Meyer-Jeffries Real Estate. How are you doing today?" a woman asks.

It takes a beat for me to recognize the name of the real estate company that handled Alexander's purchase of the building outlined in the papers in Brielle's safety deposit box.

"I'm doing fine. How can I help you?" I ask.

I dig through the papers to pull out the documents in case I need to cross-reference any information. Since they are legal documents, I know it's likely she won't be able to give me all the details I may want, but I'm hoping to at least get something valuable out of her.

"I got a message from you inquiring about a specific piece of property. You were asking what type of business was being operated out of Thirteen Liberty Manor," she says.

"Yes. I am a private investigator working on a rather complicated case, and information about that property came up in the course of my research. I'm just trying to figure out what type of business it is and if it might have any connection to my case."

I figure being honest about my motivation is the best way to illustrate the urgency of my call and maybe encourage her to be more open with me than she may have been with just a curious caller. But I'm careful not to give away too much. I don't want to risk her mentioning this call to Alexander or compromising what Brielle was trying to protect.

"That may explain it," she says. "I was confused when I got your message, because that property is not a business. It's a home."

"A home? Like a house?" I ask.

"Yes. An original Gothic revival that was dismantled in its original location and painstakingly rebuilt in Maryland amidst authentic landscaping. It's gorgeous. A truly unique find. But most certainly a house."

"Could it be operating as a bed-and-breakfast? Or a short-term rental?" I ask.

"No," Kimberly says with a distinct note of distaste. "The area doesn't allow for any kind of business like that to operate out of the homes."

"I guess I'm confused too, because the paperwork has a business listed as the purchaser," I say. "Magnolia Enterprises."

"Privacy laws prevent me from giving out specific information, but I can tell you that many times businesses will purchase properties as investments. Individuals may also use a business name as a way to protect their privacy and interests when purchasing real estate," she tells me.

"Thank you. I appreciate you getting back in touch with me. I'm sorry for the confusion," I say.

"Not at all. I'm glad I could help in any way I may have. If you have any other questions, don't hesitate to call me back, and I'll help if I can. And if you're ever interested in purchasing a new home, I'd be happy to help you with that as well."

I hang up feeling like I've just extricated myself from the middle of a commercial and with just as many questions as I had going in. Maybe even more.

"Who was that?" Xavier asks, coming back from his visit to what Sheridan calls her library but is essentially just a bedroom packed with as many books as she could shove in. The haphazard arrangement doesn't seem to have bothered Xavier, who is now carrying an armful of various volumes.

"That was the real estate company that managed the purchase of that piece of property from Brielle's paperwork. Turns out it isn't a business. It's a house," I tell him.

"A house? Why would she have the paperwork for a house in with Alexander's business papers?" Xavier asks.

"I don't know. He's never mentioned owning additional property or other homes besides a small lake house that has already been thoroughly checked. Could this have something to do with money laundering? Obviously, this fake business has been linked to that address. Maybe he's using it as a cover. The loan was taken out in Alexander's name, but the property agreement itself has this Magnolia Enterprises name listed. The property was purchased under the guise of a business venture, but according to the real estate agent, none of the homes in that area allow for any type of business operating out of them.

"I'm sure there's flexibility for people who work from home or have home-based offices, but that doesn't really count. Those people are just working at home. The home itself is not considered a business. This agreement implies the property was purchased for the purposes of the business. Though she did mention that some people will establish business names and use them when buying property to protect their own identities and their privacy."

"Like Walt Disney," he says.

I slide my eyes over to him. "Has he been buying up a bunch of houses recently?"

"I certainly hope not," Xavier says matter-of-factly, setting the books down and coming over to the table where I've spread everything out. "But when he was getting ready to open Disney World, he knew he couldn't just go down to Florida and buy up a bunch of land using his name. People would automatically know his worth and jack up the price. Plus they would start leaking information about his project. So he didn't just buy one big piece of land. Instead, he bought a bunch of smaller adjoining pieces under various different names. Eventually, people figured it out, but he was able to keep things under wraps for a pretty long time."

"I don't think Alexander is planning on opening a theme park in Maryland. But I guess there could be a reason why he doesn't want people to know he bought another house. I mean, if even a fraction of the shady deals and backstabbing I'm noticing in these papers actually turns out to be something he did, I would probably want to get out of town and not have anybody be able to find me either. All it's going to take is one little slip, and he is going to have some very powerful and very angry people after him."

Xavier leans down a little to get a better look at something. "Hmmm."

"What?" I ask.

"Just something I didn't notice before," he says. He pushes the loan paper toward me. "The signature."

"What about it?' I ask. "It says Alexander Bardot."

"That's what it says, but that doesn't mean it's his signature. Look at these other papers. The signatures are different."

I pull one of the contracts over to place it beside the loan agreement so I can compare the two signatures. At first glance, they look exactly alike. The closer I look, however, the more I start to notice differences in how the letters are formed and the way they come together in the names. The differences are slight, but they are there.

"Someone else signed either the contracts or the loan agreement," I say.

"Look at the letters he signed or memos to people within the company," Xavier says.

We compare several more signatures and notice differences that create three categories of signatures.

"Something like a contract is much more likely to be signed in the presence of somebody else. Either the person that you are making the contract with or a notary. I would guess the signature on those contracts is Alexander Bardot's authentic signature. But I would also say it's very likely he was in the habit of having somebody else, probably his secretary, sign things for him occasionally to save him time."

I grab my phone and dial Alexander.

"Dean, good to hear from you. I feel like it's been a while," Alexander says when he picks up the phone. "What do you have for me? Have you heard from Owen?"

There's concern in the question, but it doesn't sound like that of a worried parent. I feel like he's less concerned about his son's safety than he is about not having everyone in his life carefully controlled.

"I don't have any information to give you just yet," I tell him, bypassing the question about Owen. "I'm actually calling with a question for you."

"Oh?" he asks.

"Nothing serious. Just routine to make sure I'm looking at everything correctly. I've been going over some of the personal papers and correspondence and things that you gave me, and I just wanted to make sure that you are the only one who signs papers. Is there anyone else who ever signs anything for you at work or anything?"

"What do you mean?"

"I've worked with a couple of businessmen who just don't have the time to stop and sign everything that crosses their desk, so they entrust an assistant or someone else close to them to assign basic papers so they don't have to worry about it," I explain. "I'm just making sure because I don't want to notice differences in signatures and think there could be something wrong. I haven't yet, I'm just laying the groundwork."

"Makes sense," Alexander says. "There are definitely times when work is so crazy I just can't stop and read another memo to the company or note to a client or work order approval. I used to have my secretary do it for me, but in the last few years, it's been Brielle. I figure if there's anybody in the world I could trust, it would be my wife. Besides, she's seen my signature so many times she could replicate it without even thinking about it." He lets out a sigh. "You know, I've gotten really good at convincing myself she's still here. When I'm at work or doing something away from the house, I can just pretend she's back at home and I'll see her soon. But then I think about things like that, and it hits me all over again. It's those kinds of things I really miss. Is that odd?"

It does strike me as very odd, but probably not for the reasons he's asking.

"Well, I'll let you go. Thanks for your time," I say.

"You'll let me know if you notice anything that might be concerning, right?" he asks.

"Of course. That's why you hired me."

"That's right."

I end the call and toss my phone onto the table in front of me.

"Something isn't right with him. I've been suspicious of him pretty much since the beginning, and nothing I find out about him is making that any better. I'm not sure what all he is up to, or if he had anything to do with what happened to Brielle, but I am sure about one thing. He isn't the one who bought that house. She did."

"Do you think he knows about it?" Xavier asks.

"No, and I think that was her entire point for handling it the way she did. I need to go to Maryland and check this place out."

CHAPTER FIFTEEN

The drive to Maryland is only a couple of hours from Sheridan's house, but it would be at least ten from Magnolia Glen. That is far too much distance for a weekend country home, and I can't imagine that there would be any reason Brielle would feel the need for a vacation house in Revel, Maryland. As we drive through it, I can see it's a lovely place. Nice houses, quiet streets. But it is definitely a place to live, not a tourist destination.

Xavier's face is pressed to the window observing the sights, and I'm running through the case out loud—mostly to order my thoughts rather than expecting any particular feedback.

"She was planning on leaving him. That's the only thing that makes sense. She was collecting all of that evidence against him, and she bought a house several states away from him in a way she knew would keep him from knowing what was going on. He let her sign things for him, so she was able to replicate his signature easily. And he had so many business deals and his fingers in so many things he couldn't possibly keep up with all of it all the time. She knew he wouldn't notice the loan payments coming out of the bank account because he would just think they were something he had authorized.

"She had been building this escape route for a long time. And then something happened, and she never got to use it. But I don't think Alexander found out about the house. I don't even think he knew she was making copies of documents. If he did, he would have found a way to cover it up or mentioned that so if I did find it, I wouldn't be surprised. This was still her secret when she died."

The GPS brings me along a long road and directs me to a driveway that leads up a small hill. A large, black iron gate at the road and a curve in the driveway obscure the view of the entire house, but I can see the top of it looming on the horizon.

When it was rebuilt, it was positioned so the face of the house is at an angle that allows anyone looking through the windows to see the meticulously designed landscaping and wooded grounds rather than just the driveway and street below. From here, I can see a large glassed-in greenhouse and a massive balcony with intricate iron detailing.

There's something at once foreboding and enchanting about the mansion. Looking more closely at the gate in front of me, I realize there's no lock on it. Instead, a keypad on one of the pillars controls the opening and closing with a code. I drive up to get a better look and see that no lights are illuminating the buttons. Usually, a pad like this would have indicator lights to guide the process of putting in the correct code, and would flash green or something when the lock disengaged.

But this one is dark. I touch a couple of the buttons and hear no response. The screen doesn't light up; there is no chirp or alarm to indicate any kind of system is attached. I get out of the car and pull on the gate. It's heavy, but it opens. I quickly get back in the car and drive through the gate, stopping just inside to close it again.

I drive quickly up toward the house to avoid being noticed by anyone who might venture down to this part of the street, though each of the houses is arranged in such a way that they seem isolated and separate from one another. I can't imagine there's much of a view of any of the neighbors from the other houses, but I don't want the risk.

The house is even more incredible as we drive around to the front. A massive fountain just outside sits dry and empty. A garden to one side features several monuments and statues that almost give it the impression of a graveyard. A chill goes down my spine at the comparison. Xavier and I get out of the car and look around. While I walk around the circular drive in front of the house and begin to make my way around the perimeter, Xavier heads up the front steps toward the entrance.

It's been a couple years since Brielle bought the property, and I wonder if she ever actually came here. I'm looking for anything that shows she's been here. Anything that suggests she was building another life that could have made her happy. Even though the thought of her being so brutally cut down before she could ever get out of Alexander's grasp and come here is excruciating, there's also a sense of comfort that comes with the idea that she had that hope to hold on to. If she was upset or angry or afraid, she could think of this house and what she was looking forward to, and maybe it took some of the edge off. I want to think that even though this place never had the opportunity to fulfill that dream for her fully, it merely existing gave her moments of happiness.

"Dean!"

I come back around the side of the house and head for Xavier's voice. We meet in the center of the front steps. I can see there's something in his hand.

"What's that?" I ask.

"I found it caught just under the bottom of the rocker. It's a receipt. Somebody had a pizza delivered here less than a week ago."

I take the paper out of his hand and look at it. The receipt looks like it's from a local restaurant and shows that a medium pepperoni and sausage pizza with a side of garlic bread was delivered here just a couple of days ago. A notation at the bottom suggests the order was made online and paid for in cash when it arrived. The name on the order says Brielle Adair.

I have to temper myself when I see that name. Everything in me wants to believe there's some way it's true. If this was a movie, this would be the moment when Brielle would come sweeping through the front door of the mansion, looking happy and content, having extricated herself from a life she didn't want by faking her death and setting up her criminal of a husband for a fall. I want that to be what's really going to happen. My skin tingles. My heart pounds a little.

And if I hadn't stood in the house in Magnolia Glen and seen her bloodied, ravaged body, I would let myself sink beneath the suggestion. It would be so easy to live in that hope and let it buoy me for a little while. But I know it isn't true. I found her murdered. I watched her body come out of the house on a gurney and get put into the back of the medical examiner's truck. There is no chance she's alive. Her name appearing on the receipt is a farce, but I have a strong feeling it was also absolutely intentional.

"Have you tried the door?" I ask, tucking the receipt away in my pocket.

"No," Xavier says. "It looks like one that's going to open itself." I give him a disbelieving look, and he gestures toward it. "Which it clearly isn't going to do, but also means I'm not going to touch it."

I shrug. "Fair enough."

"Though a door that opens itself..." he murmurs, and I know the house in Harlan may soon feature yet another wholly unnecessary but fantastical feature. At this point, I essentially live at Hogwarts.

I try the door, but it's locked. Peering into the windows on either side does little good because of heavy curtains covering all but a narrow gap in the middle. But even squinting through that shows me very little within the darkened house.

We get off the porch, and I continue my progress around the perimeter, trying to look in every window we encounter and shaking doorknobs along the way. We've just passed the back door when I hear a door close quickly followed by a voice.

"What are you doing here? You're trespassing."

I look up and see someone standing on the upper level of a multitier patio that had been added to the original structure of the mansion. He's glaring at me, but I don't care about the bitter expression. All I see is Brielle's eyes. I've seen that face staring at me from dozens of pictures by this point. I know exactly who it is.

"Owen," I say.

He pivots and heads back inside the house. Pressing my hand to the railing of the next level of the patio, I launch myself over the barrier and run up the steps toward the door he just went through. I don't stop for a second thought before wrenching it open and rushing inside.

"Owen!" I shout to him. "I need you to come talk to me."

His face appears around a corner, his eyes like ice and his jaw set so hard the muscles on either side of his face are twitching.

"Get out of my house," he demands.

"I need to talk to you," I say.

He darts off, and I chase after him. He has an advantage over me in that he knows the layout of the house and can navigate it much more easily than me, but I follow right behind him. Before I can get him to stop, he runs through another door and out into the grounds.

"Leave me alone. I don't want to talk to you," he says.

I chase him, quickly catching up with him and curving around his side to cut off his progress. He tries to pivot out of my way, but I bounce backward again, cutting him off.

"Owen, stop. I need to talk to you. I'm Dean Steele," I say.

"I know who you are," he says through gritted teeth. "And like I said, I don't want to talk to you. I need you to stop following me. Stop trying to find me."

He moves away from me and starts to run again, but I call after him.

"Your mother asked me for help," I say. "Brielle called me just before she died and told me something was happening, she was scared, and I was the only one who could help her."

Owen's steps slow, and he finally stops. He stands with his back to me for a moment, like he's trying to decide whether he's going to trust me. I don't know what he's heard about me other than the fact that I've been following him. I don't put it past Brielle's parents to have continued insulting and criticizing me even after all these years. They probably decided to have at least some discretion by not detailing our relationship, instead just spewing their vitriol toward me without context. But that would be for no other reason than to try to revise history. They would rather no one know how low their daughter sank and how close she came to completely destroying the reputation of the entire family.

Only Brielle herself needed to hear the constant reminders of what she did and how much they had to go through because of her. I don't know any of this for certain, of course. I've happily lived without having to hear either of their voices or see their faces since I was a teenager. But it would fit right in with what I know about them. They want to have both the ability to pretend our relationship never happened and to hold it over Brielle's head as a source of shame and leverage.

If I'm right, that means Owen has heard my name before—likely followed by a barrage of insults, accusations, and judgments. He would have an entire perspective of who I am without ever coming into contact with me. Now I'm trying to track him down when all he wants is to be left alone, and he's having to decide if he's going to follow what he's heard from his grandparents or what I'm telling him about his mother.

Finally, he turns around. "Why did she need your help?" he asks.

I shake my head. "I don't know. She didn't tell me. All the message said was that she needed help and I was the only one who could help her. I got to her as fast as I could, but..."

"She was dead," he says coldly.

"I'm so sorry for your loss," I say. "I know how painful it is."

"I hate when people say that," Owen says angrily. "Just because you're an adult doesn't mean you know everything. You can't possibly know how I feel."

"I don't know because I'm an adult. I know because my mother was murdered too. I was even younger than you are. So yes, I do know how painful it is."

"Sorry," he grumbles, looking at his feet.

I'm struck by how familiar he seems. It's like I know him even though this is the first time I'm speaking to him. It's more than just knowing what he looks like because of all the pictures I've seen. It's like I can feel the part of Brielle that's in him and I already know it.

"Look, I'm not here to cause you any trouble. But I need you to talk to me. I need to understand what's going on."

"Did Dad send you?" he asks. "I know you're a private investigator."

It's hard to find the right answer for that. I don't want to seem like I'm lying to him by not telling him Alexander hired me, but I also don't want to get into anything that I've found out about him recently either. The connection between Owen and me is extremely tenuous at this moment, and I don't want to chance breaking it and him disappearing for good.

"Your father did hire me to look into the circumstances around your mother's death as well as your disappearance. But I'm here because I was worried about you and I know your mother would want someone to be sure you're safe. Not because of him."

"He doesn't know I'm here?" Owen asks. He sounds cautious, but I can feel that I'm starting to break through.

"No," I say, taking a step closer to him. "I didn't tell him anything about this place. And he doesn't know you called me either. I haven't told him anything. I am operating under the belief that you had a very good reason for leaving without letting anybody know where you were going or where you've been. All I have to support that is knowing your mother and knowing what I experienced when I was your age. But if I'm going to continue to think that way, and if I'm going to continue to not tell your father what I know, I need you to be honest with me. Can you do that? Do we have a deal?"

"Do you need me to write something up really fast?" Xavier mutters under his breath, his head suddenly appearing next to my ear over my shoulder.

"I don't think that's going to be necessary, but thank you," I say.

Owen gives him a quizzical look, and I gesture toward Xavier. "This is Xavier."

Xavier waves. "How was your pizza the other night? Good? I was thinking pizza sounded good."

Owen's eyes snap at me. "You've been watching me?"

"We found the receipt on the front porch," I say.

"You really should be more careful with your littering," Xavier adds. "It's not good for the environment."

"Thanks for the tip," Owen says.

"I have plenty more," Xavier chirps.

"He really does," I say.

Owen's eyes meet Xavier's. "It's my favorite pizza. They put extra garlic on the bread too."

"Did you hear that, Dean? Extra garlic. We should order dinner from there," Xavier says.

Owen lifts an eyebrow.

"I really love garlic," I say. "Xavier says when I make garlic bread, you can smell the garlic through the house for days."

Owen lets out a little grunt of laughter. "That's how I like it too." Owen glances around like he is trying to confirm I'm telling the truth about not telling Alexander about the house or coming here. "How did you find me?"

"I'll explain it, but I need you to talk to me first."

He gives a resigned nod. "Come in."

He walks around me to go to the steps at the back of the house. We follow him back inside and into the kitchen. He opens a cabinet and takes out a cup to fill with water. Looking at us, he lifts the glass and raises his eyebrows in a silent offer.

We both accept, and he fills our glasses. He sets them in front of us, then takes his and walks out of the kitchen into the living room. Rather than this feeling like he's trailing us around or demanding we follow him, Owen seems more dazed, like he's going through motions but not all of them are connecting. Finally, he sits down and stares down into his cup of water. Xavier and I take seats on the furniture around him and wait.

"I didn't kill my mom," Owen says after a long pause. His eyes lift. "I know people think I did."

I nod. "Some do. But I don't. That's why I agreed to look for you but haven't said anything to your father. I want to hear from you what happened and what you've been doing."

"Right now, all I can tell you is, I had nothing to do with her death. I'm trying to distance myself from the whole situation. I need to protect myself and my sister and find out what happened to my mother. I didn't leave Colleen because I was being selfish or didn't care about her. I know she's safe there, but she wouldn't be if I was there. I can't explain it more than that right now, and I need you to accept that," he says.

"Can you tell me if you feel that way because you might know something about your mother's death, or at least what might have led up to it?" I ask.

"I might. But I'm not sure yet and can't say anything until I am."

"I might be able to help you," I say.

"And when I think there's something for you to help me with, I'll tell you," Owen says. "For now, I can't say anything else."

I nod to show my understanding. "What about this house? What's the story about this place?"

"Mom bought it a couple of years ago. She didn't tell anybody about it when she first bought it, but about a year ago, she took me aside and told me about it, gave me a key, and explained she'd set it up so that the utilities are automatically taken out of a fund she put aside. The mortgage payments come out of Dad's account," Owen says. "He's not very good at things like money management, so he always had Mom handle most of the banking. He looks over it every now and then, but I honestly don't think he has any idea what he's looking at most of the time. And he'd gotten so many loans for so many things he wouldn't notice if there was another payment coming out. If he did, Mom would just explain it away as being for something he knew about."

"So she'd been thinking about this for a while," I say.

"Yeah. When she told me about the house, she said she always wanted to make sure that my sister and I were safe and taken care of. No matter what, she wanted us to know that we would be okay, and this house was part of that. It made sense to me. I've had suspicions for a long time about Dad's clients."

"What do you mean?" I ask.

"The most important things to Dad are money, power, and reputation. That's it. He's always been very aware of not being on the same level as his family or Mom's family. I think it really pissed him off that they didn't give him a cushy executive job in one of their companies when they got married."

"I thought he wanted to build his own career and make a name for himself," I say.

"That's the line he tells people. He wants people to admire him for how hard he works to make his own way or whatever. But it's never really been that way. He would argue with Mom about her convincing Grandpa to give him a position in the company that would pay him more. He said he deserves it for what he's done and that he would think they would appreciate him more," Owen says.

"Do you know what he meant by that?" I ask.

He shakes his head. "No."

"What about his actual work?" I ask, not offering any details about the papers Brielle left or my suspicions about Alexander's business practices.

"The one thing he has worked really hard on is finding as many ways as possible not to work hard. He's never been good with money and, according to Mom, has never had the ambition or business skills to find legitimate clients and build up a good reputation. So he makes himself available to the kinds of clients that pay well but carry a lot more risk than a bad review if things don't go their way," he says. "You get what I'm saying?"

I nod. "I'm beginning to think so. But do you have anything tangible about who he's working with and what he's doing?"

"I know my mother had a lot to do with the banking, and she would help him out with the occasional legitimate client that came his way, usually through my grandparents. But that doesn't explain why she would leave the house with files of papers and come back without them. Or why she would go to such extremes to make sure there was a place for us to go. When she was first talking about it, I thought she'd bought it for all of us. She didn't come right out and say it, but I figured she was putting a safeguard in place just in case someone got mad at Dad and we needed to leave.

"But then she told me I was the only one who knew about the house and that I couldn't tell anybody. I couldn't mention it to Colleen or to Dad, and if he asked, I was supposed to act like I didn't know what he was talking about. She'd never told me to lie to him before, so I knew it had to be something else. I tried to get her to tell me more, but she just said when I needed to know, she would tell me, but that this was her making sure everything was going to be okay. Then I guess a month or so later, she gave me the information for the bank account she had set aside and gave me a card so if I ever needed to use it, I had it. It felt like she was getting ready for something and just wasn't telling me what."

"Did you notice a change in her over the last few months?" I ask. "Other than her telling you about the house and the bank account?"

He lets out a breath and looks down at his hands, rubbing them together as his arms rest on his knees.

"She was different. I knew things weren't great between her and Dad. They barely spent any time together, and when they did, there just wasn't a lot of connection. When I was a kid, they were a lot closer. Never really like all over each other in love or anything, but that's how it is with like my friends' parents and stuff. It's like you know they like each other, but they don't want to really show it. They don't hug and kiss or hold hands all the time or anything. But they were closer.

"I didn't even realize there could be some other way to be in a relationship until I went over to a friend's house and saw his parents. They were making dinner together, and his father put some music on. They started dancing around the kitchen. Like he was twirling her around and dipping her and stuff. The kind of thing you see in movies. I didn't think people actually acted like that. My friend just kind of rolled his eyes, and I realized they weren't doing that for show. It was just normal for them.

"But things were just kind of the same until a little while before she told me about the house. After that, she seemed like… like she was under a lot more stress, and she was always on edge. I don't think Dad even noticed. She always did everything she could to seem put together and to make sure that my sister and I had everything we needed. That's when I really started to realize she wasn't putting things in place so that the whole family could relocate or get away for a while. It was just for the three of us. And that's when I started looking more into who Dad was working with and what he was doing."

"You said she set up a bank account. I'm guessing that means everything else is joint?"

"They have a joint account, and she has one of her own. That's one of the things I've heard my grandmother lecture about. Women should always have their own bank account that they can spend at their own discretion. Of course, that doesn't actually mean it's private. I know for a fact my grandparents checked in on what she was doing with her bank account all the time. So did Dad. He's not good with money, but he's very good about keeping his nose in other people's business. And when you have last names as powerful as Adair and Bardot in this town, privacy laws don't really apply anymore.

"As long as he felt like their joint account was adding up and things were getting paid, that was all that mattered. But he would have noticed and been furious if she did it with her own money. Especially within the last few years, he was in so far over his head that sometimes he would barely know what was going on if Mom wasn't there to tell him he was getting payments deposited into the account and bills were getting paid. I also think he did some favors for some of his clients, so not all of the money going through the accounts or the transactions that were being done were actually his. And Mom figured that out."

This confirms some of what I've been thinking about Alexander. It's very possible he's been laundering money as just one piece of his shady dealings with his less-than-reputable clients. It lines up with Brielle buying the house through the deceptive signature. She didn't want Alexander or her parents to trace the spending if she just did it with her own account or if she was to get the mortgage in her name. Instead, she used his signature and made sure the payments were made automatically out of the account that was already used for countless other automatic drafts and temporary holdings.

Brielle knew he was getting himself so wrapped up in these clients that he couldn't keep up. Another loan or contract crossing his desk or going through the account wouldn't set off any alarms as long as they were paid and didn't cause him any trouble. She'd make sure that was the case.

I take a breath. "I'm going to ask you a question, and I need you to be completely honest with me. Knowing I'm not going to call the police or do anything like that no matter what you say. I'm asking because I need to know all the information for my investigation."

"We didn't break into those houses," Owen says before I can even ask. "I know people think the guys I was hanging out with aren't worth anything because they don't come from the rich neighborhoods, but they're just normal guys. That's what I like about them. I don't like watching the people around me constantly trying to compete to be the most impressive, the most influential, the most… whatever. You can just fill in the blank. Kids who grow up in my neighborhood are constantly competing and showing off, and the ones who are in the wealthier neighborhoods aren't impressed and make fun of them, which just eggs them on. It's exhausting and really annoying. Hanging out with those guys was just hanging out. We didn't talk about stupid shit like who was going to be the first one to get the new model of car that wasn't supposed to roll off the line until the next year or who pulled what strings to get good tickets to a concert. We talked about stupid shit like… I dunno, like normal kids. That was all I ever wanted."

"A couple of them did have bad reputations, you have to admit that. Police records."

"I know. But so do you," he counters.

Xavier slides closer to me, his eyes locked on Owen but talking out of the corner of his mouth. I'm never sure if Xavier is aware that people can hear him when he does that and it doesn't work like an aside in a play.

"Did you tell him that?" he whispers.

"You're right," I say. "I do. And I'm not judging them. People encounter all kinds of things in their lives, and they handle it how they handle it. That doesn't mean they always make the right choice or what they do is justified, but it does mean everybody has a story. I sure as hell do. I'm just pointing out that people aren't just basing what they think of those guys on where they're from. That's part of it—of all people, I can't argue that—but there is a good reason for them to assume they might be involved in crimes. Especially when people are saying they were seen in the area."

"I know. But I'm telling you, it wasn't us. The neighbors saw us around the area because I live there. When the guys came over to hang out, they were in the neighborhood. But we didn't break in anywhere. At least not any of the houses the police say we did." He pauses and looks at me through slightly tilted-down eyes. "You said you're not going to call the police or say anything to anybody, right?"

"Unless you're about to give me a detailed account of what happened that day so I can go make sure the person responsible was arrested, then no. I might be technically working for your father, but my loyalties lie with Brielle. Always. And now that I know what you've been telling me, I know she would want me to think of you and your sister well before I think about your father, or even her. If you think I need to know something, then tell me," I say.

"Sometimes when we wanted to blow off some steam, we'd go to the other side of town and break into abandoned houses or people's sheds. A couple of times we broke into gas stations after they were closed. Nothing major. We didn't cover the walls with spray paint or break everything up or anything. We might have caused a little damage in the abandoned houses and stolen some little stupid stuff, but it wasn't anything like what happened to the houses in my old neighborhood."

"You know, Glen is in jail," I say, referencing the only one of the group of teenagers accused of the break-ins who has been arrested and is being held.

Owen nods solemnly. "Yeah. I feel really bad about it. But he doesn't know where I am. I didn't tell any of the guys where I was going because I didn't want them holding on to that. That way they didn't have to lie. And if they knew I was here, they would probably come to try to find me, and then all of us could be in some serious shit. And I wouldn't be able to keep looking for who hurt my mom. I tried to figure out a way to get him out. I even called up a bail bondsman in the next town over and offered to pay his bail just to get him out. But it didn't work. I don't know what's going on, but I'm worried about him."

"Your father went to see him. Do you know why he would do that other than to ask if he knew where you were?"

Owen looks confused and a bit alarmed. "Glen's dad's boss has worked with my dad before. But I don't know what he did for him. I don't know why that would have anything to do with him being in jail or why he would go to see him."

"That's something I'll find out," I tell him. "That's what I do."

He nods. "What else do you do?"

"What do you mean?"

"You're a private investigator. You've worked on some pretty serious cases. I did my research. And I know you agreed to work with Dad just so you could help my mom. It isn't like you're hurting for work. So what else are you doing?"

I hesitate, and he leans forward to put his cup down on the table in front of him.

"I just want to think about something else. I've been running and holed up in hotels and this place for weeks. I just want to think about something else. Just for a little while."

The pain and sorrow are evident in his eyes now. He's done well in building up a wall around him and not letting anybody see what's actually going on beneath the surface. But he's reached his limit. For right now, he just needs to separate from what's crushing in around him and think about something else.

I oblige by telling about Rose Doe and the Garden of Bodies case. He listens with close attention as I describe my hopes for the genetic genealogy and the meaning I'm trying to find in the similarities among the murder victims.

"This whole thing reminds me of Dad," he suddenly says.

I raise an eyebrow at him, and he shakes his head.

"Not that I think he's a serial killer. Just that feeling of manipulation and overdoing things to create an image he wants the world around him to see."

Those words stick with me as we continue to talk about this case and some of the others I've worked on. He doesn't ask me about his mother or how we knew each other. He doesn't mention anything else about his father or his sister. For now, all that has been put aside, and he's just letting himself exist.

A while later, I glance at my phone and see it's getting late in the evening. I haven't realized so much time has passed, and my stomach is rumbling.

"I think it's about time we grab something to eat and get going," I say to Xavier. "We've got a couple of hours of drive ahead of us, and I'm starving."

"Why don't you stay here?" Owen asks. "You're already here, and Xavier wants to try the pizza. It's not like there isn't enough space."

I'm surprised by the offer but don't hesitate to latch on to it. I've been searching for this boy for weeks, and now I finally know he's safe. But he has something locked inside him that he's not willing to share yet. I'm hoping I may be able to build up enough trust that he'll tell me.

CHAPTER SIXTEEN

We order pizza and spend the rest of the evening hanging out and watching TV. We talk about mundane things, but that seems to delight Owen, who I discover smiles like his mother. He's directed us to spare bedrooms but falls asleep on the couch. I cover him with a throw blanket before we head up to bed.

"It's so weird," I say, glancing back in his direction as we go up the stairs. "I feel like I know him. I mean, I know I've seen his picture and have been talking about him, but it's more than that. I guess it's just because he's Brielle's son. I felt a connection to Colleen too. They're a part of her and all that's left."

"It's not weird," Xavier says. "I feel a pull toward him too. Like I already know him in a way."

I go to bed with Owen's words about his father still going through my head. I close my eyes and see his against my lids. Right before I fall asleep, they change to Brielle's.

When we wake up the next morning, Owen is gone. There's a note in the kitchen explaining he has to keep moving and that while he trusts I'm not going to say anything, he doesn't feel settled yet. He doesn't want Alexander to know where he is or that I've seen him, and he doesn't want to risk that anyone will stumble on the existence of the house and surprise him. For now, he has to keep moving around and looking into his mother's death. There's no promise that he'll contact me again and no information on how I can get in touch with him. I can only hope this is not the last time I'll see him.

A bright green sticky note stuck to the front of the refrigerator tells us the kitchen is stocked and to help ourselves to whatever we want since he doesn't know when he'll be back around here. I decide to take him up on it, making breakfast while Xavier calls Nicole and I check in with Sheridan so she knows we'll be back a bit later. I checked in with her last night to tell her we wouldn't be back so she wouldn't worry something had happened to us, and I want to make sure she knows we haven't left yet. There hasn't been any sign that our investigation has ruffled any feathers, but when delving into the world of a serial killer, awareness and touchpoints with other people are a safeguard that shouldn't be skipped. I've gone through enough myself and watched Emma face enough that I understand the importance very clearly.

The breakfast I manage to piece together isn't elaborate, but nothing got burned, and I take that as a win. If my life when I was younger has taught me anything, it was that things aren't always going to be there when you need them, so appreciate them when they are, even if they aren't exactly what they should be.

"Why didn't you tell me about Brielle before this?" Xavier asks when I put his plate in front of him and sit down at the island in the center of the kitchen.

"Just going to dig right in, aren't you?" I ask.

"It's a logical question, Dean. You've told me about everything else. But I'd never even heard of Brielle until you got that message."

"Why didn't you tell me about Mirabel?" I ask, trying to deflect the question.

"Trauma and compartmentalization," he says without hesitation.

"Oh. Well, can I use that answer too?"

"No."

"All right. I didn't tell you about her because I didn't really want to think about her. That part of my life was really difficult, and she was a big part of that. Not her, specifically, but her parents. I told you about them and how they treated me. You know the story," I say. "I went through some of the worst times of my life right around then. Just before and just after her. It's not really a time I want to go back to. It was better for me to just put it out of my mind and not have to think about it. There wasn't any occasion for me to tell you about her," I say.

"She made you happy, didn't she?" he asks.

"Yes," I say. I don't want to elaborate any further than that, and he doesn't ask me to. "So I guess that means I shouldn't have totally shut off that part of my past. I should be happy to have those memories, hang on to them, and think about them because they should still be good."

"Not necessarily," he says.

I'm surprised by the ease and certainty in the words.

"Not necessarily?" I ask.

"I know people say it's better to have loved and lost than to have never loved at all, but I don't think that's always true. In fact, I've found it very rarely to be true. At least when those people are alive, just not part of your life anymore. I think if most people were honest with themselves, they would admit that they don't get any pleasure out of thinking back on the memories of people who left their lives. It hurts to think about them because thinking about them automatically brings up the pain of them not being around anymore and whatever precipitated them being gone.

"If you had someone in your life who you were very close with, who you connected deeply with, who you felt you shared something special with, and then something bad happened between you that ripped that completely apart, that's what's going to stay in your soul. It isn't the good thoughts. Those feelings are fragile, and once they're shattered, they're like pieces of glass. The shards get on everything around them and cut you if you get close. Thinking of something you once did with them, or fun you used to have with them, can't bring up those good feelings anymore because those feelings are gone. All that's left is the pain.

"When that pain is because that person was taken from you, like with Mirabel, it can be worth it. I might let her exist away from my conscious mind because that's where she wants to be, but when I think of her, I take the hurt because it comes with the joy I can still feel about her. I wouldn't trade my sister away to make that pain not exist. But if it's someone who betrayed you or chose to leave you without any regard for how you felt, or what you shared, that pain isn't worth anything you could have ever had together. It would be much better to never have those memories at all than to have them and feel the pain that comes with them." He pauses.

"But maybe that's just me. And maybe in the end, I'm lucky. I don't connect with many people. Some, yes, but not many. I don't get attached. So I can make good memories with them and then walk away and not feel any pain when I think about them. It seems so much harder to have a lot of people entangled in your life. To let them in is hard enough, but to tear them out and have that raw, open space..." He shakes his head. "People may not understand me, but I don't understand how any of you can survive what the world does to you."

The words dig into my heart, the calm way he says them as he eats making them more devastating.

"I think a lot of people would feel the same about you," I say.

He takes another bite and shrugs. "Then I guess it's good we ended up who we did."

"I guess it is," I say.

My phone chimes beside me, and I glance at the screen. All thoughts of breakfast leave my head when I see the message that the genetic genealogy search has produced a hit on Rose Doe's identity.

I immediately call Lyle Walker, the genealogist who works with law enforcement to help with murder investigations and other crimes through the use of genetic testing. He's handling this case for us, and I'm eager to find out what he has to tell me. I'm not building myself up that he's going to be able to give me her name right off the bat. If it were that easy, she would have come up before. His message didn't tell me he had her identity specifically, just that he had a hit on it. But that's enough. I'll take even the smallest nudge in the direction of the truth.

My conversation with Lyle is short. All he's able to give me is a single name: Paula Anderson. Her name popped up on an ancestry site because she submitted her DNA to find out about her heritage and build a family tree.

"There are several people connected to her on the tree, but none of them come up as having any kind of familial link to Rose Doe, which means they are from a different side of her family," I explain to Xavier. "Lyle messaged her on the site and briefly explained that we needed to speak to her about a missing person and asked for her contact information. I don't know how many details he gave her, he said he kept it really vague, but I don't know how she's going to feel about talking to me."

"Do you want me to talk to her?" Xavier asks.

I give him an incredulous, questioning look. "You're willing to call her?"

This is a man who is unwilling to order a pizza over the phone and has been known to not even answer when Bellamy or Eric calls because of the extent of his dislike for the phone. With very few exceptions in his life, he is uncomfortable talking on the phone to anyone for any reason, and really has to build himself up in order to do it. Sometimes the effort just isn't there for them.

"I did not say that," he says, dashing my hopes a bit but falling back into line with my expectations for him, which, in a way, is far more comfortable. "I asked if you want me to talk to her. Bring me to her, and I will tell her what's going on and get her to call you."

"If we're there talking to her, why would she need to call me?" I ask.

"Because that's how you were going to get in touch with her," he says.

"That was before it was a thought that we could just go find her and speak to her in person," I say.

"Can we just go find her and speak to her in person?" Xavier asks.

"No," I say.

"Then doesn't that mean you have to call her?" he asks.

I take a breath. "I'm going to call her."

"If you can get her here, I'll talk to her."

I take my phone with me and walk out of the kitchen. The phone rings a couple of times before a wary female voice answers.

"Hello?"

"Hi, my name is Dean Steele. May I speak with Paula Anderson?" I ask.

"This is Paula," the woman asks. "Are you that private eye who wants to talk to me about some missing person?"

"That's me. I appreciate you taking my call," I say.

"Well, when that guy called and said my name came up in an investigator's case, I figured I didn't much have a choice but to talk. I don't know what I could have to do with a missing person. I don't know anyone who is missing," she says.

"Did Lyle explain how we found you?" I ask.

"Yeah. Comparing some woman's DNA to mine," she says. "So how did you get that DNA if she's missing?"

"To be honest with you, Lyle misspoke. The case is not really about a missing person. The DNA came from a murder victim," I say.

This is obviously a woman who is used to things coming straight at her and doesn't like sugarcoating. I can tell it's going to be easier to talk to her, and I'm more likely to get useful information out of her if I am just upfront and honest with her.

"Oh my god," Paula says. "A murder victim? Someone in my family was murdered? Who?"

"That's what we're trying to figure out," I explain. "This murder happened about ten years ago, and the victim has gone unidentified since then. I was asked to investigate her murder after evidence was found that links her murder to the deaths of six other women."

"I just don't understand. Nobody has gone missing from my family. I was certainly old enough ten years ago to remember if something like that happened. Do you have a picture or anything?"

"No. Unfortunately, her body was so badly damaged when she was found that there were no pictures of her face available. All I'm able to tell you is that she was in her late teens or very early twenties. Dark hair. Average height. I know that isn't particularly helpful. It sounds like most people. But it's what we have to go on."

"And she was found in Virginia?" Paula asks.

"Yes. On a piece of old farmland near Mineral."

"Mineral," she whispers like she's trying to give the word context.

It's such a small place it's unlikely anyone not very familiar with the area would be able to place it. Considering she lives halfway across the country, I can't imagine it's a place she knows.

"Right now, we don't have enough information to know whether she was originally from Virginia or if she was brought there," I offer.

"None of that sounds familiar to me. But I do know we have quite a few extended family members I could get in touch with for you. I have a whole side of my family I was essentially cut off from after my parents got divorced. That was a long time ago, and I didn't really have much relationship with any of them for a long time, but I got back in touch with one of my cousins not too long ago. He might know something I don't."

Paula gives me the contact information for her cousin Seth Roberts and tells me she'll get in touch with him to give him a heads-up about the situation. I thank her and start to end the call, but she interrupts.

"If you do find out who she is, will you let me know? If she was family, I'd like to know what happened," she says.

"I'll let you know anything I find out," I promise and hang up.

I want to give Paula time to reach out to Seth and let him know I'll be in touch, so Xavier and I clean up and head out. It feels strange continuing to stay at Sheridan's house, but it's the most convenient option considering her proximity to where Rose Doe was found, her grave, and the people who worked her case originally.

We get back to Sheridan's house to find it empty and a note on the kitchen counter telling us she left food in the refrigerator. I take a shower and change to use up some more time, but finally, the anticipation gets the most of me, and I have to call Seth Roberts.

CHAPTER SEVENTEEN

"DO YOU REALLY THINK IT MIGHT BE HER?"

The first words out of Seth Roberts's mouth are abrupt and heavy. There's no desperation in them, nothing urgent or anxious like he's been frantically searching for something and thinks it may be right within his grasp. Instead, he sounds almost burdened by the thought, dragged down so he's struggling just to contain it.

"Who?" I ask.

"Sienna Roberts," he says. "My sister."

The words stun me for a second. I was expecting another spiraling conversation explaining the whole situation and trying to decipher who this person might be. Instead, Seth seems to be handing her identity right to me.

"We don't have any confirmed identification information," I tell him. "That's why we ran the DNA test through the ancestry systems. The hope was to zero in on a family tree that might allow us to pinpoint the right person."

"I know. Paula explained it to me. But I can't think of anyone else it could possibly be. It has to be Sienna." He takes a shuddering breath, new emotion starting to rise to the surface. "I didn't think it would turn out this way."

"Where are you located?" I ask.

"Just outside of Myrtle Beach," he tells me.

"All right. I'm in Virginia right now. If I can catch a flight and get there this evening, would you be willing to meet up tonight or tomorrow and talk about your sister?" I ask.

"Sure. If you think it would help, I'm willing to tell you everything I know," Seth says.

"That's great. Thank you. I'll let you know when I have the arrangements made."

"You're going to have to stop making up excuses to hang out with me," Zara Stein says ten minutes later when I've finally gotten ahold of her to find out if she is available for a private flight to South Carolina this afternoon. "I'm seeing you more often than I am Emma."

"You're just too charming to resist," I tell her.

"Yeah," she says with a hint of a snort in her laugh. "That's it. But you're cute, so I'll let it slide. It also so happens I have a clear schedule today. Where's the closest airfield to you?"

Zara is a former high-priced call girl-turned-FBI informant who now owns her own private plane. She owes Emma a favor—I have no idea what—but she's come in handy when needing to fly out at a moment's notice.

It takes a couple of minutes to triangulate the place where it would be most convenient for her to pick me up, and we get the plans in place. She already knows the payment information for the bank account Emma set up for these types of expenses using the money unexpectedly left to her by Greg Bailey. Xavier has added to it, resulting in a single fund we can use for work travel and other needs. I argued with Emma when she first told me about it, insisting I was fine paying for things on my own, but she pushed right back. The vast majority of her expenses when she is on a case are covered by the Bureau, and the windfall from the loss of her former boyfriend was a complete shock. Both because she never thought he would leave anything to her after the way their relationship ended, and the sheer amount he left her. Emma donated a considerable amount of it to the community center project in Sherwood, and she wanted more of it to do as much good as possible. Making it easier to handle our investigations fits that requirement.

Xavier and I are packed and out of the house before Sheridan has gotten back. I leave her a note next to the one she left me and call Emma on the way to let her know what's going on. We make it a habit of keeping each other aware of what we're doing and where we're going when we are involved in a case. Along with the tracking devices Xavier designed for us, keeping the family aware provides another layer of security. It's easier to know when one of us might have gone missing or be facing some sort of danger when we know locations and schedules.

Zara is already waiting with a cheery, flirtatious grin when we get to the airport, and we're in the air not long after. It's a very short flight, and by the time we land, I have a text with Seth's address and an invitation to come over whenever we land. We don't even bother to stop by the hotel. As soon as we are in our rental car, we head for the quiet neighborhood that sits well outside the tourist area but close enough to the beach for there to be sand toys and piles of seashells on virtually every front porch along the well-established streets.

Seth greets us at the door and ushers us inside.

"You got here fast," he says.

"We got a good flight," I tell him.

"Can I get you something to drink?" he asks. "Water? Coffee?"

"Coffee would be great," I say, feeling the effects of all the travel and high adrenaline of the last couple of days.

"Me too," Xavier says.

"Be right back. Make yourself comfortable."

We sit down on the overstuffed blue faux suede couch, and I look around the room. There's little decoration in the space, but a few pictures in mismatched frames fill the surface of the mantle over the fireplace on the far wall. I get up to look at them. There's no caption or context to them, but it looks like the pictures chronicle the lives of a family across many years. Some are formal portraits like from school or a studio, and others are snaps from vacations, holidays, and parties. I examine each of the pictures carefully for faces of girls whose ages might line up with Rose Doe, possibly Sienna Roberts.

"I don't know how you take it, so I brought some milk and sugar."

I turn around and see Seth coming back into the room with three mugs of coffee, a juice glass full of milk, and a rolled-down bag of sugar. This is definitely not a man who puts a lot of stock into the appearances he puts up for people who come by.

"Thank you," I say, taking one of the mugs and carefully tipping milk from the juice glass into the coffee.

"How positive are you that these results were accurate?" Seth asks when he sits down with his own mug.

"Positive," I say. "The DNA run through the system was taken from the body when it was found. It connected directly to Paula."

He nods, taking a breath and then a dip gulp of his coffee. "When I was ten my parents adopted a three-year-old little girl. They told me they'd always wanted three children, but after having my older sister Lucy and then me, they weren't ever able to have another. So they adopted Sienna."

I shake my head. "Wait. Adopted? That doesn't make any sense. The DNA connected directly to Paula. She said you are her cousin on her mother's side. Is that not right?"

"It is," Seth says. "Have you heard all the complaints people have about those websites? They are really great for connecting distant family members and helping trace their lineage. But they also bring out a lot of family secrets. Things people never wanted anyone else to know. Turns out my family has some of those secrets."

"Just let him tell you his story," Xavier says.

"I'm sorry. Go ahead," I say.

"Everybody was really happy when Sienna was adopted. At least, at first. It seemed like our parents were right, and she was supposed to be there all along. We all babied her, and for a couple of years, we really did have a happy family. We were one of those families that did everything together and never got sick of each other," Seth says.

"An orange juice family," Xavier says with a tone of absolute confidence like anyone who heard it would instantly understand his meaning.

"A what?" Seth says.

"An orange juice family," Xavier repeats.

"Like the people in an orange juice commercial," I interpret for him. "The ones that look really happy when they're just sitting around the breakfast table together drinking orange juice and then they go out and do some sort of outdoor activity together in slow motion still smiling a lot."

This is a comparison I have heard before.

"Oh," Seth says. He thinks over it for a second, then nods. "Yeah, that's pretty much it. Then Sienna got really sick. We really thought she was going to die. She needed a lot of treatment, including emergency surgery. When that happened, my parents were forced to tell us the truth. Sienna was adopted, but it wasn't as simple as a typical adoption process.

"Looking back on it after everything came out, I realized I'd never heard them talk about the possibility of adopting. They'd never said anything about filling out any paperwork or meeting with anyone. There were never any home visits. But none of that was anything I'd think of as a ten-year-old kid. I didn't know the legal process of adopting. If you'd asked me back then, I probably would have said there was just a field of babies and little kids somewhere and parents got to go pick one out like when you pick a pumpkin. I didn't know. It just wasn't something I'd ever thought about. I didn't know anybody who was adopted or who had adopted siblings or anything.

"I don't know the entire story. I don't know everything that happened after we found out Sienna was sick and that she was going to need a lot of care. So I'm not sure exactly why everything unfolded the way it did. All I know is, we found out, and then there was a lot of tension and anxiety in the house for a few days. Then my parents sat me down and told me the truth about my little sister.

"They explained to me Sienna was Lucy's daughter. She was born when my older sister was only fourteen. It would have been a major source of shame for the entire family, and my father was convinced he would lose his job because he worked for an extremely conservative company. That sounds crazy now, but it was a lot different then. Companies had a lot more space to just send you out on your ass if you did something they didn't like, and my dad was positive that would have happened to him if anybody found out Lucy got pregnant that young. After they told me, I remembered she'd been homeschooled for a couple of months that school year because my parents said she was sick and couldn't go to school. I didn't really notice anything different about her, but she was in her room almost all the time and wore baggy clothes."

"And she was your sister," I say. "You were just a kid. You wouldn't have thought to notice something like that."

"Exactly. Then all of a sudden she was better for when it was time to go off to summer camp. We'd gone to the same camp together the year before, but that year my parents said we were going to go to different ones because I was seven and she was fourteen, so we needed different things. She was gone all summer and then came back and went right back to normal life. I didn't know she had actually gone and had a baby. My parents arranged for the adoption and originally planned for it to be closed. They weren't even going to find out if the baby was a boy or a girl because they didn't think it was going to do any good.

"But at the last minute, they all changed their minds and decided to do an open adoption. Everything seemed fine, but then before she even turned a year old, both of her adoptive parents were killed in a car accident. She ended up in the foster care system. It took the next two years for my parents and my sister to get her back. But of course, Lucy's parental rights had been severed. She wasn't technically her daughter anymore. So my parents had to adopt her.

"When the truth came out, it was horrible. It was this massive scandal and created a rift in the family. There are relatives I haven't seen since. I didn't really understand how other people could be so mad about it. I knew I was hurt that I didn't know the truth. I didn't like the feeling that they had lied to me. But at the same time, even at that age, I could understand that sometimes, even if we're told to always tell the truth, secrets need to be kept. They told me it would have caused massive damage to the family, so I believed them. And I guess they were right. I thought people should just be happy that Sienna was going to live because she could get the treatments that she needed. And I thought it was kind of fun to find out she was actually a blood relative the whole time.

"Even though I knew from then on that Sienna was my biological niece rather than my sister, it didn't change how I looked at her. I still saw my little sister. She didn't find out until years later. My parents and my sister asked me never to tell her about it because they wanted to be able to tell her in their own time, in their own way. I figured that was their right, and I never said anything. But she found out accidentally when she was going through some paperwork," Seth says.

"How old was she?" I ask.

"About twelve," he says. "She asked me about it, but I had promised my parents I wasn't going to say anything, and I didn't want to break that, so I told her she had to talk to them. There are times when I really regret that. I know I made that promise, but I was her big brother. I was supposed to take care of her, and she was supposed to be able to trust me. Instead, she ended up feeling like I betrayed her.

"She went to our parents to find out what was going on. I think she was hoping she was wrong, like she had read the papers wrong or something. But they told her the truth. She was so angry and upset. She said everybody had lied to her and she was completely humiliated by being the only one who didn't know who she actually was. That was the start of things going badly for her. She was really young, but she started to get into trouble. She wouldn't listen to our parents anymore. She started running away and staying out late, smoking and drinking. She was doing the kinds of things people my age were getting in trouble for, and she was still so much of a kid.

"She cleaned up a bit for a while, then it got worse again. It went through cycles like that. She had a history of disappearing for stretches of time, and nobody would know where she was or what she was doing. Everybody knew she had really bad substance abuse problems, but she never ended up serving any time for it. It would have been so much better if she had. If they had just taken her off the streets and forced her to get clean, I really think everything could have turned out differently."

"They would have been able to ID her more quickly," Xavier offers.

"X," I say under my breath.

"No, it's true," Seth says. "I'd hoped that if she had ended up in jail a couple of times for getting high or robbing people to get money for drugs, then she would have cleaned up, but that might not have happened. And even if it had, she still might have ended up like she did. We don't know what happened, so it might not have mattered either way. But if she had been arrested, her DNA would have been taken, and she would have been identified as soon as she was found. We wouldn't have been waiting for ten years to know what happened to her."

"Can you tell me what happened the last time you saw her?" I ask.

"It was right after one of her worst episodes. She'd gotten herself into a really bad place and called me to come get her. I'd always told her anytime she needed anything, she could trust me to help her in any way I could. It didn't matter to me if I had almost nothing myself, I was going to do whatever I possibly could to help my sister. By this point, Lucy had essentially washed her hands of her, and that had only made the situation worse. My parents were always worried about her, and it was killing them, but she didn't want to call them ever. Partly because she knew how much it hurt them and partly because of how much they'd hurt her.

"I picked her up that night, brought her back to my apartment, got her cleaned up and fed. She was in rough shape. But after a couple of days, she seemed more lucid than I'd seen her in a really long time. It was like no matter how much help we offered her, it didn't really mean anything until she'd smashed into rock bottom herself. Then she was willing to come out of the fog and really talk about what was going on in her life. She told me she had been struggling with her identity and feelings of abandonment. She said she never felt good enough because Lucy hadn't kept her calm and the only reason my parents came back for her was because she was in foster care and being treated badly.

"She told me she was having flashbacks and nightmares that she thought were memories from what she went through between when she was born and when my parents adopted her. She didn't have any real concrete memories of anything that happened in foster care but was really traumatized and would have panic attacks when certain things happened. I know my parents know more about what happened to her during that time than they ever told me, but honestly, I don't want to know. All that ever mattered to me was that she was home with us and she was safe, but during that time, I realized it really wasn't that simple.

"She told me she wanted to get better. That she really wanted to make more of a life for herself and that she was going to make the family proud. She felt really bad for all the stress and heartache she caused all of us, but especially our parents. Even though she struggled a lot with being lied to and not really understanding all the decisions that were made, or who she really was, she also knew my parents didn't have to go back for her. They could have just kept it as a closed adoption and never thought about her again. But they did go back. And she had a far better life than she ever would have without them. She wanted to show them they didn't have to regret bringing her back into the family," Seth tells me.

"How long did she stay with you?" I ask.

"A couple of weeks. Long enough to really clean up and even do a little bit of miscellaneous work at a couple of places to earn some cash. Nothing permanent. There weren't really a lot of options in our town at the time, and I think even if there were, she would have still wanted to leave. She wanted to prove she wasn't depending on us anymore. That she could stand on her own two feet and we didn't have to feel like we were constantly trying to run around waiting to catch her. One morning she told me she was ready to go, and she left. No other preparation than that. That was the last time I saw her. That was about thirteen years ago."

"Did you talk to her at all after that?" I ask.

"Yeah, actually. For a while, she was contacting us pretty regularly. She was traveling around, just trying to find her footing in life. She did a lot of odd jobs and temporary stuff. Just anything she was able to get with her limited experience and having barely finished high school. She started talking about wanting to get into a community college and find a good career.

"We kept telling her if there was any time she needed help or if she just wanted to come back home and keep building on her progress here, she could. That we were proud of her and that there were a lot of things she could do here to help her along. At one point she said she was going to take us up on that. She had looked into doing some online classes and thought it might be good to reconnect and make a new life for herself where she had made all the mistakes before.

"But that never happened. Instead, she told us that she was just feeling scared when she said that, and she was really determined to make it on her own. School was going to have to wait for a little while so she could save up some money, but she had gotten a really good job working for some sort of sales group."

My eyebrow twitches up at that. "What kind of sales group?"

"I don't really know," Seth admits. "She didn't give us a lot of information about it. Just that it was a good job and she was going to save up money before going to school. But she sounded really good. She sounded healthy and happy. Like things were finally going well for her. Or at least far better than we thought things would ever go for her.

"Contact with us slowed down, and we hoped it was just because she was busy and things were still getting better. But then she stopped communicating with us at all. She stopped calling us. She didn't have any kind of social media or anything, so we weren't able to check on her or get in touch. All of us were hanging on to the hope that one day we were just going to pick up the phone and it was going to be her saying she was on her way, or she was going to show up at the door and say she was ready to be home and find out where life was going to take her next. Ten years later, we are still waiting," Seth says.

"Did you file a missing persons report about her?" I ask.

"Yes. After a couple of months of not hearing from her, we contacted the police. Because she had so much history of disappearing, we didn't want to just jump the gun and automatically assume something was wrong. Especially because things were going better for her in her life. She was a full-grown adult and had the absolute right to just live however she wanted to live without checking in with anybody. I know my parents hated it, but they were used to her antics, and I think they were worried if they pushed too hard or caused trouble for her with her new job or any new friends she might have, it would just tip her back over the edge into her addictions and chase her away again.

"It had just been too long, though, by the time we talked to the police. We tried every way we could think of to get in touch with her, but we couldn't. We finally found the sales group she was talking about working for in Virginia, but the head guy of the group denied ever having anything to do with her. He wouldn't talk. He just acted like he couldn't possibly know who came in and out of his company because there were so many people. He wouldn't help us." Seth's voice suddenly sounds emotional. He hung his head and raked his fingers back through his hair.

"I'm sorry you're having to go through this," I say.

"I just want to know what happened to her. It's been so many years, and I have gone over every scenario in my head. There were times when I clung so stupidly to all the hope in the world that she was out living a wonderful life and had just decided it would be better to cut ties so that she wasn't still hanging on to the past.

"Then I would think about that again, and it would make me really angry to think she would just turn her back on us and walk away without ever letting us know she was all right. She knew how much we worried about her, and we had had that whole conversation. I hated the idea that she was just willing to let all of us worry even more and never know where she was or what she was doing, no matter what her justification.

"Then that's how I started to be afraid, because that just didn't sound right. I couldn't see her doing that to us. I couldn't believe that after all the progress she made, everything she said she wanted to do, that she could be so cold and callous toward the family. Even if she had decided she needed to separate from us, even for a little while, she would have said something. If she honestly believed that was what was best for her and the way she was going to achieve the life she really wanted, she would have told us. She wouldn't have just let us hurt, coming out after so many years of damage she had done to the family.

"But I never wanted to think about it that way. Because if I let myself do that, if I let myself feel that fear, I had to admit that something had happened to her. I could easily believe that even with all of her progress, all her work, all her ambition, she could still have gotten herself wrapped back up in her old habits. She had said it herself many times. She was the type of person who believed once you had control over a vice, once you were clean and had your life together, you could occasionally indulge without it being a problem. Someone recovering from severe alcoholism could occasionally have a glass of wine. Someone who quit smoking could light up during a celebration or a particularly difficult time.

"We had all tried to tell her that it doesn't work that way with harder drugs. It doesn't work that way with the other things either, but it is especially dangerous to think that about the kinds of things she was into. We explained once you were an addict, you were always an addict, and just a little bit could very quickly turn into another full-blown binge. Sometimes it seemed like we'd gotten through to her about that and she wasn't going to dabble. Sometimes it was like she was teetering right on the edge and only said she agreed because she wanted to make everybody happy. Or to make us shut up. Both are very possible," he says.

"So you started to worry she got on her feet and celebrated by letting loose a bit," I say. "You thought she might have slipped into her addiction again and gotten into a dangerous situation."

"Yes," he says. "But I made myself stop thinking about that. I told myself she had come so far and was doing so well she wouldn't let that happen again. Even if everything I'd seen suggested otherwise, it felt like if I let myself keep thinking that, I was giving up on her, and that was something I couldn't do. I couldn't let myself even believe that because then I wasn't sending enough good thoughts to her, I wasn't supporting her. Like that would make a difference.

"And as soon as I forced those thoughts out of my mind, other ones came. Plenty of people get hurt or killed when they aren't doing anything wrong at all. They have never touched a glass of alcohol or a drug, and they still end up picked up and murdered. Maybe something else happened to her. After everything she went through, she finally got herself together and still ended up…"

Emotion catches in his throat again, and he stops to look down between his knees again as he sucks in breaths.

Without saying another word, he stands up and walks over to the cabinet where the TV is sitting. He opens a drawer at the front and pulls something out. When he comes back, I see that it's a small stack of pictures. He looks down at them affectionately, sifting through them for a moment, then hands them to me.

"That's Sienna. Paula said you didn't see her face," he says.

"We haven't," I tell him.

I look through the pictures, feeling a tightness in my throat at the sight of the dark-haired girl smiling up at me. My eyes go back to Seth.

"Thank you."

He nods. "Thank you for finding me."

"I want you to know she was never forgotten. I'm sorry the system failed your family and her missing persons report was never connected to the reports of her death, and I'm sorry so little has been done to try to get you answers. But you should know there have been people looking out for her and trying to advocate for her since she was found. My friend Sheridan has a group of friends who researches and discusses crimes, and when they heard about your sister, they were immediately attached. They've spent the last ten years investigating her death, speaking out for her, holding vigils and memorials, trying to get the police to do more, and making sure no one ever forgot her. They even got her a grave and a marker in a cemetery near Sheridan's house so she wouldn't have to be put in a potter's field with just a number. They visit her regularly." I take a breath. "The anniversary of her death was just a few days ago."

Tears finally spill from Seth's eyes, and he takes a second to get a hold of himself. When he has calmed a little, he lifts his head again.

"I need you to tell me what happened. When she was found. Everything." He hesitates, and a slightly confused look flickers across his face. "You said they got her a stone."

"Yes," I say.

"What does it have on it? They didn't know her name or when she was born."

"They put the date she died," I say. "And the name Rose Doe."

Breath catches in Seth's throat. "Rose Doe?"

"Yes. She was wearing a bracelet with ..."

"A rose on it. I know the case. Not the details. Not everything about it. But I've heard of it." He rubs his hands over his face. "Oh my god. I watched news reports about my sister being found dead, and I never knew it."

"You couldn't know," I say. "She was in a different state, and there wasn't enough identifying information for you to reasonably think it was her. You can't blame yourself for that."

"Have you seen her grave?" he asks.

"I have. I went there with Sheridan," I tell him.

"I want to go. I want to see it," he says. "And I want to be able to bring my parents there. We should be allowed to bring her home. She should be here with the family, not out somewhere she barely knew without anyone around who loves her."

"I'll make sure you can do that soon," I tell him. "For right now we need to focus on finding out the truth behind what happened to your sister. First, we'll have to get a formal identification made. We'll need a conclusive DNA match or dental records, something that will prove it really is Sienna so the Rose Doe record can be amended."

"I'll call Lucy. I don't know if she'll cooperate, but I'll try. I'll also call my parents and see if we can get her dental records."

"Great. That will be really helpful," I say.

"Promise me you'll keep me up to date on everything that happens," Seth says.

"I will. And I promise I will do all I can for Sienna and for your family."

CHAPTER EIGHTEEN

Zara has flights scheduled for tonight and tomorrow, so I book the next available commercial flight. It's not until morning, so Xavier and I settle into a hotel for the night. There's so much going on in my head that I don't think I could possibly go to sleep, but I don't even remember turning off the TV after putting my head down on the pillow.

I sleep heavily that night, any dreams I've had completely forgotten by the time my phone alarm wakes me. Xavier and I have just enough time to eat breakfast before getting to the airport, and before noon we're back at Sheridan's house. She's leaning against her kitchen counter stirring a cup of hot tea when we walk in, and as soon as she sees us, she straightens, her eyes widening as she takes a step closer.

"How did it go? I want to know everything," she says, the sentences tumbling out of her mouth as a stream of sound rather than individual words. As soon as she says it, she takes a step back. "I'm sorry. I know you just traveled, and you probably want to take a second."

"Yeah," I say. "It's been kind of a lot these last couple of days."

"Can I make you tea?" she asks.

"Sure," I say. "I'm going to just put this stuff upstairs."

"Xavier?" Sheridan asks as we both head for the steps.

"Hmm?" he asks, turning back to look at her.

"Tea?"

"Is it chamomile?" he asks.

"Yes."

"No, thank you."

He continues on, and I look at her. "He only drinks peppermint hot tea."

Sheridan glances around. "Ummmm… I have some soft peppermint sticks I could put in it."

"I don't think it works that way."

"I could put them in hot chocolate?"

"Yes." I turn away, then turn back, holding up a hand imploringly. "Just don't call them candy canes."

"All right," she says, sounding wary.

"X, peppermint pillows in hot cocoa?" I call up the stairs.

"Sold!" he shouts back.

I flash Sheridan a double thumbs-up before continuing up the stairs. Our drinks are waiting for us when we get back down, along with a plate of cookies and another of cheese and crackers. Sheridan is milling around the kitchen chopping vegetables and seems to be preparing a tray with a bowl of dip in the center.

When she catches sight of us, she shrugs. "Some people stress-eat. I stress-cook. Or stress-prepare, I guess." She takes a bite of the carrot in her hand. "So I can stress-eat." She chews. "Tell me what happened. Who did you go see?"

"A man named Seth Roberts. We don't know everything yet," I tell her. "He told me what he could, but there are some things we still have to find out. But at least for right now, I can tell you her name, and I can show you what she looked like."

Her breath catches. "You have a picture of her?"

I nod and take the pictures Seth gave me out of my pocket. I glance at them again before holding them out to Sheridan.

"This is Sienna Roberts," I tell her.

Sheridan's hand comes up to cover her mouth, and tears glaze her eyes. She stares at the first picture for a long time before moving to the next. For a few quiet minutes, we look at the pictures, each of us aware of the significance of just being able to see what this young woman looked like in life and finally have a name to call her beyond the description given to her in death.

When Sheridan is ready, I tell her about my meeting with Seth and a brief overview of what I found out about Sienna.

"While I was on my way back here, Seth sent me some extra information. He said the name of the group she was apparently working for when she disappeared was Bright Horizons Opportunities. He described it as somewhere between a temp-worker-type group and an underprivileged youth and young adult outreach program. The man he spoke to who said he never had anything to do with her and that she wasn't a part of the group is Art Bellinger," I tell her. "I'm going to call in some favors have some people I know to look into Sienna's life as much as I can, as well as this Bellinger guy and the BHO group. I want to see if I can trace where they overlapped, if they actually did."

"What do you mean if they actually did?" Sheridan asks.

"I know you have a very close attachment to this case, but it's really important from this moment moving forward that you remember you aren't talking about Rose Doe anymore. This isn't a fictional character or some abstract woman you've envisioned in your head for these last ten years. We're talking about Sienna Roberts, a real person with a real life and, unfortunately, a real past. I don't want to hurt you, Sheridan, but you're going to have to start accepting that there are things about her you might not like and might not want to hear.

"One of those things is that she had a checkered history that included a lot of deception, lying, and manipulation. It came from a deep place of hurt and trauma, but it was still there, and her family suffered a considerable amount because of it. She went off on her own to try to prove to her family that she could take care of herself and that she could make something of herself without her parents or her siblings, in any configuration considering their complicated history, helping her along or saving her again. She wanted to make them proud.

"If she went out there and started facing really hard times that forced her into some bad decisions, or she just made those bad decisions on her own for whatever reason, she wouldn't want to admit it. She'd refused their offers of help over and over, saying she could do it herself. And she was probably too embarrassed or too proud, or a bit of both, to come back home and ask for help. Even if they said over and over that they would support her. The history there would have been too much to deal with. She wanted everything to seem perfect, so she told her family it was perfect.

"So with all that in consideration, I also have to follow up on what Art Bellinger said. We have to find out all the details we possibly can and find the truth in them. So I'm going to do as much digging as I can and find out everything about both of them. Hopefully, now that we have her name and where came from originally, we'll have more of a chance of finding the answers we need to the rest of our questions."

Sheridan holds up the pictures. "Can I hang on to these long enough to show the others? I think they would really like to see her face and know her name. I can take a picture of them and send it to Barrett too."

The officer has to go back to work, and it seems Sheridan is missing him more than she wants to admit.

"Absolutely," I say.

"Thank you."

The next day I head for the closest library to research. Simply running Sienna's name through the search engine for her hometown brings up articles and police reports detailing her spiraling behavior. In South Carolina, DNA is automatically taken when someone is arrested for a felony or under charges that could result in a sentence of five years or more. Unfortunately for me, though, Sienna isn't present in any of these databases.

While it seems she spent a good chunk of time waltzing in and out of jails on a multitude of charges, she never crossed the line over into felony territory and was never actually brought to trial. She managed to avoid it all, including having her DNA taken. What she likely saw as a lucky break was actually her slipping through the cracks.

All this hits extremely close to home as I think about my own struggles and the difficulties I faced after my mother's death. Scenes from my life, including a long trail of decisions and actions I never should have made or taken, flash in front of me. The very stark reality that I could easily have faced a fate similar to Sienna's is never far from my thoughts.

The paths I went down weren't far from the ones she walked, and some of mine were arguably worse. I ended up behind bars on several occasions. I'd love to say that straightened me out and made me the man I am today, but that would be a lie. Each stint was like getting picked up and shaken, but rather than rattling me into behaving, it made me angrier. I walked out clean and sober, but agitated and bristled against anything and anyone who thought they knew what was best for me.

Looking back on that time now, I know there were benefits I didn't see at the time because I was too young and too full of bitterness and pain. During those years I didn't process the fact that angry or not, bitter or not, every stretch I served was time I wasn't on the street. It represented negative connections I didn't make. It meant influences I didn't follow and things I likely would have done that I didn't do.

I didn't change because of my time in jail. That came later in the form of a young girl's horrific murder and the terrifying thought that in the midst of one of my unexplainable blackouts, I could have been responsible for it. But those sentences very likely did go a long way in saving me from myself in the long term. In the short term, it made things much worse.

I don't know how things could have changed for Sienna if any of her troubles from the time she was twelve until she left home had actually resulted in a conviction. Maybe, like Seth thinks, it could have saved her. But not necessarily, because it would have stopped her from doing the things she wanted to do. From even the slivers of information I'm able to get from her and the way Seth talks about her, I can tell Sienna was an extremely headstrong woman. If she wanted to do something, she was going to do it. That might have meant wholly and completely ignoring the warnings and consequences.

At the same time, hitting that form of rock bottom might have been just what she needed. It's impossible to know.

The difficult information about Sienna's life occasionally brightens with something about her life before the harsh realities took over. Like the smiling pictures that Seth has given me, images of her enjoying what looks like a normal, happy life strike as a hard contrast to what I see later on. She shows up several times in school yearbooks and in blurry, angled photos on an old, abandoned social media site that hadn't been updated for years before her death.

I feel like I know her better as I shift the focus of my search to Bright Horizons Opportunities. It sounds less generic than Magnolia Enterprises, the fake company Brielle made up to cover the purchase of the house in Maryland, but still not particularly explanatory. When I finally find the most recent, active version of their website, I find out why.

"The job Sienna got was basically a scam," I say.

"How?" Xavier asks.

I sigh and show him the website. "This site is working really hard to make it look like it's a really legitimate opportunity for people who need help getting back on their feet or improving their lives. What it actually boils down to is essentially one of those groups that drop people off in different neighborhoods to go door to door selling magazine subscriptions and newspapers while also soliciting donations to 'help the community and the mission.' All they're doing is trying to bilk people out of money.

"This group takes it to another level. There's a forum page dedicated just to people who spent time with the group and left. Some of them say it started as a great experience. They were making money, being treated well. Art even helped them find places to live and supported them. But it went downhill after they were committed. Rather than just doing magazines and newspapers, this group essentially sells anything they can get their hands on. Random products, meat, services. Whatever they can scrape together to make money, Art makes them do. And if they don't, they don't get money, they can lose their home. They've heard of worse things happening to some people. A couple of people on the forum even talk about Art becoming enraged at times and being really scary. People would come and go, and sometimes they didn't know what happened to the people when they left. They just weren't there anymore."

"Those people who just weren't there anymore, were they ever found again?" Xavier asks.

"Seems like most of them do get back in contact with the people they met in the group. But there were a couple who they never heard from again. Including one named Sienna," I say.

"So she did get a job with that group," Xavier says. "She wasn't lying about it. Art Bellinger was."

"And I want to know why."

I'm actually surprised the contact information listed on the website is accurate. I had a feeling it was more for show, but it must mean Bellinger is actively seeking new employees for the "opportunities" he's promising.

He sounds slick and friendly on the phone, undoubtedly part of his ability to convince so many to follow his schemes, but the instant

I tell him who I am and that I want to talk about Sienna Roberts, his tone changes.

"Are you fucking kidding me?" he explodes. "Excuse my language, but it's been, what, eight years? Nine?"

"Twelve," I provide.

"Twelve. Even better. After all these years, you people want to come back and start bothering me about that girl again? This is ridiculous. I got hounded enough back then, and I don't feel like talking about it now. I said my piece, and that's all any of you are gonna get out of me," he says.

"Actually, it's not that simple. Because you didn't tell the truth back then, and Sienna Roberts was just identified as a murder victim found ten years ago," I say.

"Murder victim?" he asks. "No. Oh no. You're not going to pin some murder on me. I didn't have anything to do with her getting herself killed. I'll admit I lied to the police when they came to talk to me about her, but there's no way you're going to get me to say I had anything to do with her being dead."

"Why did you lie when the police asked if you knew her or if she had ever been employed by your company?" I ask.

"To try to get myself out from under the bullshit of the police constantly hounding me about my business and the people who come to me for help. I told everybody I had nothing to do with her and had never met her because they came to me saying this girl had gone missing and I had no idea what happened to her. I didn't want to be pegged with something I didn't do, so I said I didn't know her. I mean, she ran off. I don't know why. I didn't know where she was or what was going on with her, so I didn't have anything helpful to tell them. That's all. I didn't think I needed to be harassed and accused of something when I didn't do anything. Employees ghost me all the time. This isn't exactly new."

"It isn't?" I ask.

"No. Look, I work with people who aren't exactly employable in other circumstances and not in the best phases of their lives, which means they aren't always the most dependable bunch. They come to me looking for a new start and thinking they're going to have this whole new life, but sometimes their old ones still have a hold of them. As soon as they get a little bit up on their feet and have some money in their pockets—or they see an opportunity for some fast, easy cash—they're off doing what they've done to end up in the dirt in the first place.

"That's not on me. I do what I can to help these people. I go out of my way to try to get them out of the hard times. And that puts me at risk of getting screwed over. That's what happened with Sienna. I really thought she was different. I thought she was going to be someone special, and I was going to be able to really get her somewhere in life. I did everything I could for her, and what I got in return is her stealing a bunch of money from me and running off," Art says.

I make a mental note of that. It's the first time I'm hearing anything about her stealing money. "This was so long ago. I'm sure you have a lot of people pass your way every year. How do you remember her so clearly?" I ask.

"You're right. I do go through a lot of people. And I don't remember all the details about that situation, but what I do remember is because Sienna did stand out so much. Then she dropped me so hard. That girl caused me a lot of grief, you know? You don't easily forget being robbed blind and then having the thief's family come after you with the police blaming you for her being missing.

"I didn't know she was dead. I was mad at her for taking everything and running off on me even after I helped her get on her feet, making sure she had an apartment, her bills got paid, everything. There were a lot of other people in the group who were jealous of her because they thought she was getting a lot of special treatment. But she didn't care. I gave her a good life, and this was how she thanked me."

"Did you look for her after she left?" I ask.

"Of course I did. I wasn't just going to let her get away with it if I could find her. I went all over and dropped by her apartment just to see if she might show up. She was never there, but I was able to at least make some restitution for what she'd taken from me," Art says. "I figured if she really wanted that stuff, she would have taken it with her. And she owed me."

My immediate reaction is to feel like this guy is a solid lead. The way he talks about the people who come to him for help is far from respectful and caring, and it's obvious how much disdain he still carries. Even after telling him Sienna is dead, he seems upset only because I'm coming to him about it rather than the fact that she lost her life.

Even still, I'm not completely convinced. Art seems genuine in his anger, though him describing Sienna stealing money and running off doesn't strike me as completely honest. It doesn't track with what I know about Sienna at the time of her life when she joined the group, especially her efforts to turn her life around. Though it is true that people frequently slip backward in their efforts to get on a new path in life, her pattern was always to resurface after going through a bad patch. The fact that she never did tells me there's something more to that story.

"Do you remember the address of her apartment?" I ask.

"Yeah, but it's been a long time. I don't know what you think you're going to find there," he says.

It's a prickly sentiment I tuck away into the back of my mind.

"That's the fun of my career, Mr. Bellinger, I get to look for things no one else knows about all the time."

I get the address from him and let him know he should be prepared to hear from me again before ending the call. As soon as I'm off the phone, I input the address into a search. Somehow I had envisioned a large city apartment building. Instead, the image that comes up is of a squat, blue building that seems to contain only four units arranged in a row. At the edge of the image is what looks like a white cube of a brick building. I look through another few images until I find one that shows the entire building. Hand-painted black lettering spells out "Office" on the side of the door.

The images of the apartment building, even those meant to advertise it, have a heavy, sad feel. They show a run-down building sagging under the weight of years of neglect. This is the type of building offered to low-income residents by unscrupulous landlords who then barely pay attention to the building or the tenants' needs. They skate by with the absolute minimum, sometimes even not doing that much because they know the desperation in the lives of the people living in their buildings. And according to them, these people should be grateful for whatever they have so it doesn't really matter if they put a lot of effort into maintaining the buildings.

The thought of that makes me angry. I have plenty of my own experience struggling through life and through difficult patches I thought I would never get through. I know what it is to feel like you have slipped down into a pit and are just trying to crawl your way out of it in any way you possibly can. When you're going through a time like that, all you can hope for is that you will look up and see someone standing at the edge reaching down to pull you up. Instead, it's very often that someone is kicking the dirt down on you while they watch you struggle.

I turn the computer screen towards Xavier.

"This is what he considered giving Sienna the good life. This picture was taken ten years ago according to the time stamp. When Bellinger told me about her leaving, he said she ran off about eleven years ago. That means Sienna lived here a year before this picture was taken. I have very strong doubts it went tremendously downhill in one year," I say.

"That also means there's a year unaccounted for," Xavier says.

I look up at him from going through more of the images of the apartment building, morbidly fascinated by the management company's efforts to make the units look even close to appealing.

"What?"

"Seth said Sienna left home to find herself thirteen years ago. Bellinger said she joined his company twelve years ago," he says.

"Remember, Seth said she spent a while traveling around trying different things, having odd jobs. That could have easily taken a year," I say.

"And then she ran off from Art eleven years ago," Xavier points out.

It takes a beat for his point to settle in.

"She was found ten years ago," I say.

He nods. "Which means there is a year unaccounted for. Either he managed to concoct the story of Sienna running off, convince everybody who knew her that she was gone, and keep her hidden away for a year before killing her, or he really didn't have anything to do with it."

"Either is possible," I say. "You know that. We've seen people kept out of sight for years. Owen is managing to prove just how easy it can be to slide undetected through life even now. Art may be telling the truth about her stealing from him and running. Or maybe he's telling the truth about her stealing from him and he retaliated by holding her hostage hidden away somewhere. Or maybe she didn't steal anything at all and that was just his cover story because he did have her captive for those months. I still don't know enough to be sure about anything.

"I want to talk to the property manager for this place. If it's the same person, maybe they remember Sienna and can provide some information. Not that I think it would have been much of a priority for her to leave a forwarding address if she was on the run, but they might remember if she had specific people over frequently or if there was any kind of disruption just before she left. If anything, just remembering her and giving us some sort of window of when she left would be helpful," I say.

The apartment building is close, less than an hour away from where Sienna's body was found. Rather than bothering to call up to the office, I decide to just drive over to the building and see if I can get a hold of the property manager.

Other than a coat of paint that is already weathered but deepened the shade of blue on the walls, the apartment building looks largely untouched since the picture from so long ago. It's like the whole place was locked in time from that moment. There isn't a specific driveway or paved parking area. Instead, some of the small yard surrounding the building appears to have had the grass removed and a sprinkling of gravel laid down at some point.

For the most part, it just looks bare, almost like it was just worn down that way by years of vehicles driving in and out. Seems to be a pretty apt metaphor for the place.

I park close to the white office building that looks even more like a cinder block shed now that we're standing in front of it. The door to one of the four apartments opens, and a man's face pops out for a brief second. He looks at me, then disappears back behind his door. A second later, I notice two slates of broken blinds hanging from the single window associated with that apartment on the front of the building part as he peers between them at us.

Xavier and I walk up to the door of the office, and I knock.

"It's open," a gruff voice says from inside.

I open the door and step in. The tight dimensions of the interior of the building are further exacerbated by the cluster of mismatched, oversized furniture stuffed into it. A desk takes up one half of the space while the other has a love seat, two chairs, and a table. The furniture is ratty and a little scuffed, but at least it seems clean from where I'm standing. I'm assuming the door at the far end of the building leads to a bathroom.

There's a strong smell of apple pumpkin, and I have a feeling this man's wife is a fan of seasonal candles. My eyes sweep the room and very quickly fall on the jar burning away on a tiny table I've barely noticed tucked between the two chairs. The man sitting behind the desk snorts a little, and when I look back at him, I see the smile on his face and realize the sound is a laugh. He gestures at the candle with his pen.

"My wife just can't get enough of those things. Every couple of weeks, it's a different smell, and she says they're all lined up with holidays and stuff. They're all over the house. Now she has them in here. I guess I'm just destined to always know exactly what the month is supposed to smell like," he says.

"I hope you make sure to blow it out anytime you're not going to be in here," Xavier says. "Last thing you want is for this place to go up in flames in the name of seasonal sensory stimulation."

I don't ever presume to know exactly what's happening inside Xavier's brain, but at this moment I am fairly certain we're sharing the same thought. If the candle did somehow spark a fire, everything in it would go up like a tinderbox, but the structure itself would just go right on standing.

"Don't worry, I am very conscientious about putting it out," the man says. He stands up and finally extends his hand. "Danny Caldwell."

He's closest to Xavier and seems to be expecting Xavier to take his hand, but the chances of that are right about the same as the chances that Sienna Roberts's apartment has been left fully intact since the day she disappeared and I'll be able to dig through it. Instead, I take a slight step closer and take his hand.

"Dean Steele," I tell him. "That's Xavier."

"Good to meet you. What can I do for you?" Danny suddenly puts both hands up in front of him like he's surrendering and lowers himself back into his chair. "Now, I'll tell you right up front I don't have any available units here right now. In fact, all of my properties are full for the time being. I have a feeling there are going to be a couple of openings really soon though, if you want to look around and get on a waiting list."

I shake my head. "No, thanks, but that's not actually why we came here."

"Oh," he says. "Well, what can I do for you?" he asks.

Danny Caldwell is coming across as surprisingly friendly and helpful, which is far from what I expected. I'm having a hard time reconciling the condition of the property with this man being the one running it.

"I'm a private investigator. I'm looking into the disappearance and murder of a woman who used to live here," I say.

Danny looks shocked by the revelation. "A murder victim? Who?"

"She lived here a good while ago. How long have you been property manager for this building?" I ask.

"A long, long time," he says. "I'm not just the property manager. I'm the landlord. I own this property. I bought it about twenty years ago when it was already distressed and have been workin' my tail off to keep it from just crumbling into dust since."

"It doesn't look like it's in great condition," I say.

"It is what it is," he says. "Maintaining an apartment building, even if it is only four units, is a major risk. You have to be responsible for anything and everything. I've been called because there was a bug in a woman's kitchen in another building I own, and she felt it was my job to come out and get it for her. A single bug. The point is, being responsible for it means spending a lot of money to deal with things like broken appliances, leaks, infestations. It's expensive, and very frequently, it feels like the moment one thing gets fixed, something else falls apart immediately."

I want there to be something else attached to that, but there isn't. I decide the best thing to do is to just move on with the conversation while I can still cling to some shred of respect for the man.

"So you owned the property eleven years ago?" I ask.

"Yeah," he says. "Who are we talking about?"

"Her name was Sienna Roberts. Early twenties. Dark hair."

"I remember her," Caldwell says without hesitation. "She lived in apartment C." He shakes his head. "She's dead? Shit. Oh sorry. Excuse my language."

"It's fine," I say. "I generally believe anytime a person is murdered, especially as brutally as she was, it's worth a bit of profanity."

He nods, his eyes slightly widened as he seems to think back through the years to when Sienna lived here. He suddenly looks directly at me. "I don't understand though. Like you said, she lived here eleven years ago. Why are you coming to talk to me about her murder?"

"I'm working it as a cold case. She was found dead ten years ago," I tell him. "We only recently identified her body."

"I didn't know. I had no idea she was dead." He sounds almost panicked, and I hold up a hand to stop him.

"We don't think you had anything to do with her death. I'm only here because I'm trying to track her movements before she was found. Do you remember when she went missing?"

"Yeah, I do. I mean, it's not like she's the first one to just kind of disappear on me. People ducking out of this place isn't all that unheard of. But I didn't really expect it from that one. And I'd been keeping an eye on her for a bit. I was worried about her."

"Why is that?" I ask.

"When she first moved here, she was bubbly and friendly. She just seemed really excited to have her own place and be kind of settled. The guy who came with her to sign her lease explained he was helping her get her life back on track, and I could see she was really trying to make it. Anytime I saw her, she would smile and wave. She wasn't around very much, and I wouldn't say she was particularly social with her neighbors, but there was always a smile on her face, and she would chat with them if they happened to be outside at the same time.

"But then that changed. She got quieter and more withdrawn. It got to the point where she wouldn't even look my way. Walked kind of hunched over, you know. Like she was trying to close her shoulders in on herself. She just didn't seem like her. Then she was gone. I thought she had just decided it was time to move on. Maybe something else was going on with that guy trying to help her and she got herself in a tight spot. I really didn't know. But it's not my business to pry into people's lives," he says.

"Is that why you never called the police?" I ask.

"I didn't think that was necessary. I didn't see anything that I would describe as a crime. It's not like she ever showed up back here all beaten up. She never asked for my help. And when she disappeared, it looked like she just walked out of her apartment. There wasn't stuff broken all over the place or blood everywhere. Like I said, it's not unheard of for people living in places like this to just up and leave in the middle of the night. That's what I figured was going on."

"What did you do with what was left in her apartment?" I ask.

"According to the law, I have to follow certain rules when personal belongings are left behind after somebody abandons the apartment. I'd like to just shovel it all out into the trash, but I'm not allowed to do that. I have to give them until either the end of their lease if it's the last month or when they've missed enough rent payments to be evicted. I have to try to contact them to come get everything. Then when all else fails, I have to pack it all up and keep it stored for a set period of time before I can toss it. Fortunately, the guy who secured the apartment for her came by a couple of days after the last time I saw her and took a bunch of stuff out," Danny says.

"Why would you allow that? Those things belonged to Sienna, not him. If you're held to laws regarding how you manage personal property, wouldn't you have to make sure you released that property only to the tenant or to a next of kin?" I ask.

"Most of the time, yes. But since he signed on the apartment too, he had rights to it. And he was around all the time, so I figured I couldn't really argue with it. Besides, it saved me hauling all that stuff to storage and then to the dumpster when she inevitably didn't come back. For all I know, everything he took belonged to him or he had bought it for her, so I couldn't really argue with him. Besides, when he came to get it, he was pissed. He stomped in that place like he was on some kind of mission, and I wasn't about to get in his way. I'm not risking getting into it with someone that angry over a couple of armfuls of stuff out of an apartment," he says.

"I guess I can understand that," I say. "When you were packing up everything he left behind to put in storage, was there anything in there that stood out to you? Something that seemed strange or out of place?"

"Not that comes to mind right off the bat. It was all basic stuff, if I remember correctly."

"How long did you keep everything before you threw it away?"

"Actually, now that I'm thinking about it, I don't know if I ever did. That guy stripped that place pretty bare, not that there was a ton in there to begin with. I was able to put everything left in I think two boxes. I don't remember getting rid of them. It was a long time ago, so I might have just forgotten, but there's a chance it's still in the storage space," he says.

"Where's that?" I ask.

"Under the building. Want to go take a look?"

CHAPTER NINETEEN

Sienna

Eleven years ago

COLD RAIN RUNNING DOWN MY BACK WAS ENOUGH TO CHILL me down to the bones. I woke up this morning hoping for sun. Last night was the last I could pay for in the motel I'd been staying in for the last couple of weeks, and I knew if some sort of miracle didn't come my way, I'd be bunking out on a bench or under a tree somewhere until I found a way to get another room.

It wouldn't be the first time. I was very familiar with setting up a makeshift camp wherever I needed to. When your entire existence was focused on chasing that next thrill, that next high, that next thing to fill the void and ease the pain, things like having a solid place to live didn't seem nearly as important. Not until you woke up to pelting rain and the little TV sitting on an old dresser told you it was going to be just a few degrees above freezing for the next couple of nights.

I wasn't even living that life anymore. It had been a long time since I gave in to the cravings and impulses that had controlled me for so long. I barely even felt them anymore. Sometimes when I was feeling particularly low or, on the other hand, especially good, it was still my instinct to reach for something to either soothe me or to celebrate. But that was just compulsion. Habit. I didn't want it anymore. I hadn't in a year. When my brother snatched me back from the edge of finally dying because of my stupidity, I decided right then I was done with it. I wasn't going to do it anymore.

For once I was going to live my life rather than trying to drown it out.

That meant trying to make it on my own. He offered to help me. Everybody did. But that wasn't what I wanted. They'd been dragging me back up to my feet for years, and I didn't want to see that in their eyes when they looked at me anymore. That look that said they were glad I was still breathing but were just waiting for the next thing I was going to do to humiliate them and spit on everything they'd done for me.

I wasn't going to do that again. I was going to leave everything I knew, all the temptations and bad influences, and actually make something of myself. They'd be proud of me.

And I ended up here.

It had been a year since I walked out of my brother's house and promised I would be all right. He always sounded relieved when I called him to check in and let him know what I was up to. Every few days, maybe once a week or so, I'd let him know where I'd found myself and what I was doing. I told him all the good things, and for months it was almost all good. I didn't get right off to a running start or anything, but I did what I could. I moved around, took odd jobs, found people who were moving around like me, and teamed up with them for a while.

But I'd hit a stumbling block. Everyone I'd hooked up with along the way had dissipated. I couldn't find enough work to keep me going. I'd already made the decision that I wanted to go to school and try to make something of myself that way, but I couldn't ask my brother or my parents to get me back home. I hadn't told them I was struggling, and I wasn't going to. I didn't want them to think I was saying I wanted to enroll as a ploy to get them to pay for me to get back and put me up without just saying I needed them to do that. I wanted them to know I really had gotten to that place in my mind and was ready for the new start.

And then the rain came.

I had a few crumpled-up bills in my pocket I was hanging on to for food when I couldn't take it anymore, but it wasn't enough to pay for a place to stay. I needed work fast. Something that would pay me daily. Ahead of me through the driving rain, I saw what I was aiming for. The glow of the diner's neon sign was like a beacon. One of their fliers was in a worn binder full of local businesses in the hotel room. I'd never been a waitress, but I figured it couldn't be that hard. And they got tips, so I might be able to scrape together enough for a room after a day or two.

Until then it was going to be back to my old ways of birdbaths in public restrooms and trying to find nooks and crannies where I could be warm and safe during the night. Out in the open might work for summer or mild weather, but when it was cold and wet, I was going to be relying on alternating between sleeping in doorways and dipping into twenty-four-hour businesses to thaw during the night. Maybe I'd save my cash to use on the bus and just sleep while I rode around.

But that would only be for that night, I told myself. Maybe the next. I was going to go into the diner and get a job, and it was going to get me through. Soon I'd be able to tell my family I was on my way home.

I walked into the diner and took a second to try to smooth my hair and shake off some of the raindrops clinging to me. There wasn't a lot I could do to salvage my appearance after walking half a mile in the pouring rain, but I wanted to look as presentable as possible.

There weren't many people inside at that time. I'd lingered in the hotel room as long as I possibly could, knowing I was going to have to leave, and in that time I was soaking up the warmth of the heater and taking down as many cups of coffee from the in-room maker as I could to at least give me something to go on; the breakfast rush had passed. It seemed like lunch should be starting soon, but right then it was a lull. A small group of people sat at one booth toward the back. Another handful were scattered individually down the counter, reading and drinking coffee or staring into their plates like the food was going to tell them all the mysteries of the universe.

Clanging sounds and loud voices came from the open kitchen along with warm, greasy, salty smells that made my stomach rumble. The doors swung open, and a woman with a white apron with her hair tied in a massive bun on the back of her head swept out carrying three plates and a carafe of coffee. Watching her move effortlessly out from behind the counter and to the booth where she set the plates down without a hitch before refilling coffee mugs and giving a friendly parting smile told me I might be underestimating the challenges of working here.

But I could do it. She had me by several decades, all of which were probably spent right here doing exactly what I'd just watched her do. She was going to have more skill than me. I didn't need to be the sweetheart of the diner or sling plates at the speed of light. I just needed to make enough to get through a few weeks.

She went back behind the counter and turned to me, taking a pad and pencil out of the pocket of her apron.

"What can I get for you, honey?" she asked.

"I'm not ordering anything," I said. "I actually came in to see if you're hiring. I'm looking for a job." I tried to sound confident and hopeful rather than desperate, but I wasn't sure I was pulling it off.

She gave me a sympathetic little smile. "Sorry. We're all full. This time of year everybody's looking for a job."

Without another word, she stuffed the pad back in her pocket and headed into the back again. A second later the door opened, and another woman in the same uniform as the first came in quickly followed by another. As if their appearance heralded the beginning of the lunch rush, several cars pulled up, and the booths started filling. I knew I should leave, try to find the next place to ask, but the waitresses who just arrived had come in shaking even harder rain off their umbrellas and the meager light that had been outside when I walked to the diner was gone. I couldn't bear the thought of walking out into that quite yet.

I slid into the nearest stool and let out a long breath. The waitress came back out of the kitchen and eyed me.

"Did you decide to order something?" she asked.

"No," I told her.

"Sorry, hon, but people are starting to fill up this place. If you're not going to order, you're going to need to free up a seat," she said.

I started to get down, my heart heavy, when I heard a voice from off to one side.

"No, she is going to order."

I looked over and saw a man smiling at me. He'd been sitting along at the end of the counter flipping through his phone and eating breakfast from the time I walked in. Now his plate was nearly empty, and he was sliding a menu toward me.

"No, I…" I shook my head. "I can't."

"Of course you can," he said. "And Lucy here will put it right on my ticket. Won't you, Lucy?"

My heart clenched painfully in my chest at the mention of the name. *Lucy*. I hadn't heard that name in a long time outside of my own mind. My family tended not to say it around me. *Lucy*. My older sister. My mother. The woman who turned her back on me and pushed me aside even when it was what she did that made me the way I was.

"I guess if there's something she wants, I can do that," the waitress said.

"How 'bout it?" he asked. "Can I buy you breakfast?"

I wanted to turn him down. This was exactly the kind of thing you learned to be wary of really quickly when you navigated life on the fringes. Time on the street can make you tough and unreachable, but it also makes you vulnerable. You want to hang on to anything that's offered out to you because you might not see it again, but you learn not to trust anyone who seems like they are being nice for no reason. My instincts told me to thank him and leave. I had no idea who this guy was, and he looked to be at least ten years older than me.

But he was looking me right in the eye when he offered. And he knew the waitress's name, which meant he came in here a lot. She didn't seem to have any hesitation about him. My stomach rumbled again. I'd been trying to conserve my money for days and was barely eating. The smell of the kitchen was too much. I finally nodded.

"Good. Look over the menu, and pick whatever you want. Seriously. Whatever you want." He leaned toward me and lowered his voice, like he was sharing some kind of important secret. "I highly recommend the lumberjack platter. It's my favorite." He gestured over his mostly empty plate. "As you can see."

He went back to eating and scrolling through his phone as I scanned the menu. What I wanted was to order one of just about everything. What I settled on was his recommendation: a massive meal consisting of eggs, pancakes, sausage, bacon, biscuits and gravy, toast, and fruit with a cup of coffee and a glass of orange juice. It sounded like more food than I'd had in a week. It sounded like heaven.

After taking the menu from me, Lucy headed for the kitchen, and I got up to walk over to the man.

"Thank you," I said. "You really didn't have to do that."

He looked up at me and smiled. "I know I didn't have to. That's why I did it. Where's the fun in doing something for somebody when you have to? I'd much rather do things I want to."

He smiled a little wider, and the infectious grin made the corners of my mouth twitch up just a bit.

"I really do appreciate it."

"Well, you're welcome. It looked like you were having kind of a hard morning, and my mama always told me that the best way to have a good morning is with a good breakfast. And I figure you should always listen to Mama," he said.

"Good words to live by," I say, wishing in a raw place deep inside me that I'd followed that bit of advice a long time ago.

Behind us, the group that had been sitting in the booth slid out of the way.

"Come on," the man said, grabbing up his plate and mug and rushing over to the table.

Another waitress was still cleaning it off as we slid in on either side. I could hear people standing at the door grumbling about us snatching away the table when we'd already had seats at the counter, but the man didn't seem to notice. Or maybe he just didn't care.

"You're going to start a riot in here, Art," Lucy said, coming up to the table with my coffee and juice. "People are serious about their lunch breaks."

"And they will get done faster if they're sitting at the counter. Really, I'm doing them a service."

Lucy scoffed and headed back toward the kitchen, looking over her shoulder to talk to me as she went. "I'll be back with your food in just a couple of minutes."

"I hope you don't mind me mentioning it, but I couldn't help but overhear you a few minutes ago. You're looking for a job?"

The juice went down cold and sharp, and I suddenly felt a little more awake.

"Yeah. I've kind of found myself in a bit of a rough spot and was looking for something to get me over the hump. But it seems like everybody had the same idea as me."

"Well, maybe that's a good thing," he said.

"I really doubt it. Not being able to pay for another night in a hotel and trying to figure out how many meals I can make out of a vending machine it doesn't really feel like a good thing," I said.

I didn't know why I was telling him that. I wasn't usually one to open up so easily. And definitely not so quickly. But there was something about him that made me feel at ease. He carried himself without any pretension. There was no judgment in the way he looked at me. He sat perfectly comfortably on the other side of the table, looking at me like he was actually listening to what I was saying.

"No, I can agree with you there. That definitely doesn't sound like a good thing. But perhaps not becoming a waitress here is. It just so happens, I own a company," he said.

"You do?" I asked.

"Yes." He reached into his pocket and pulled out a business card, handing it across the table to me. "Bright Horizons Opportunities. We're growing fast, and I'm always looking for new employees who are willing to work hard, but for amazing returns. I went through some pretty difficult times myself when I was younger, and since then I have made it a commitment to try to help people find their way back. If you're interested, I'd love to tell you about it."

My heart swelled and I nodded. "Absolutely," I said.

"Good," he said with a grin, reaching his hand across the table toward me. "I'm Art Bellinger."

My food arrived, and I waited until the plates were all arranged in front of me before taking his hand.

"It's nice to meet you. I'm Sienna."

CHAPTER TWENTY

Now

DANNY OPENS THE TOP DRAWER IN THE DESK AND GRABS A SET of keys hanging from a black lanyard. He walks around the desk toward the door but stops when Xavier clears his throat loudly. We look over and see him tilting his head toward the candle, his eyes snapping back and forth between Danny and the flame.

"Ah. Yes," Danny says, walking over and setting the glass lid on the jar to snuff the flame.

Xavier stands still, watching the orange flicker die down until it is fully extinguished, before following us out of the building. Danny locks the door to the office building and then leads us across the grassy space to the back of the building. The man is no longer peeking through his blinds, and I wonder how long he stood there watching before he decided it was enough.

The grassy area behind the building shows a few more signs of life than the front. Some toys are scattered around, and a couple of old grills sit on smooth cement slabs behind each of the four doors. Positioned in the center with a set of two doors to either side is a gap and a set of concrete steps leading down. We get to the bottom where bare bulbs beside each of the two doors provide some hazy illumination.

Danny turns to one of the doors and pushes a key in the lock, shaking it to try to get it to turn. He bounces his head back toward the other door.

"That's the laundry. There's a little bit of storage area down there for each of them too. But they don't tend to keep much down there. Some Christmas decorations and stuff sometimes, but nothing significant. I keep everything I need stored over on this side."

The lock finally gives way, and he opens the door. The familiar dank smell of a basement rolls out at me. Even when Danny hits a light switch just inside the door, the space remains shadowy.

"Absolutely not," Xavier says. He retreats back from the door and up several of the steps.

"It's fine down here," Danny says. "Nobody else has a key. The exterminator comes every other month."

"Nope. I'll stand guard out here."

"X, what are you guarding against?" I ask.

"I don't know, but whatever it is, like me, won't get in there," he says.

I shrug toward Danny, and we go inside. It definitely isn't a pleasant feeling down here, but not much different than most of the unfinished basement areas I've been in. There's just something about a subterranean room comprised mostly of cinder block, cement, and dirt that isn't enjoyable no matter what is down there or why you've ventured to find it.

"Should be over here somewhere if I still have it," Danny says, heading toward the far back corner of the space. "Since I use this front space for my lawn stuff, tools, and things, I got to keeping the stuff that belonged to tenants who abandoned their apartments way back in the corner here."

We walk past wooden shelves of tools, paint cans, gardening implements, and various odds and ends. There are a couple of bikes propped against one wall and a few electronics that look like Danny may be skimming off the top of the abandoned property the way Art Bellinger did rather than just disposing of it all at the end of the mandated storage period. By the time these items come to Danny Caldwell though, that is within his rights. He is allowed to try to make up for lost rental payments by liquidating the property after it goes unclaimed. Bellinger was just scavenging for scraps.

The back corner of the room has a few stacks of boxes, and Caldwell sifts through them.

"You all right down there, Dean?" Xavier calls from his post outside the door.

"Yep," I call back. "You all right?"

"I'm fine."

Caldwell glances at me. "He always like that?"

"He's gotten better, actually," I say without any further explanation.

He sets aside a box and grabs another. Turning it so he can read what's written on it in black lettering, he turns and hands it to me.

"Here you go. There's this one and…" He leans down to pick up another, smaller box. "This one."

"That's it?" I ask.

"Yep. Like I said, she didn't really have much to begin with, and there was even less when that guy finished with it," Caldwell says.

"Thanks. I appreciate your help," I say.

"Sure. I'm sorry I can't tell you any more than that. But if you think of any other questions or anything, you can give me a call," he says.

"I will."

We get to the door, and I see Xavier standing right where we've left him. I hand him one of the boxes.

"Done?" he asks.

"Yep. How did it go? Did you have to ward off any potential intruders?"

"There was a wasp that was a little touch and go for a second, but I sent him on his way," Xavier says with a determined nod. He raises a stiff hand like he karate chopped the insect away. Knowing him, he probably did.

"Well done. Ready to go?"

Even though we aren't far from Sheridan's house, I decide to get a hotel for another couple of days so I can be close to the area to further my investigation. As soon as we're checked in, I bring the boxes up to the room and start going through them. I don't have a tremendous amount of hope for what I'm going to find inside, and it seems my assumptions are completely accurate. There's little in the boxes except for some clothing, a couple of random little knickknacks, and some old pictures. I set the pictures aside so I can bring them to Seth. I can't imagine he would be terribly interested in having her old clothes and a stack of junk mail, but I'll offer it to him just in case.

I do find a copy of her lease with Sienna's signature alongside Art Bellinger's. At the bottom of the box, I find a note. There are several pieces of paper with handwriting on them that matches the predominant handwriting on the lease and looks like it corresponds with Sienna's signature, making me assume that is her handwriting. This note, however, doesn't look like hers or Bellinger's.

"'*The rain wont' last forever. Sometimes you have to be your own sunshine*,'" I read.

I show the note to Xavier, who takes it and examines it.

"A bit trite. A little saccharine. But motivational," he says. "If grammatically incorrect."

"Why?"

He shows it to me, pointing out the placement of the apostrophe. "It's transposed. It shouldn't be after the *t*."

"Maybe it's just the handwriting," I say.

"You are a kind and generous person, Dean," he says.

He hands the note back to me and goes to the bed at the far side of the room. Hopping onto it, he grabs the remote and starts flipping through channels. I go through everything that's in the boxes again, hoping there is something I've missed or something that has additional meaning that didn't stand out to me at first but will suddenly click. There's nothing.

I put everything back in the boxes, making sure the pictures are on top so they are easily accessible, and set them aside. Sitting on my own bed, I take out my computer and run another search. I still feel like something has to be going on with Bright Horizons Opportunities and Art Bellinger. The whole thing just feels so shady, and he was extremely jumpy and defensive throughout the entire conversation. It's been a long time, I understand, and I'm sure it's a shock for Sienna to be brought up after all these years, but it struck me as very strange that he would be so anxious talking about her.

Up until now, I've only used fairly conventional search tactics to try to find out as much information about the company and Art Bellinger as I could. Just basic, straightforward online searches anyone could do. Now I need to go deeper than that.

My more aggressive search reveals another layer of the people who have spoken about their time with the company in terms that are no less than frightening. On these hidden forums, people share horror stories of the abuse they've encountered at the hands of Bellinger when they didn't do as he said. Others describe being used for his own personal indulgences or being offered up to others in exchange for more cash. Several describe getting out of the group as 'escaping.'

I find a long discussion about why he has managed to stay out of trouble all this time, why no one has ever gone to the police, or why they've never charged him with anything. The general consensus is that he is manipulative and crafty, able to convince anyone of anything, including the police. Because he hires people who are at the lowest point in their lives and don't have anything else to rely on, he immediately has them trapped. He can leverage their homes, food, and physical safety. And the people working for him know as well as he does that the police aren't going to take the word of people they have likely arrested before. They see criminals, liars, and wastes of space. They don't see humans.

Bellinger knew that then, and he knows it now.

"Hey, X," I say when I find a comment that stops me cold. "Listen to this. An anonymous user in this group asks, *'Whatever happened with that 911 call? Didn't the police talk to him about some girl running away from him?'* And another one answers, *'I bet it was Sienna.'*"

CHAPTER TWENTY-ONE

THE 911 CALL IS CHILLING. A MAN AT A GAS STATION TELLS THE dispatcher he just watched a half-naked girl scramble out of a van and run across the parking lot, looking terrified. He says she looks like she has blood on her. At the end of the call, he sounds almost frantic, saying a man has come out of the building and is shouting after her, looking like he is going to follow her, but stops when he realizes people are looking at him.

A post by the owner of the gas station who had been shaken up by the entire incident contains footage from his security cameras from that night. He isn't very vocal in the conversation, but it's clear he is disturbed by nothing coming from the incident. He makes it very clear he is familiar with "Mr. Bellinger," noting he comes into the shop regularly and has always seemed friendly but that there is something just beneath the surface that always makes him feel a bit uneasy.

He posted the security footage to make people aware of what was really going on. I watch it, going back to the beginning and replaying it over and over, trying to catch every detail. It was recorded on security cameras that were already old technology even ten years ago, which resulted in grainy, time-lapsed footage. Rather than just watching what happened in one smooth stream, the camera recorded in bursts every couple of seconds.

Though it isn't very clear, I'm able to see a van pull up to one of the gas pumps. The driver's side door opens, with the angle of the camera not showing the driver's face. A figure walks away from the van, and a few moments later, the passenger door opens, and a young woman tumbles out. It looks like Sienna, barefoot and in seasonally inappropriate, torn clothing, escaping from the car and running, terrified, across the parking lot.

She disappears out of frame, and at the top of the screen, the figure I am assuming is Art Bellinger runs out of the gas station. He pauses next to the van, looking around with emotion that seems somewhere between frantic and infuriated. People approach him from either side, and I see someone clutching a phone to their ear. I'm assuming it's the man who made the call I'd listened to. Less than a minute later, the police arrive, and there are a few moments of them talking to Art before the footage shuts off.

I watch it through a couple of more times before calling him.

"Why didn't you tell me the police were called after someone who looked very much like Sienna Roberts escaped from your van at a gas station?" I ask without any form of greeting when he answers the phone.

Art lets out a heavy sigh, making it very obvious he has no interest in talking to me. About this or about anything else having to do with Sienna.

"I figured if you were any good at your job, you would have found out about the incident yourself," he says. "Besides, it didn't turn into anything. They didn't even bring me to the station. I told them exactly what happened, and they let me go. Just that simple. The guy who made the call even had to apologize to me."

Somehow I very highly doubt that last part is true, but I'm not going to mention it.

"You might not grasp the difference between a private investigator and a detective, but I don't just get handed records like that. I have to search them out. And even if I was in law enforcement, assuming you don't need to mention something like having police contact after a girl who was later reported missing escapes from your van bloody and half-naked makes you look seriously fucking guilty," I say.

"She wasn't bloody," he says. "And she might have not been wearing a ton of clothes, but that was Sienna. She was an adult. She could do what she wanted. And that night she wasn't on duty for work, so she didn't have to dress professionally. If she decided she wanted to wear next to nothing, that was on her. I tried to get her to see that it was going to make people look at her a certain way and that they weren't going to take her seriously, and it might even put her in danger, but it didn't matter to her. I guess it caught up with her though, didn't it?"

"Don't you dare," I say through gritted teeth. "Don't you dare blame her for what happened to her. I don't care what she was doing or what she looked like, there is absolutely nothing that would make her deserve what happened to her."

"You can think what you like."

"And what I think is that you are an arrogant ass who uses girls up and spits them out when he wants to. She ran from your car scared out of her mind, and you watched it happen. What was going on before that to make her do that?" I ask.

"She didn't escape," he says angrily. "She got out of the car and ran because that was the night she stole all my shit. What you're watching in that security footage, since I'm assuming you saw the same footage I did, is her getting out of the car and running away. There were no shackles on her. She wasn't chained. She wasn't tied up. She opened a car door and left."

"She fell out," I say.

"So she was clumsy. That's not my fault either."

"Where did she go?" I ask.

"I don't know," he says with a sarcastic rise in his voice. "She probably had somebody waiting for her somewhere and they picked her up. What matters is, I talked to the police that night, and they didn't see anything worth arresting me for."

"Did you let them search your car?" I ask.

"Why would anyone let an officer search their car?" he asks coldly. "They already think way too much of themselves. I wasn't the one who did anything wrong that night, so I wasn't going to let them dig around in my personal space just because they wanted to."

"It wasn't because they wanted to. It was because somebody reported a terrified girl running away from the van. Did you tell them her name?" I ask.

"I told them her name was Sienna," he tells me.

"Why not her last name? If you are so upset about her supposedly stealing from you, why didn't you give the officers her full name and her address so they could try to get everything back?"

"I'm not stupid. I know how things like this work. They weren't going to find her. She wasn't going to go back to her apartment knowing I could find her so easily. And like I've told you before, I work with people who aren't in the best place in their lives. They don't exactly have a lot of trust in the police. If I start having cops around, I'm not going to have any employees. I handle things for myself. And that was what I planned on doing.

"Besides, it was embarrassing to admit that I'd gotten taken by her. She got everything and ran so fast I figured she'd planned it all along and had some accomplice waiting for her. That was why she was running so fast and going right for the road. Think about it, if she was so scared and needed help so much, why didn't she run right to one of the people parked in the lot? Or even go inside? I was in there, but so were the employees," he says.

"How would she have an accomplice waiting for her? How would she know you were going to be at the gas station at that time that night?" I ask.

"Because we went up there to get gas and buy lotto tickets, cigarettes, and beer a few times a week. She would know the schedule."

"You're trying to clean up people's lives, and you're bringing them along with you to buy cigarettes and beer?" I ask.

"My life doesn't need cleaning up," he replies smugly.

"So even when her family and the police came to you and said she was reported missing, you didn't think it might matter enough to admit you knew her? Knowing you had lied to the police about her name? Knowing you hadn't given them the information about where she lived? You just thought it was perfectly fine to keep on lying?" I say.

"They came sniffing around months after that night. It wasn't like it was immediate. She was perfectly fine that night. Whatever happened to her after that wasn't my fault, and I didn't want anything to do with it," he says.

I can't tolerate another second of talking to him, so I end the call.

"Less than helpful?" Xavier asks.

"That's an understatement," I say. "Someone needs to go after him. He's gotten away with this for far too long, and someone else is going to end up like Sienna."

I watch the footage again.

"She isn't carrying anything when she gets out of the car. I guess she could have stolen cash and cards, some jewelry or something else small, and stuffed it in what little pockets she has, but I would think she wouldn't do that while still sitting in the car."

I scan back and click through the footage slowly to watch her run across the lot, hoping to see which direction she's going. She disappears out of frame before she makes a move in either direction, but I do notice something I didn't before.

"Look," I say, pointing at the edge of the screen. "Headlights. She ran out into the road when a car was coming. They pause for a second, then they leave the frame."

"It looks like someone picked her up," Xavier says.

"Which is what Art said he thought happened. Like he had seen it and that was why he made that guess. Only, from where he's standing, he wouldn't have been able to see the road. Is it possible someone picked her up and turned her back over to him?"

CHAPTER TWENTY-TWO

I HAVEN'T GOTTEN ANY FURTHER WITH ART BELLINGER OR BRIGHT Horizon Opportunities the next morning when Sheridan calls. I figure she's checking in to see if I've made any more progress, but she surprises me.

"I just got a call from the family who owns the farm."

"The farm Sienna was found on?" I ask even though I can't think of another farm it could be.

"Yes. Remember I told you the two people who were living there at the time she was found didn't actually own the land? Well, I just heard from the people who do. Lyra Richard and Lynn Booth. They're the ones who gave my group permission to come to the land and tend to the grave and everything. We've been in contact a couple of times over the years, just briefly. They pretty much gave us blanket permission as long as we didn't do any damage to the land or start doing any kind of tours or anything," she says.

"Considering her body was found there and then the woman was beaten to death, not to mention that farm is just scary as hell, I can understand why they would make that specification with you," I say.

"So can I. But we convinced them that's not the point of our group or why we would want to be able to go on the land, and they just said we had permission and would leave us alone. They didn't want anything to do with it," she tells me.

"So why did they call?" I ask.

"They want to talk to you."

She gives me Lyra's contact information, and I promise I'll fill her in on everything as soon as I can before getting off the phone. I immediately dial the number and wait through three rings for a woman to answer.

"Hello?"

"Is this Lyra Richard?" I ask.

"Yes," she says.

"Dean Steele. Sheridan Morris told me you want to speak with me about the Rose Doe case."

Now that I know her name, it feels strange to refer to Sienna that way, but I also know that will always be the way her case will be remembered. It's been her name and the only way anyone could refer to her with even the slightest amount of humanity for a decade. I'll say her name as many times as I can, but there will always be people calling her Rose Doe.

"Mr. Steele. Yes. Thank you for getting in touch with me," she says.

"Call me Dean," I say. "What can I do for you?"

"My brother and I heard the girl whose body was found on the property was identified," she says.

"She was," I confirm but don't offer any additional information. Until I know exactly why she and her brother are reaching out to me, I am going to keep the details to a minimum.

"And there is a new focus on the case?" she says.

"Yes. Her disappearance and murder are still unsolved, and I've been asked to look into it," I tell her. "With the new information that's been uncovered and some additional issues that have come up very recently, it's more pressing than ever that we find out what happened to her. But I also feel it is well within my grasp."

"That's good to hear. As you can probably imagine, knowing that something that gruesome happened out on land our family owns has haunted my brother and me for a long time. We weren't kids when it happened, but that's not something you ever shake no matter how old you are," Lyra says.

"I can attest to that," I say.

"We've kept our distance from the whole thing all this time because there was never any progress and we didn't think there was anything for us to offer. But now that she's been identified and there's more of a chance of finding out what happened, we think it's important to be involved. We want to help in any way we can."

The words sound good, but her voice is unsure.

"You sound hesitant about that," I tell her.

"It's not that we're hesitant to help. If there's anything we can do to give a family answers, that's what we want. But you have to understand, there is a lot of anxiety related to that farm. A lot of drama and pain. We don't have anything to do with it anymore and haven't been out there in many years," she says.

"I can appreciate that, but would you be willing to go out there and talk to me about it?" I ask.

She takes a second, and I hear her swallow. "Yes. We can do that."

"Great. Are you busy today? Maybe we could meet out there in a couple of hours?" I ask.

"I'll talk to my brother, but that should be fine. I'll let you know when we have a time," she says.

"That's fine with me. I'll talk to you soon."

I'd intended on staying at the hotel for a couple of days to look around the area and try to find out more about Sienna's time here, but this is a much more pressing chance, so Xavier and I load up the car. We stop by a little diner to grab some breakfast while I wait for Lyra to call back. The booths are full, so we take two available seats at the counter and grab well-used menus from where they're propped between a napkin dispenser and a large glass sugar shaker.

We've only been sitting there a few seconds when a woman steps up in front of us.

"Can I get you some coffee, gentlemen?"

Before we've even answered, she's setting white mugs on the counter.

"Yes, please," we both answer, and she smiles as she tips hot, dark brew into both.

"Do you know what you want for breakfast?" she asks.

"Banana nut pancakes, fried eggs, and bacon," Xavier says. "Do you have sourdough toast?"

"Sure do."

"And some of that," he says.

I don't know how he has managed to lift that off the menu in the short time we were looking at it, but there's also a chance it isn't on it at all. The waitress didn't ask what we wanted to order; she asked what we wanted. Those things are not the same to Xavier. But she also didn't blink when he told her, so either it is an actual option or she is going to work some diner kitchen magic for him.

"How about you, hon?" she asks, turning her attention to me.

I look up at her and see her nametag. Lucy.

"I think I'll have the lumberjack," I say. "It's cold out there, and I'm hungry this morning."

She gives me a warm, friendly smile I'm sure has won the loyalty of countless locals.

"You've got it. How can I get those eggs for you?"

"Fried, please."

She takes up the menus. "I'll get that going."

She walks away, leaving Xavier and me to glance around and take in the atmosphere of the clearly loved restaurant. The food comes quickly, and we have a chance to fill ourselves as much as we can before Lyra sends me a text letting me know they'll be at the farm in an hour and a half. It doesn't give us much time to get there, so we pack up what's left of our food, leave cash for Lucy, and head out.

We manage to pull up into the tire grooves at the front of the property exactly on time, and as we get out of the car, another pulls in behind us. It parks, and the two people inside talk back and forth for a couple of seconds before getting out. A tall woman with cropped sandy hair comes toward me first. She extends her hand to shake mine.

"I'm Lyra."

"Dean," I tell her. "This is Xavier." I glance over my shoulder to indicate him, but he has already walked away. "I think he's with the cats."

She gives a single nod of acknowledgment. "There are a lot of them." A man who looks similar to Lyra comes over. "This is my brother, Lynn."

"Dean Steele," I say, shaking his hand. "It's nice to meet you. Thanks for coming out here and talking to me. Like Lyra shared with me, I'm sure having something this horrific happening on the property you own isn't easy."

"It definitely isn't," Lynn says. "But we think it's important that you understand the whole story. Starting with how we ended up being the ones here talking to you."

"Okay," I say.

"You see, we don't actually own this land. Our mother does. It's been in our family for a very long time. Something like four generations. She didn't have it because she wanted it. In fact, she was never particularly interested in it at all. But after it was passed to our grandmother, her mother, it was left to her. There was a stipulation in our grandmother's will that her much younger sister, Mae, be allowed to live on the land even though ownership would stay with our mother.

"Mom and Aunt Mae had a very tense relationship growing up, and it didn't get any better into adulthood. I can only remember a very small handful of times I actually spent any time even in the same house with her on holidays or anything. My mother ended up taking on the bulk of caring for my grandmother during the last years of her life, and as you can see, Mae didn't do anything to respect or care for this land. Even though Mom didn't want it, it made her really angry too to see how it was being mistreated.

"There was a lot of tension and bad blood between them. It really became a problem when Mom became completely obsessed with a church group she had been spending time with and decided she wanted to sign the land over to them for their use. This erupted into a huge argument. There were a lot of threats. Mae's husband Benjamin made it very clear they had no intention of leaving the land, and we had to call out the sheriff several times.

"There was a lot of difficulty surrounding it because of how the will was worded and the laws about property and ownership in Virginia. It got really nasty and further exploded after Rose Doe was found. My mother immediately blamed Benjamin, saying she knew he had been abusing Mae all this time and that he was so obsessive about making sure that no one came on the land because he was doing awful things on it. I'm sure you already know he was an immediate person of interest, and the police investigated him pretty thoroughly but ended up clearing him," Lynn says bitterly.

"Yes. Sheridan gave me all the background on the case," I tell him. "What happened after he was cleared?"

"Mom was despondent about the whole situation and ended up leaving the state, telling us we needed to deal with the land now," Lyra says. "Just a few months later, Benjamin was arrested for beating Mae to death. The land has been sitting here empty except for the cats and Sheridan's group ever since."

"Why haven't you sold it?" I ask.

"It's too much hassle, honestly," Lynn says. "My mother won't even talk about it, and she would be the one who would have to go through with the process of selling it since she's the one who technically owns it. She wants nothing to do with it. And because of the gravesite, even though the body isn't there anymore, we haven't felt right trying to force her into it. It's like we told Sheridan when she first contacted us. We don't want people to see this place as some sort of haunted trail destination. It's a horrible thing that happened, but this is still private land, and we're not going to allow it, or her, to be a spectacle."

"I respect that," I tell him. "I think there are a lot of people who forget that there are human beings, families, and lives behind murders. It isn't just a story to tell or a morbid place to visit. There's too much of a blur in the line of what is entertainment and what is far too real."

"That's exactly how we felt," Lyra says. "So we just essentially walked away. We pretend this place doesn't exist as much as possible. I don't think either one of us thought about it for a long time before we started hearing about the case again on the news."

"I know you don't want to be thrown right back into the middle of this. And I don't want to cause you any more stress or difficulty. So I really appreciate you being willing to help."

We walk around the farmland, and the siblings give me more details about the complex family relationships that led to what sounds like a horrific several months after a lifetime that was already tense and unpleasant. Ownership of the property was a major source of contention between their mother and their great-aunt and uncle, as well as their cousins, them, and the courts. It became an aggressive battle that only ended when Benjamin was arrested for murder.

They mention the church group their mother was a part of again, saying they didn't know why the property wasn't transferred to them after the arrest, but it never was, and my mind goes to the church right next door to the farm.

"Was the group part of that church?" I ask.

Lyra and Lynn shrug, exchanging glances like they are checking to see if the other has any information about it.

"I don't really know. Mom wouldn't tell us much about it. She was very secretive when it came to the things in her life that were really important. She used to tell us that her marriage to our father was all about being in the public eye because he was a really successful businessman who was very popular around the community. Then the divorce put her under even more scrutiny. Everything she ever did or said was judged and picked over. So when that was all over, we were adults, and she had the chance to really live her life for herself, that was exactly what she did.

"She kept things close and didn't share them with people. It was her way of being able to enjoy it without feeling like she needed to answer for it. So we never got to hear much about it. All she ever really said was how much that group meant to her during all the terrible family conflicts. I was glad she had something that made her feel better," Lynn says.

"How did you feel about her wanting to sign the farm over to them?" I ask.

"It's hard to answer that question," Lyra says. "This property is the only real inheritance we have from past generations. We didn't spend a lot of time out here when we were young or anything, but we always knew about it, and since my mother is an only child and we are her only children, we always knew we were going to inherit it eventually. There were even times when we talked about the kinds of things we wanted to do with it when we did eventually inherit it.

"We honestly never really thought about Benjamin and Mae living on it. That was just a reality that was kind of in the back of our minds. Because she was so much older and, to our understanding, the living agreement was only meant to apply to her, we figured they would be long gone by the time it was our property," Lyra explains. "We thought about starting a Christmas tree farm. Or a pumpkin patch. It was really happy to think about. So in that way, yeah, it was painful to think that our mother just wanted to get rid of it.

"At the same time, those were just dreams of really young people. As we got older, we didn't really have anything to do with the farm, and neither of us was living lives that we could just pick up and move to live out in the middle of nowhere. And the thought that Mom could take this piece of land she never really wanted in the first place and do something that made her so happy made us happy. I just hated to see that become such a source of pain for her."

"But it wasn't that she wanted to sign it over to a church group that bothered you?" I ask.

"No," Lynn says. "Not at all. If she felt like that would be a good use of her property, something she could feel good about, why would I have a problem with it?"

"We didn't feel like the church group was a problem, if that's what you're asking," Lyra interjects. "Not at that time anyway. She was really protective of it, but like we told you, that's how she was. She took tennis lessons for almost two years before we ever knew. That's just the kind of person she was. There were plenty of other things she always shared with us and that we did together, but every now and then, she just wanted something all to herself, and we didn't see anything wrong with that.

"It never seemed like they were controlling her or changing what she believed or anything. It all seemed pretty normal. It wasn't until after everything and we didn't hear from the group, still didn't see them, and Mom decided she needed to move, that we thought there might be something going on. We tried to find out more about the group, but we weren't ever able to trace them."

"How did you try to trace them?" I ask.

"I was at Mom's house once and found some brochures and things that looked like they had to do with the group. I figured I should read about them and see what they were all about since they were so important to her. I hung on to them even after she left."

"Do you still have them?" I ask.

"I should," she says. "I'll look around and see if I can find them."

"How about the church next door? Are you at all familiar with them? Have you ever met anyone from it?"

"As far as I know, it's been empty for a few years. The congregation started making plans to move pretty soon after they found Rose Doe and then Mae's murder. They never came right out and said that was the reason for it, but there were enough calls for prayer and giant signs posted outside asking for donations that were creatively worded to get the point across," she tells me.

"Would you have a problem with me trying to get in touch with them to find out if the group your mother was a part of was associated with them?" I ask.

"Go ahead," Lynn says. "I'd hope if it were, though, that they would have at least come over to talk to us when we were over here or made contact with us when Mom moved."

"It's possible she asked them not to," I suggest.

He nods, the faint look of a hurt, disappointed child briefly crossing his face. This is a man who has told himself he is perfectly fine with his mother's decisions but still hasn't quite come to terms with them.

The siblings leave, and I walk around until I find Xavier. He is pulling weeds out of one of the old planting beds and carrying on a conversation with the horde of cats sprawled around him.

"X," I call over to him. "Come on, buddy. We're going over to the church."

"Is this a formal service? Because I don't think I'm dressed for it."

"We're not going *to* church. We're going to check out the church next door. I want to see if I can find someone to talk to about Lyra and Lynn's mother."

He tosses a handful of weeds over into the trees, brushes his hands on his pants, and comes over to me, high-stepping through tall grass and tangled vines, working hard to take back over the briefly cleared field. Rather than drive the short distance to the church, we decide to walk through the property to see how they connect. The land isn't uniformly shaped. Most of it goes toward the back and in the opposite direction, making the distance between the trailer in the church only a matter of about five acres.

Despite it not being that far, the overgrowth makes the area feel like we are in deep woods impossibly far from anything. We go a short distance in this direction with the siblings, but as we push further, we find even more evidence of the destruction the elder couple wreaked on property I can tell was once beautiful and well-tended. It's heartbreaking to see the abandoned vehicle parts, rusted barrels, and chunks of cinder block and stone scattered throughout the trees. We have to be cautious not to run into any of the abandoned barbed-wire fences still standing where they once corralled animals. At the same time, it's humbling to see the sheer power of nature, forcing its way back through and covering up the scars left by the people.

We walk through an area that dips down slightly with more sparse trees and evidence of lush grass that would fill the space in the warmer months. Another tree line then finally opens out into the cemetery behind the old church. It's eerie walking out into the collection of tombstones, knowing these graves have been left here with the church empty, no congregation to come each week to worship and to acknowledge the lives of these former members. Some faded flower arrangements sitting atop a few of the stones show that at least some of the families haven't fully forgotten their loved ones, but others look as though they haven't been visited in years.

We roam around looking at some of the graves before reaching the building. It's a quintessential country church down to the little front porch and big double doors, which I'm sure have seen countless newlywed couples burst out and pause for a quick kiss before running off into their futures.

A sound inside the church makes me pause.

"And I don't even have my equipment with me," Xavier whispers from behind me.

"It isn't a ghost, Xavier," I tell him.

"Well, I'm never going to know that without my K2 meter and my REM pod, am I?" he asks.

"Yes," I tell him. "You know right now that is not a ghost."

"Do I need to remind you about the campground?" he asks.

No. He definitely doesn't need to remind me about that. I will never forget the horrifying night spent back at Arrow Lake and how close I was to losing Xavier and Emma. But that's not his point, and I know it.

"That was not a ghost, Xavier."

"But wasn't it, Dean?" he asks, his head tilting and his eyebrows going up.

I turn around to face him. "We have talked about this, X…"

Before I can continue, the door at the top of the brick steps opens, making me whip back around. A startled-looking man stops and stares down at us.

"Hello," he finally says. "This building no longer holds an active congregation. But if you need the comfort of the sanctuary, you're more than welcome to come inside."

"No," I start.

"I am," Xavier says, rushing past me and up the steps.

It's an old building. I should have been prepared for this.

"Apparently, he does. But I'm actually here looking for somebody I could talk to about some previous members of the congregation… or possible members of the congregation."

"I suppose I'd be the one to talk to about that. I'm the caretaker around here now that the congregation has moved. I make sure the building is taken care of and the grounds are maintained. But I'm also an elder and have worked with the church office," he says.

"That's amazing," I say. "Can I come in to talk to you? Or would you rather…" I gesture behind me to indicate he could come join me.

"Of course, you can come in," he says with a smile. "The congregation moved, but it's still a church."

"All right. Thank you," I say, following him up the stairs.

He steps back into the building, holding the door open for me to step inside.

"I'm Howard Masters," he says.

"Nice to meet you. Dean Steele," I say.

He gestures for me to walk ahead toward the doors leading into the sanctuary right ahead of me.

"You know, Dean, I almost didn't come out here today. I knew there were a few things I needed to take care of on the grounds, and the church was due for a bit of tidying up I do every month or so, but I had a list of other things I was going to do and decided I was just going to put it off until tomorrow. But something told me I needed to come out here today. I guess now I know why." He smiles, and I can't help but return it.

When we step into the sanctuary, I notice Xavier sitting in the front pew, calmly looking ahead. I'm not sure what he's looking at or what may be going through his mind, but he seems peaceful, so I decide to let him be while I talk to Howard.

"So, Dean, you said you need to find out about some people who might have been members of the church at some point," he says as we sit down.

"Yes. I'm a private investigator, and I'm working on a case that has to do with the adjoining plot of land. The owner no longer lives in the state, but her children oversee the property and met with me to talk about it. They mentioned their mother wanted to transfer ownership of the property to a church group she was involved with a little more than ten years ago. Does any of that sound familiar?" I ask.

He thinks for a second. "I know of the family from that property, but I can't say I know them well. As far as I know, none of them were ever members of the congregation here. And I've been going here since I was born. I know a couple of their family from generations ago are buried out in the cemetery, but that was based on proximity, not on them being members of the church.

"Way back, when the church was still fairly new, this building wasn't even here. All the church had was a baptismal and a graveyard. They held services in a clearing in the woods. I've seen some pictures, and it was really gorgeous. I know being able to be inside a building and climate control is nice, but there's something to be said for worshipping right out in God's creation."

"I think we walked through that area on the way here," I tell him.

"You probably did. That area was on land that's technically part of that farm, not owned by the church. But because the family allowed the congregation to use it, they reciprocated by offering space in the cemetery."

"But none of the family members in recent history were members here?"

"None that I can recall," he says. "As far as I know, the woman you're talking about, the actual owner of the property, didn't live there."

"That's right," I say. "And you would know if that property had been given to the church."

"Oh, absolutely. We certainly would have utilized it. I've also been an elder for twenty years. I would have known about a discussion of acquiring any type of property. That's something we would have had to pray over and vote on. There would have been a lot more that went into it than just her signing papers."

"Thank you," I say. "I appreciate your time."

"Absolutely," Howard says. "Here." He hands me his card. "If there's ever anything else I can do for you, don't hesitate to call." He looks over at Xavier. "Even if he just wants to come sit in here for a spell."

Softness washes over me when I look at Xavier again. I know the torment he goes through, the challenges that he faces daily that other people could never begin to understand simply by the merit of being born with a typical brain. I try to balance that for him and help him navigate when he is struggling to connect, but there are some things I can't do for him, things I can't fix for him. In some ways, he is within himself in a way that can't be fully reached by anyone. And then there are moments like this when something does get into that place. Something that may not be what others see or what is expected from that moment but is meaningful only to him. It gives me peace to know these moments happen and that sometimes he can just exist.

CHAPTER TWENTY-THREE

I SPEND THE REST OF THE DAY AND THE NEXT RESEARCHING PROPerty and court records, trying to get a better understanding of the whole conflict over the farmland. I discover several filings and court cases related to it, including the petition with the court asking that Mae Jackson be removed from the property and put into a proper care home so that ownership of the land could be transferred. The filings don't specify who Tamara Booth wanted to transfer the land to. The process didn't get that far.

A court order stopped any possibility of transferring ownership based on an argument from Benjamin, stating he and Mae had the absolute right to remain on the property through the rest of their lives and the land could not be sold or otherwise change hands while they were still alive and living there. Arguments from Tamara's attorneys pointed out that the will only said Mae had the right to live there and only if she was in good health and condition and the property was properly maintained.

Benjamin's side fought right back, producing a letter signed and notarized a few years after the preparation of the will stating both Mae and Benjamin had a lifetime right to live on the property. This created a heated fight over whether that constituted legal life tenancy, if Mae's older sister had enough mental faculties at the time of writing that letter to truly be able to give that consent, and if the wording of the will regarding Mae's health and the land's care and maintenance should be considered more pressing than Benjamin's rights to live there.

It's a dizzying situation more than a decade down the line, and I wasn't even a part of it. I manage to find a few articles from local newspapers talking about Sienna's body being found and a couple reference the ongoing legal battle in the family, suggesting it worsened considerably when the body was found.

Though the case was not meant to be public, information about it got out, and soon everyone was talking about Tamara wanting to give the land over to a church group no one knew anything about. It was apparently no secret that many people believed she was being scammed. There was almost the suggestion that the murder of Rose Doe and the subsequent questioning and imprisonment of Benjamin Jackson for the death of his wife had a silver lining in that it ended the court battles and evidently got Tamara out from under the sway of this church.

Reading all that gives more context to Tamara Booth's decision to leave town. It wasn't just a decision on a whim. She was not only grappling with the horrors of what happened on her family's land as well as a heated and extremely tense court case, but everyone around her was starting to whisper that she had fallen under the control of a con artist. I can imagine that left her not feeling at home in the area anymore. It gave her the desire to go somewhere else where she could start fresh; where no one would know any of the stories she left behind.

I meet with Lyra to pick up the materials she found about the group and chat with her for a few minutes about her mother. She gives me a phone number, though she warns that she hasn't even been able to get in touch with her in quite a while. This makes me nervous as soon as I hear it, but Lyra clarifies that she knows Tamara is alive because of live videos she has posted on her video-sharing site and things she puts on social media.

I try the phone number Lyra gave me as I'm driving back to the hotel, but it goes to voice mail. As soon as I'm back in the room, I send her an email explaining briefly who I am and asking her to get in touch with me.

That done, I start going over the materials about the church group. Referred to simply as the Comfort Circle, the group is described vaguely and generically. It could have been written about any church or religious group. All the right phrases and sentiments are there, but there's nothing that sets it apart from other organizations. Without any specific leadership names or points of contact, the material seems less like it was produced as a form of blanket recruitment designed to catch attention and draw people in, and more like it was given to those who had already expressed that interest and were looking to become members.

I look up the Comfort Circle and don't find it. At least, nothing specific about it. There is a defunct website that has not been updated for over twelve years and appears to have been wiped of nearly everything. There are a few basic statements of faith and a general mission statement claiming the group is designed to provide a place of rest and solitude for those wearied by the challenges of life or a place of reassurance and connection for those who want to celebrate the goodness in life while remaining anchored. Whatever that means.

There's one reference to a meeting held at the library not far from the church, but nothing else. I call Howard back to find out if he has ever heard of the group and may be able to direct me to the organization it is either affiliated with or absorbed into after apparently disbanding.

"Can't say I've ever heard of that gathering," he says. "Of course, I don't know every group from all the churches around here, so it could have been from one of those, but I'd think there would be a reference to the parent church in the materials."

"Yeah, I thought so too."

"I can see how that would make Benjamin Jackson even angrier about her trying to get him off that land though," Howard says.

"Why is that?" I ask.

"He fancied himself a preacher. He used to like to talk about his church and how he was ministering to those who really needed him. Only, he had no congregation, no meeting space, no events. When I first heard him talking about being a man of the cloth, I thought he might use the old grove to meet with a small flock like the church used to, but I quickly found out that wasn't the case. According to him, he did his sermons online and broadcasted them to people because those who listened to him were so afflicted and in so much need they couldn't possibly be expected to come out to him," Howard tells me.

"But they could access the internet to watch his sermon?" I ask.

"Apparently. And there was no shortage of donations coming in either. Love offerings, he called them. A few years before the dispute over the land, things were a bit better over there, I think. I was never invited over, mind you, but I stopped by, and so did other members of the congregation to try to make connections with them. He would never even have a civil conversation with us. But we saw women come and bring prepared food, bags of groceries, bakery boxes. He checked his mail once and had a stack of checks addressed to 'Pastor Jackson.'

"I'm sure it didn't sit well with him when his own family wouldn't follow him, only for him to find out he might lose his home to another preacher. I don't like to talk badly about anyone. Not a single one of us is perfect. Every one of us has had bad times, made mistakes, done things we never should have done. It's not my job to stand in judgment of anyone or to encourage anybody else to judge them by talking about it. But I'll admit I have a very difficult time finding anything redeeming about that old man. He wasn't just a fraud. He was cruel and aggressive. He treated everyone who crossed his path horribly unless they were doing something for him or he was trying to impress them, like those people giving him those love offerings.

"The truth is, I wasn't surprised at all to hear he killed his wife. I wish there was something else I could have done, but as soon as I heard the news, my first thought was that it was a matter of time. And no matter what anyone else says, I still think he had something to do with those girls."

CHAPTER TWENTY-FOUR

HOWARD'S USE OF THE PLURAL INSTANTLY CATCHES MY ATTENTION.

"Girls?" I ask. "More than one?"

"You didn't know there was another body found on that land?" he says.

"What other body? What are you talking about?"

"A couple of years before Rose Doe, there was another young woman found out there. She was discovered during a controlled burn on a piece of the land that was incorrectly associated with a neighboring property because the boundary lines hadn't been correctly outlined. A man had recently inherited a small farm right up against the old airfield and was trying to clean it up so he could see if there was anything he could do with it or if he could just sell it. He found a dilapidated old building, thought it was on his property, and hired a local guy to come burn it down," Howard says.

"Burn it?" I ask. "Isn't that dangerous? Why wouldn't he just dismantle it?"

"That takes a lot of time and manpower. And depending on the size of the building and the materials, it can be more dangerous to pick it apart and carry off the debris than just burning it. It's pretty common out here. Usually, people hire professionals who know what they're doing to keep it as safe as possible. But sometimes they just rely on a friend or a farmer who's experienced with it. This guy hired a mechanic from up the road who mentioned he had done some burns before. And when the building was gone, they realized it had uncovered a body. As far as I know, she was never identified either."

I'm stunned I haven't heard anything about this case, and as soon as I'm off the phone with Howard, I plunge into investigating it. I call Sheridan to find out what she might know about it. She admits she has never heard about it either, and the frustration in her voice is palpable.

Having explored a good portion of the land and recognizing the odd shape of its boundaries, it's easy to see how someone unfamiliar with the area could get confused and assume a piece of land is theirs when it actually belongs to the other farm. What I don't understand is how the deaths of two unidentified women found within a few hundred yards of each other could have possibly never been linked.

Reading over the information available about the case, I discover the woman, who was thought to be in her mid-twenties, was never identified and no DNA was preserved from her body. That immediately tells me we can't pursue genetic genealogy the way we did with Sienna, making the obviously necessary effort to identify her more difficult.

The police department considers her case closed, making the official declaration that she was a junkie who wandered into the woods and ended up overdosing. Burns on her body suggested she had started a campfire for herself and fell into it during her stupor. This instantly strikes me as a completely ridiculous, throwaway conclusion considering the body went unnoticed even as a team of men were lighting up a fire around her, meaning it had to have been concealed in some way. She couldn't have rolled around in the fire, overdosed, and then concealed herself. It had to have been done by another person.

The presence of another body on the land makes Benjamin look even guiltier, just as Howard said. But there is no direct evidence, and the investigation that did happen after Sienna was found concluded he was not present at the farm on that day, so he could not have been the one to commit the murder.

I get back to Sheridan's house the next afternoon disappointed after a visit to the police department.

"They wouldn't give me access to the investigation records," I tell the group gathered in the living room. "They said the case is closed and they weren't going to release information to someone outside of law enforcement. All they would give me is a redacted version of the medical examiner's report. Essentially what they would give a reporter."

"Does it have anything interesting in it?" Sheridan asks.

I get a drink from the refrigerator and sit down with them. "Depends on who's looking at it. According to the police investigators, all it does is confirm she was some transient hippie woman who ended up dying in the woods. But that's not what I see.

"The medical examiner discovered that she was in the early stages of pregnancy. There also was evidence of burns to her body that were not related to the controlled burn. Now this does make the theory of the campfire and her falling in it make a bit more sense," I say. "But honestly, I still struggle to believe someone could fall into a fire, suffer burns all over their body, and not alert anybody anywhere in the area with their screams or the fire that would continue burning."

"It also still doesn't explain why her body was hidden," Grant points out.

"You're right. It doesn't. The medical examiner believed she died within a couple of months of being found, which would mean her body would be visible to the people managing the controlled burn if she wasn't very well hidden. There wouldn't have been enough overgrowth or leaves falling or anything like that to completely conceal her if she was just lying out in the middle of the woods. Not to mention there are predatory animals out there."

"The cats alone would have done a number on her," Xavier points out.

Everyone stares at him, but Sheridan shrugs.

"He's not lying. Cats are known for consuming parts of their owners after death. But beyond the cats, there are foxes, raccoons, possums, wolves, bears. All of those are pretty prevalent in the area. If there was a body just lying out in the woods, it would have been ripped apart. They wouldn't have been able to find it just neatly lying next to the building, probably under some wood and leaves."

"There's also a note on the report that suggests the presence of sage and other herbs on the body," I point out.

"That links her to the other victims," Cara says excitedly.

"There's one more thing," I say. "The ME circled a particular marking on the diagram of the body and wrote a note next to it. 'Burn? Flower?' It was on her arm."

An hour later I'm off the phone from my call with Keegan. It took some convincing, but she told me about the personal effects found in the vicinity of the body. I look at each of the group members in turn.

"They found a bracelet with a charm of a tulip."

Emma would be extremely proud of the massive roll of white butcher paper I find at a local craft store and tape to Sheridan's wall. There's too much information to try to process it just by talking. With so many interlocking stories and seemingly disconnected details, I need more of a visual approach to take in all the details.

Using a thick black marker, I start making notes as we lay out the similarities among all the murders.

"They don't all share all of the same characteristics," I say, drawing eight bubbles at the top of the page to indicate the victims. "But there is a lot of overlap in some of the details. There are similarities in their clothing, their hairstyle, their stomach contents when that was identifiable, and the presence of burn patterns."

"And the herbs," Emily adds. "The large bundles of sage found with some of them could be an indicator of some sort of purification. Sage is used to remove negative energies and cleanse areas."

"But didn't they also find some traces of other herbs too?" Emily asks. "Like when they swabbed their skin?"

"Yeah," I say. "There were a few compounds they found in all of them."

"Skin treatments," Emily says like the thought is just occurring to her. She looks at Cara, who nods at her. "The hairstyle, makeup, and skin treatments… it's like they were put through a preparation before they were murdered."

"That's good," I say, jotting the thought down on the corner of the paper. "Of course, we can't forget the most obvious of the shared details among the women. The bracelets and their flower charms. These bracelets are clearly a key feature in the murders."

"But they aren't all the same," Wyatt argues.

"They aren't," I agree. "We now know that Sienna wasn't the first victim. She died years after the unidentified victim."

"Tulip," Sheridan says. "I hate calling them 'victims.' They're more than that. Call her Tulip."

"If these bracelets really do have something to do with the killer, should we be calling her by something he chose for her?" Emily asks.

"It's all we have," Sheridan says. "It's better than just calling her 'the unidentified victim.'"

"How about neither?" I say, wanting to keep the disagreement from escalating any further so we can move on. "We'll call her TD. Short for Tulip Doe. It gives her a name for us to call, but we're not actually referring to the flower."

Emily nods, and I bob my head in return.

"Okay. Hers is different than all the others. Sienna's was similar to it. But then the other six are all alike except for the type of flower. They are similar to Sienna's, but pretty distinct from TD's."

"The flowers aren't there," Grant reminds me. "In the garden, each of the types of flowers that show up on the bracelets were planted near the bodies."

He sifts through the files we've spread out and finds images of the Garden of Bodies before all the graves were emptied, and then one of where Sienna was found.

"There weren't any roses where Sienna was," Sheridan points out. "Were there any tulips where TD was found?"

"I've only seen two pictures of the scene from after the body was removed, and I didn't see them in either."

"Forget-me-nots," Xavier says.

We all look at him, and he traces a fingertip along clusters of blue flowers at the Garden of Bodies as well as near Sienna's initial grave. I remember pops of blue in the image of TD's resting place and realize those flowers were there too.

"They're near each of the bodies."

"Those grow wild though," Grant says.

"Yes, conceivably, there could be wildflowers near the graves, but it would be extremely coincidental for the same flowers to be growing near all the women's bodies. And their name. Forget-me-not. That means something," I say. "They're there for a reason."

"What I don't understand is why Sienna and TD were alone," Sheridan says. "The other six were all together in a clearly planned location. The graves were carefully dug, there were flowers planted. It was obviously done with a lot of attention. But then Sienna and TD were each found by themselves, separated from each other and far from the rest of them."

"And look at this," I say, stepping back to examine the web I've been creating by making connections between the details of the deaths and the women who exhibited them. "Sienna doesn't have as many of the features as the other women. Even without having a specific grave for us to examine and there being a completely different way her body was found, it looks like TD has more similarities in a lot of ways with the other six women than Sienna does."

"Something went wrong," Xavier says. "Plans were in place for TD, and then something happened with Sienna. The plan worked for the subsequent murders, but they had to be in a different place."

"That hunter interrupted the killer when he saw the smoke. Some of it would have had to have been done before, but the process was already shaken up," I interpret for the rest of the group. "Something happened that made him completely change his approach, and I think it's more than just the hunter walking up on him."

My phone rings, and I glance down at it where it's sitting on the side table.

Tamara Booth.

I snatch it up and hold it so the group can see it. "I need to take this."

The room is buzzing with them going over ideas as I rush out to the porch so I can hear her but no one else can.

"Hello?"

"Dean Steele?"

"Yes," I say. "Is this Tamara Booth?"

"It is," she says.

"Mrs. Booth, thank you so much for getting back to me. I am ..."

"I know, Mr. Steele. You told me in your messages to me, and I have heard of you. I know that you're involved in the case having to do with my property that's bubbling back up after ten years," she says.

"The investigation into the murder of the woman found on the property has never formally closed," I tell her. "But you're right, it has heated up considerably recently. She was identified, and now I'm working to find out what happened to her. I spoke with your children ..."

"Mr. Steele," she says, stopping me again. "I want to make myself very clear right now. I am not trying to stand in the way of any investigation or obstruct anything. I've been forthcoming and helpful ever since that day. The reality is, I don't know anything about the girl, her death, or anything else. That time in my life was truly horrible, and I really just want to be left alone about it.

"As for you speaking with my children, I'm sure they had some creative things to tell you about what was going on with the land ownership conflict and how I disappeared out of their lives. What you need to understand is, they were right in the thick of the entire thing, fighting and making the entire thing far more difficult than it even needed to be. They always had these foolish ideas about that land. They talked about building houses out there, raising their children, growing crops. Then it turned into building one big house and having that be the family center for holidays and vacations. Then it turned into a bed-and-breakfast with special holiday activities," she says dismissively. "It went on and on. And I knew it was all just talk. But I let them do it. I had never wavered on the fact that I was not interested in the land. My mother left it to me because I was her only child. It was left to her because she was older and more sensible than Mae. I saw the entire complicated agreement as nothing but confusion and hassle."

"Then why didn't you just sell it to your aunt and uncle?" I ask.

"Spite," she says without hesitation. "The hatred I carry for that man is something I will never step away from nor apologize for. He brought a tremendous amount of grief into my family as soon as he married her. He was not her first husband and is not the father of her children. I know for a fact he mistreated all of them. I reported him over and over and it never did any good. He took advantage of my mother, he stole from her, and he destroyed the land she loved. The only solace I had was that she never saw what they did to it. She stopped going out there after her father died because it reminded her too much of him, so she never saw the damage.

"I didn't sell it to them because I didn't want him to own it. I never wanted him to have ownership papers for that piece of land. That and I was positive he would turn right around and sell it to someone else. My aunt would lose her home, end up God knows where, and there would be nothing I could do about it. We never had a great relationship, ever, but she was still family. I wouldn't want to see her further hurt by the man who tormented her. What I got in the end was her being horrifically murdered by him."

She takes a breath. "My point is, you don't know the full story. And I'm not going to get into all of it. What I'm going to tell you is, I started looking for ways to legally remove him from the property two years before I made any filings. I contacted organizations about the condition of their home, the condition of the land, the way he treated her, and everything I possibly could, hoping to have them removed, my aunt put somewhere safe where she would get good care, and the land reverted fully to my use so I could decide what to do with it then."

"They told me about the church group you were involved in," I say, hoping a bit of suggestion that I know more than I actually do might lead her into giving me the details I want.

"Comfort Circle offered me a place where I didn't have to grapple with everything going on around me all the time. I've always had a strong spiritual connection, life just brought me in and out of it. At that time, I needed to be very much in it, and that group gave that to me. I made the decision to transfer ownership of the property to them on my own. They never asked for it. They never even suggested it. I wasn't one to talk openly about what I was going through. When I was there, I prayed silently, and I accepted their reassurance. They didn't know about the land.

"The first time I thought about giving it to them was when they started talking about wanting to find a permanent space to exist together. It would have been like one of those old utopian experiment societies, which I don't know all that much about, but I understood the desire. Most of us just wanted to pull out of regular society and have a simpler life focused on cooperation, connection with others, faith, and our connection with the Divine. When I heard that, I thought it would be the perfect use of the land. I approached Pastor Laurence and told him what I was feeling. He didn't jump on it immediately. He said to pray about it and we would come to a decision together.

"We never had that opportunity. The courts made it impossible, and then finding that woman's body tore my life apart. I know it sounds selfish for me to say that, but those were the hardest months of my entire life. My family was already at each other's throats, and now we were the focus of a massive investigation. Benjamin was the only one of us ever considered a person of interest, but that didn't stop the scrutiny we all felt. I couldn't take it. When the Comfort Circle was called to leave Virginia and establish a permanent space, I decided to go with them. I wanted to leave everything behind and start over. And that's what I did," she says.

I'm stunned at the implication. "You're still with the group? The group moved somewhere together?"

"Yes," she says. "A piece of land was made available in Pennsylvania, and Pastor Laurence took the sign from God and accepted. I didn't tell my children. Now I'm living out here. It's not like it sounds. It's a huge piece of land and we've made a nice little village out of it. We've got a meeting house, a recreation center. A library. We created our own town, and it's perfect. I don't want them to know this is what I've chosen because I don't want or need their opinions. I made the decision to keep the farmland in Virginia because it's been through enough. When I'm gone, they can decide what to do with it. Until then, I just want to be left alone and have a chance at life again."

The conversation leaves me rattled but also more sympathetic toward Tamara for all she has gone through. She deserves to have her wishes honored, so I won't tell her children the details of her new life. But at least now I have an explanation for the group's apparent disappearance. They didn't dissolve away; they left the area for something I hope is far better.

CHAPTER TWENTY-FIVE

"HAVE YOU EVER HEARD OF THE CRESCENT COVE MOTEL?" Sheridan asks when I come down the next morning.

A night made restless by thoughts that just won't quiet down has me feeling groggy and out of sorts, but I try to push it aside with the promise of coffee just a few strides away.

"Crescent Cove Motel?" I ask, making sure I heard her right.

"Yeah. It's near Fredericksburg."

"No," I say, getting a mug from the wire display rack kept on Sheridan's counter and setting the single-cup brewer to make me the strongest style she has. "Do you know where Xavier is?"

"I think the library," she tells me. "He was up early talking on the phone with someone about Poe, and then he said he needed to do some reading to calm his nerves. "

It takes a second for that to sink in. "Oh no, not Poe. Edgar Allan Dough. It's one of his sourdough starters. They're his babies. He has a pet sitter taking care of them right now, and I think it's really starting to get to him."

"Ah, I guess that would be why he left a mason jar of flour and water sitting on the counter with a note not to touch it," she says.

"That would be why." My heavy hand with milk makes it possible for me to just gulp down the coffee, and I go back for another cup. "What about this motel now?"

"Oh. Grant let me know we got a message on the site from somebody asking if we had ever looked into the tip about Rose Doe being seen regularly at Crescent Cove. Apparently, several weeks after the night of that 911 call when she escaped from the van, she showed up there and was then seen at least a couple of times a week at the motel for the next couple of months. According to this person, investigators pretty much dismissed the tip as soon as it was made because the person who left the tip just said they saw the security footage and was sure it was the same person. The police said there was no conclusive way to prove it was the same girl, so they put it aside. Now, there isn't really anything in the message to explain how this person knows about the tip or if it's at all reliable, but it's something," she says.

"It's possible that whoever sent the message is the one who made the tip," I suggest. "They were probably frustrated that they were ignored ten years ago, and now that attention is being put on the case again, they want to make sure that what they know, or what they think they know, gets in front of the right people."

"And you are the right people," Sheridan says.

"Right now as I stand here in my pajama pants and sweatshirt, my hair uncombed, my eyes only partially open, contemplating the long-term effects of a third cup of coffee within five minutes, I don't feel like that's an accurate description. But give me a little bit to wake up, and I'll get there."

When Xavier and I pull up to the motel early in the afternoon, I see it isn't quite what I had envisioned. Sheridan got me the address while I got ready for the day, so I didn't look it up, giving me no images or anything to go on. Based on the name however, I assumed it was going to be a tiny little side-of-the-road motel that's been there for decades, where motorists stopped because they were in the middle of nothingness before the area was built up.

It certainly has some years on it, but it is much larger than I expected, and the busy parking lot shows it is not hurting for business. We go into the lobby and find it bright, cheerful, and already fully decorated for Thanksgiving. Warm oranges and browns envelop the space in a cozy glow. There is even a switch-operated fireplace in the corner burning away. There appears to be only one woman helping everybody at the desk, so Xavier and I sit down near the fireplace to wait for her to get through the line of people waiting.

Xavier looks around. "It feels like we walked into a made-for-TV living room."

I don't think I ever would have come up with that description on my own, but having heard it, I feel it is, in fact, completely accurate. I try to envision Sienna here, wondering why she might have come so frequently. There are many possible explanations, some more nefarious than others, but I find myself wanting to lean toward the more pleasant ones. Maybe she had a friend who worked here with whom she liked to spend time. Maybe she actually had a job here, and the person who reported seeing her just didn't realize she was arriving at work. Until I know for certain otherwise, I'm going to try to find a good reason.

The line moves quickly, and when the last of the new guests have headed back out to find their rooms, the woman behind the desk looks over at us.

"Can I help you?" she calls across the lobby.

Xavier is transfixed by the fire, so I go up to the counter alone.

"Hi," I say.

"Good afternoon."

She smiles a bright, warm smile, the kind that puts everybody around the person at ease. Before I can say anything else, a phone rings behind her. She gives me a regretful look, apologizes, and turns to pick it up. The blouse she's wearing has gauzy sleeves, and when she twists her upper body to type something into a computer on the back table, I see the hint of a blue tattoo on the back of her shoulder.

She hangs up and comes back over to me. "I'm so sorry about that. I'm Jane. How can I help you?"

I explain the situation, and her eyes darken slightly as she realizes I'm not here for a pleasant night's stay. She looks at the picture of Sienna I hold out to her.

"I've worked here for the last fifteen years, so I was here when that would have happened, but I don't remember this girl. Now, I'll tell you this place was very different back then. It's undergone extensive renovations and improvements, and that has shifted our typical clientele," she says.

"Do you know of any reason why someone would say they saw her here a couple of times a week?" I ask.

"You said she was going through a really difficult time. I do a lot of volunteer work with the community, and especially then, I was in the habit of helping homeless people and people going through rough patches in their lives. When there were open rooms, I'd let them stay in them. I'd give them work when housekeeping positions opened up. I saved extra food from breakfast in the mornings so they could come eat. I really tried to do whatever I could. Maybe this girl was one of those people. But to tell you honestly, I didn't get to know most of them very well." She looks at the picture again. "She was so young. I can't believe someone would hurt her. I wish there was more I could tell you."

"I appreciate your time," I say.

Xavier and I go back to the car and sit while it warms up. A Black Friday commercial comes on the radio encouraging shoppers to consider small businesses and local artisans when shopping for the holiday season, and a sudden thought pops into my mind. I look at Xavier.

"I think I know a way I can track down the bracelets."

We get back to Sheridan's house, and I search through the crime scene and medical examiner's images for the best pictures of the bracelets I can find. I take pictures of them so I can send them to my computer and then run a reverse image search. It isn't a perfect approach. Usually, reverse image searches are used to find exact imagery lurking around on the internet, but the more sophisticated programs search for similarities and bring up results that could be that item or something related to it.

That's what I'm hoping for. The bracelets are dirty and damaged from their time in the ground, but I'm hoping there is enough of a recognizable design that it will trigger a result. It takes several tries and digging through a lot of unrelated products and stock images of laughing women, but finally, I find what I'm looking for.

"Here it is," I say. "This artist, Harmony Soleil, creates custom jewelry that she sells online and through in-person events. According to her bio, she's been doing it for over twenty years. That makes the time frame match up. There's also a note that she specializes in nature imagery within her work."

"Do you think that's her real name?" Xavier asks.

I blink. "I don't know. Maybe if we get to know each other, I'll ask her."

"I can find a way to slip it into a conversation," Xavier says.

While I have no doubt he could get it into a conversation, I have my very strong doubts there would be anything smooth and subtle about it. It's far more likely those would end up among the first words he said to her once he got past the social pleasantries.

I use the contact form on her site to send her an email, attaching an image of the tulip bracelet and asking if that design looks familiar to her. Just after I send the message, Xavier walks out of the room. He comes back a few seconds later carrying a map.

"Where did you get that?" I ask.

"It was in the library," he says as he smooths it out on the wall next to the butcher paper. "Sheridan told me they use it when they are talking about cases. It gives them a visual of where things happened."

"Why do you have it?" I ask.

He pulls a package of pushpins out of his pocket and starts sticking them into the map. A few seconds later, he steps back and shows me.

"Fortunately, the delivery guy came early today and brought the deluxe pin assortment I ordered," he says. "It is more difficult than I thought to find eight colors of pins. But I did it."

"You brought the map down so you could show off your pin colors?" I ask.

"If I was going to show off my pin colors, I would use blank paper and create a piece of original art. Get it together, Dean." He gestures to the pins stuck into the Virginia outline. "This pink one is Sienna, a.k.a. Rose Doe. She was found here. But she was from here." He points at the matching pink pin in South Carolina. "Now, we know she got to Virginia on her own, but look at the others. The red one is TD. There's only one pin right now because we don't know where she came from. Over here, we have the Garden of Bodies. Also in South Carolina. Not the same area as Sienna was from, but still the same state. Yet only one of the women there, our blue pin, the iris, was from the area. The other five are from different places, including the daisy, our white pin here, who was from Georgia, and the purple violet, who was from Virginia."

I stand up and walk over to the map to get a better look at it. Seeing the information displayed like this gives it more context than just having it written out.

"He didn't just find victims because he was in a certain area. He didn't go to them. He brought them where he wanted them to be. Sienna and TD are separate from the others because he got caught when he was burying Sienna. He intended for that to be his garden. He meant to have the women close together. They weren't as close as the other six victims, but that might have been his intention. Remember, there was evidence in the garden that at least one person was coming back to visit the graves regularly. They were maintained, and it looked like they were bringing items with them, like sage and other flowers.

"Maybe the plan wasn't originally for it to be one area with all of them together but distinct spaces for each. Maybe he planned to have his garden scattered through the woods so they could each be visited individually while walking through the woods, like a meditation garden. But why would he change that so drastically with the other bodies?"

"Circling the wagons," Xavier says. "He was comfortable on that piece of land and felt like no one would be able to find or disturb the graves. He had complete confidence that they would be safe and he would be able to go enjoy them the way he intended. When that changed, he realized that to protect his flowers, he had to keep them close. Even if that didn't mean he was close to them at all times, if they were all closer together, they were safer. His methods changed from his first victim to Sienna to the garden. He was responding to what was happening around him after each kill."

"Which means most likely TD was the first."

"And he just grew from there."

A response from Harmoney Soleil comes in, and immediately I know I'm on the right track.

"She remembers the bracelet," I tell Xavier. "Even though it's in bad condition, she can tell it's one of her designs from a while back. She keeps pictures of everything she makes, and she sent me this one."

I turn the screen toward him to show him the picture Harmony sent of the tulip bracelet when it was first made. At the bottom of the email is an invitation to video call her, which I do immediately. The woman who looks back at me from the screen is softly pretty, but her face looks etched with worry.

"Dean Steele," I say. "Thanks for talking to me. "

"Absolutely. I'd really like to know what's going on."

"Can you tell me when you sold that bracelet?" I ask.

"It was in my inventory from a festival I do every year. That particular one was about fifteen years ago. To be honest, I probably made dozens of sales that day, all in cash. I couldn't tell you who it was."

I hang my head. I'd been expecting this, but some part of me had hoped she'd have something.

"Did you have other bracelets with you that day?" I ask.

"Sure," she says. She holds up a binder with a page of pictures of individual bracelets. "All of these sold."

I look at them carefully but don't see any that look familiar.

"I noticed your site says that you favor nature imagery for your jewelry. I'm guessing that means you make a lot of flower bracelets?"

"Flowers show up a lot in my designs," she confirms. "Could you please tell me what's happening? You said in your message that you're a private investigator and the bracelet showed up in the course of a case. What happened?"

"Several murder victims have been found wearing bracelets with flower charms. I believe they can all be attributed to the same killer. This bracelet was found with the first victim. I need to know if there are others."

Her face drops as she pulls away from the screen, her hand covering her mouth.

CHAPTER TWENTY-SIX

Fifteen years ago

FESTIVALS FILLED ME WITH A KIND OF ENERGY NOTHING ELSE DID. There was something about the frivolity of them, the complete commitment to fantasy and belief in the fanciful surroundings. I loved every moment of them. Even when I traveled alone, which was the majority of the time. No one in my life felt the same about them.

I didn't mind. I would rather immerse myself fully in the experience without having to explain it, without having to justify it, without having to apologize for it. There were times when I'd brought people with me and realized almost immediately they weren't the kind of people who should be there. They wrinkled their noses at the clothes. They laughed at performances that weren't done for comedy. They questioned all aspects of the experience and made fun of everything from the moment we walked through the gates. It ruined what should have been a day of sheer joy.

I'd much rather be alone. When I was alone, I could be anyone. I got to choose who I wanted to be before I ever arrived and never had to explain it. The people I encountered at the festivals didn't question why I was doing it or do everything they could to try to draw me out of the fantasy. They just let me be. They met me in that space and came along with me, and at the same time, they invited me into their experience as well.

That year I went to the festival alone intentionally. I didn't even consider inviting anyone. Not that there were many people left around me to invite. Friendship had never come easy for me, and there was always a time when those I did find faded out of my life. In many ways, it was easier to just be by myself. And in others, I was constantly craving that connection everyone around me seemed to have. The kind of connection that made it so I could look at someone and they would know immediately what I was thinking and feeling. But that felt even further away from reality than the fantasy of the festival grounds around me.

I wandered along the dirt roads that wove through the grounds, admiring the different shops and booths the wide variety of vendors set up every year. Some held careers outside of coming here to offer their wares and justified indulging their desire to dip into the imaginary realm by making some extra cash across the several weekends the festival ran. The larger, permanent structures, though, belonged to the vendors who made their living through these events. For them, this was the source of the bulk of their income for the year, supplemented by online sales and special orders.

I was always impressed by the skill and artistry of the craftsmen. It was always the ones who demonstrated their abilities who transfixed me the most. Men in loose linen shirts, skin glistening with sweat through the open necklines, blowing glass ornaments and decorations. Women weaving tapestry while chatting with costumed guests. I finished watching a woodcarver create a tiny animal he sanded carefully and handed to a small child, then turned down a small alley to see what else I would discover.

The jewelry booth was the first thing I saw. A smaller display than many of the others, it drew me in with the enchanting way the pieces sparkled in the sunlight. I stepped up to the booth and looked over the pieces.

"I design and make everything myself," the woman said. She smiled at me when I looked at her with surprise.

"Really?"

She nodded and handed me a card. Harmony Soleil. A name that sounded right at home here but might not meld so easily in the world outside. I found myself wondering if when she packed her display at the end of the season and left the gates of the grove behind she arrived back at her home under a completely different name. Mary. Wendy. Sue. Jessica. Something that sounded at home with the PTA or the office grind.

Or maybe not. Maybe, just maybe, she arrived home exactly as she was here and lived her life on her own terms without caring.

I couldn't resist an unusual bracelet with a tulip charm hanging from it. After I bought it, Harmony helped me loop it over my wrist and latch it closed. I thanked her and left to continue exploring. In the deluge of stimulation around me, I all but forgot about the bracelet for the rest of the afternoon until I was sitting under a tree to take a break from the heat and a woman walked up to me.

"Do you mind if I sit there?" she asked, pointing toward the empty area of the low rock wall where I'd perched.

"Not at all," I said.

She settled down and looked at me with a wide, grateful smile, giving me the chance to see she was truly beautiful.

"Thank you. I can't believe how hot it is today. Isn't this supposed to be a harvest celebration?" she laughs, referencing the storyline of that year's festival.

"I don't remember it being this hot any other year," I agreed.

She leans back against the tree, and I notice her eyes drift over to my wrist.

"I love your bracelet," she said.

"Oh, thank you," I said, looking down at it and twisting my hand back and forth slightly to encourage a bit of extra sparkle. "I actually just bought it today."

"Here?" she asked.

She took my wrist gently in one of her hands and touched her fingertips to the chain, lightly moving the tulip charm back and forth.

"Mmhmm. In the vendor village, down one of the side alleys. The designer's name is Harmony," I said.

"It really is lovely," the woman said. She carefully rested my hand back down onto my lap. "Maybe you can show me where to find her, then we can get a drink and go over to the ring. The next match is about to start."

"Sure," I said."

We started toward the vendor area again, and the woman turned to look at me.

"What's your name?" she asked.

"I'm Shaelyn."

CHAPTER TWENTY-SEVEN

Now

"I CAN'T BELIEVE MY ART, SOMETHING I CREATED, WAS USED IN A murder. I wanted to make something beautiful, something that would make people happy, not ... this," Harmony says.

"I know this has to be painful for you. But right now what's important is finding who is responsible for this and stopping him. I'm going to show you pictures of the bracelets found on the other victims. Don't worry, it's just the bracelets. You won't see the women. Will you be able to identify them?" I ask.

"Yes," she says, nodding through growing tears.

As I reach for the pictures, she draws in a breath, pulling herself up like she's preparing herself. I show her the images, and she starts flipping through the book. It doesn't take long before she can show me a photograph of the entire collection of bracelets laid out together.

"They were all sold together?" I ask.

"Yes. A custom order. Give me just a second."

Her focus shifts to another part of the screen, and I realize she's clicking through documents she has saved on her computer. A few moments later, an email appears in my inbox.

"This order was taken in person, so the customer filled out one of my order forms to let me know exactly what he wanted, give me his payment information, and put the address where he wanted them delivered. I keep copies of all the order forms for my records. But it was paid with cash, so that can't be traced. But there's a name and an address."

I thank her and end the call. Energy buzzes through me as I look over the order form. The name on it is Fred Cory. I run the address through a search and come up with an apartment complex in Massachusetts. Seeing that dampens the excitement I've been feeling. Something is off. A call to the complex quickly reveals I'm not as close to the answers as I'd thought I was.

"The property manager of the complex says Fred Cory hasn't lived in that apartment in almost sixteen years. She never even met him. The only reason she knows that is because the company maintains records of all tenants in their online database," I tell Xavier. "He moved out before the delivery of the bracelets arrived."

"Did you get his forwarding address?" Xavier asks. "He should have had to provide that when he moved."

"I did. But it's coming back as an abandoned warehouse. This guy really didn't want to be found."

The post office won't give me any further information about the package and how it was eventually transmitted to whoever accepted delivery, so I'm going to have to find that out for myself. Property records for the abandoned warehouse lead me to the owner, who is not the man listed on the order form. But he can confirm that the building was a storage and logistics warehouse for a specialty food company several years ago. He checks his employment records and tells me Fred Cory used to work for the company. He started in the shipment department and worked his way up through the company until he was asked to head up the development of a new branch in South Carolina.

South Carolina... again. I'm getting extremely frustrated, feeling like I'm going around in circles. I have to take a second to step outside and breathe. I need to calm down and stay focused. The more riled up I get, the more likely it is I could slip into a blackout.

This is what I do, I remind myself. *I find the lost. Uncover secrets. Unravel the impossible.*

It takes the rest of the day chasing down Fred Cory to discover he hadn't stayed in South Carolina long before relocating to Virginia to start his own competing company. Anger and frustration burn in my belly when I realize how many hours I've wasted only to find myself driving to a building a little more than an hour away from the farm.

What had been a warehouse and office building during the time the bracelets were ordered has undergone extensive renovation and expansion. It is now a sprawling complex housing a community center and outreach organization. It's set back from the main road, taking up what had been an industrial park and surrounding land, giving it a sense of isolation, but without a gate or any other kind of barrier to prevent anyone from coming up to it.

I park and sit back, staring at the front of the building for several long seconds.

"Something's not right," I muse. "That order wasn't accidentally bounced around like that. It was meant as a diversion so it couldn't be tracked. Fred Cory doesn't even own this building anymore. But he did when the bracelets were ordered, and it's where the trail stops. I can't find any way to contact him. The only thing left to do is go in there and see if anyone remembers him or has a way to get in touch with him."

The glass front doors to the building open up to exactly what I'd expect from this type of place. Bordering between welcoming and corporate, the space is airy and decorated with light colors and plants but clearly designed with efficiency and careful management in mind. A large front desk seems to stand guard in an open lobby area while hallways jut off from either side. Behind the desk, another glass door leads further into the building.

"Good morning," the young man behind the desk says with a smile as we approach. "Welcome to Vision for the Future. I'm Tyler. What can I do for you?"

It's a polished, rehearsed greeting, yet he makes it sound sincere.

"Hi, Tyler," I say. "My name is Dean Steele. I'm a private investigator, and I'm currently working on a case that led me on kind of a twisted path to end up here."

I give him a very condensed version of tracking down the order, not offering any details of the case itself or why it's important to find where the package was delivered. He asks me to wait and goes through the glass door, coming back a few minutes later with two older people. They both give me the same warm smiles and introduce themselves. I tell them the same thing I told Tyler and show them the order form.

The man who introduced himself as Chuck Hanson shakes his head. "I'm one of the original employees here. I was around when we acquired this building. The man who sold it to us wasn't called Fred Cory. I knew him as Frank Cary. Definitely not the same name."

"Did he already own this building when this order was made?" I ask.

"Yeah," he says, nodding. "This is from several months before we moved in though. If it was delivered here, there wouldn't have been anyone to accept it. I'm sure it was just marked 'Return to Sender' and sent back. I wish I could be of more help."

"Do you know what happened to Frank Cary?" I ask.

"He was selling the building because his business went under and he was moving to get a fresh start. I only remember that because it seemed so lucky that we'd been looking for somewhere to get roots for our organization, to get our own fresh start, and we found it because someone else was looking for theirs. But I honestly can't remember right off the top of my head where he moved. I know it was quite a bit away."

"While you're here, would you like to know more about Vision of the Future?" the woman beside him, Belle Crane, asks. She's wearing a pale blue dress with a cardigan over it that accents the light color of her eyes.

I nod. "All right."

She smiles brighter and walks us over to a stand holding several written materials. She takes copies of each of them and hands them to us as she describes the group as a community-gathering place designed to promote personal growth, realization of potential, and creation of the future for the individual and the world as a whole. I'm not really sure if I believe any of it, but Belle certainly seems to.

"Belle! There you are. Thank goodness. I've been looking all over for you."

I glance over my shoulder in the direction of a woman's voice and am surprised to see a familiar face coming toward me: the receptionist from the hotel. She stops when she sees me and laughs lightly.

"Well," Jane says, "I'd think if you decided you wanted a room, you would have just gone back to the front desk rather than tracking me all the way here."

I laugh. "How are you?"

Belle looks between us with her eyebrows knitted, a questioning expression in her eyes.

"Dean here came into the Crescent Cove the other day to ask me about one of his cases," she explains.

"That's actually how I ended up here," I tell her.

"Same case?" she asks, the smile fading into a confused, slightly startled look.

"Yes."

"That's… odd. Is it about that girl? Was she a member here? Or possibly part of the outreach services?" she asks. "Remember I told you I'm involved in a lot of community service and volunteering to help those in need? This is what I was talking about. I help people as much as I can through the motel, but this is my primary passion." She holds up her hands, palms up, at shoulder level, and swings back and forth slightly, like she's putting the entirety of the building and its contents on display.

"If she was a member here, wouldn't you have recognized her?" I ask.

"Probably," she agrees. "Unless she wasn't here very long. You did say it was, what, ten or so years ago? Something like that? We do have members who come and go sometimes. They have a need in their lives, they come here to have it fulfilled, and when they no longer feel like they need us, they move on. In a lot of ways, that's the whole point. We want to help people embrace their potential and become what they can be, whether that's a specific goal or a lifelong journey. And we've been fortunate enough to have helped so many that I might not have worked with everyone individually."

"That makes sense. And honestly, I hadn't even gotten so far as to consider the possibility that she could have been involved in this group. Something completely different brought me here," I say.

"Oh," she says. "What?"

The gears are churning in the back of my mind as I tell her about the order and the twisted path that brought me here. As I'm finishing, the door to the building opens, and a cluster of people come in.

"Why don't we go back to my office? We can talk more there," Jane says.

Xavier and I follow her around the desk and through the glass door. It leads into another lobby area, this one round with doors around the curved walls. The one directly across is larger than the others, suggesting it leads still further into the already-complicated space. Jane leads us to one of the doors and opens it, stepping aside to let us in.

I was expecting a basic office. Instead, we walk into what feels more like a large lounge. The considerable space is broken up into different areas with collections of furniture and decor in distinct blue, white, and purple shades that offer various seating arrangements, eating spaces, and a packed bookshelf with cushions on the floor. Several small desks dot the space, suggesting this is a shared workspace.

Two other women are sitting at the desks. They aren't wearing matching uniforms, but all are wearing coordinating shades of blue, white, and purple that go along with the room. That must be a signature color palette of the organization. Having the women dress similarly helps to differentiate them from members or those being helped.

Jane brings us over to one of the sitting areas and offers us tea. We both accept, and when we're all holding our cups, we settle into a large sectional taking up most of one corner.

"I don't know as much about the very beginnings of the organization as some of the others. I was here for it, but not as one of the core administrators. At that time, I barely even knew Windham, and I was just excited to be a part of something that had so much potential. But I do remember hearing people talk about the man we got the building from. I don't know all the details, but I know there was some unpleasantness about him and why he was leaving the building so suddenly," Jane says. "I don't really have an explanation for his name change except that maybe he was trying to separate from the earlier part of his life. Trying to disappear a little, so to speak."

I try not to let her use of the word *disappear* feel significant. Instead, I redirect to the unfamiliar name she said.

"Windham?"

"Windham Debracey," she says. "He's the founder and head of Vision of the Future."

"That's a lot of name," Xavier says.

Jane laughs. "It certainly is. But he's a lot of man. He's one of those men who has the energy and personality of several people all packed into one. It's how he was able to achieve all this."

"Can I speak with him? Maybe he would remember something," I say.

"He's not here today. He's traveling with one of our outreach groups," she says. She checks the time. "Oh, I'm about to be late to a meeting. You're welcome to look around. Maybe you'll find a class or a group you'd like to join."

She hurries out of the room. Xavier and I sit for a few more moments, sipping our tea as we both seem lost in our own thoughts. Without talking about it, we both finish our tea and leave the room, drifting back into the front of the building so we can explore it more.

As we walk around, we're greeted by several people—some who seem like support staff and others who are members there for their various sessions. Each of the hallways coming off the main lobby leads to classrooms, workshops, and other spaces designed to accommodate the different activities offered by the group. The scope of their offerings and the constant movement of the space is at once overwhelming and invigorating. I can easily see how people get swept up into it and want to be a part of anything that's going on here.

Around the corner of one of the hallways, next to a large meeting room, we find a bulletin board that seems to act as a central hub for the group. Various fliers, schedules, and information sheets clutter the edges of the space while notes from Windham Debracey take up the center. One in particular mentions the trip he's on now, referencing his "ministry" and his hopes of encouraging others.

It doesn't come right out and say that they are out recruiting people, but that's certainly what it sounds like. I read over everything, feeling a growing sense of disquiet in the back of my mind. I'm not sure what it is, but something is bothering me about the board. As we're walking away from the board, I notice a small piece of paper tucked into one corner. A faint watercolor rainbow creates a backdrop for words written in elaborate script.

Good morning, sunshine.

At the end of the hallway, an open door allows the voices of the people inside to filter out into the hall. I catch Jane's voice and peek inside. She's standing in front of a small semicircle of chairs with people watching her, notebooks in their laps and pens poised to write down whatever she's going to say.

"We're looking forward to welcoming several new members in the next week as well as ushering in a new group for the outreach program. It's an exciting time, and a lot is going on, so we will need absolute commitment from all of you. We share the same vision. It's our duty to pursue it and make it a reality."

She looks over and sees us. She gives a little smile and wave before looking back at the group in front of her. Xavier and I start back down the hallway toward the exit, but I can still hear her talking.

"As you might know, Claudine was invited to enter leadership and development. It's an honor for her, but for us as well. She's an exceptional person who carries the fire for what we do in her heart, and I know she will accomplish amazing things. She'll be working with us intensively over the next several months to connect with the community in new ways and build bridges between us and prospective supporters. We look forward to seeing all she will do."

We get back to the car, and a sense of relief washes over me. What I heard Jane talking about is sticking with me. It sounded optimistic and even in line with what she told me the group does, but at the same time, it wasn't exactly what I would expect. The entire experience of being in there felt somewhat eerie. There was nothing outright. I didn't see anything frightening or even alarming. Everyone there seemed happy to be there and completely at ease. They came across as genuinely wanting to help others. But I couldn't shake the discomfort.

Maybe I'm just having a knee-jerk reaction to it that comes from my own youth and the many times I was funneled through community centers, Big Brother–type organizations, social worker offices, and other similar places in misguided efforts to keep me on track and rescue me from the dredges of society. I didn't have good experiences there, and while Vision for the Future didn't seem to be like those places, I'm still glad to be out of the building. I don't know what to think. Xavier has fallen silent, which means he is very likely thinking far too much.

CHAPTER TWENTY-EIGHT

"I DIDN'T SEE ANYONE WALKING AROUND WEARING FLOWER bracelets, if that's what you're asking me."

Barrett Courier looks agitated over the video call. He's back in South Carolina but has kept in close touch with Sheridan to stay up to date on the case as it continues to develop. I've spoken to him a couple of times, and every time he seems more on edge. It's like the more time stretches between him discovering the graves and our conversation, the more intense his anxiety gets. I know what he's feeling. He doesn't want the case, and the possibility of stopping whoever is responsible, to slip through his fingers.

"But what did you see? What was this place?" he asks.

"I already told you. It's a self-help center and community outreach program. Just like thousands of others. People who want to make their own lives better and want to make other people's lives better. A whole Hands Across America-type vibe. There was nothing about it that seemed shady or untrustworthy. Everybody we talked to was friendly and perfectly happy to talk to us. None of them tried to get us to stop asking questions or tried to hurry us to leave. In fact, they tried to find other people who could better answer our questions. I really don't know what to think about it," I say.

"Do you think it's possible Sienna crossed paths with them?"

"Do I think it's possible?" I ask. "Of course I do. I've learned to think just about anything as possible until I've been shown they're not. But I haven't found any connection. I've already traced her as far as I possibly could, and her trail ends at the apartment she apparently abandoned. There's no cell phone data or financial records to continue following her from there. From the night she ran from Bellinger to the day she was found, there's almost a year unaccounted for. Until we find some way to conclusively identify where she was and what she was doing, that time is lost."

"Did you ask about membership records? Or records of the people who they helped with their outreach programming?" Courier asks.

"I didn't have a chance to. But I'm gonna go back and talk to them specifically about Sienna. Right now, I'm interested in Fred Cory. Or Frank Cary. Whoever he actually is. Jane hinted at some unpleasantness in his past, and the fact that he was trying to get away, so I'd really like to know what was going on with that."

"You said he had connections to South Carolina?"

"In theory, yes. It came up when I was trying to track down where that delivery went," I say.

"Let me see what I can do trying to find him here. You focus on other places he might have been. Let's see if we can find this guy faster."

By the end of the day, Barrett and I have uncovered that Frederick Lee Cory, originally of Missouri, lived a fairly mundane and predictable life right up until his success in business really took off. Then he came under suspicion for various crimes and served time for assaulting at least one woman. Accusations of further sexual assaults and potential white-collar crime led him to shut down his business, alter his identity, and move back to Missouri.

We were able to trace him to locations near the Garden of Bodies, and we already know he had connections to the general vicinity of the farm with the warehouse building he sold to Vision of the Future. Taking that information, I dig further find his contact information. My phone call does not come as a welcome surprise for Mr. Cary.

"He was pissed I called," I tell Barrett on our follow-up video chat the next day.

He's eating lunch in his car to keep any of his coworkers from hearing our conversation. I decided to join him and am putting together a sandwich as we chat.

"He didn't want to talk about any of it. He readily admitted everything that happened and the charges he was accused of, and was very unhappy the past was coming back to get him. Which seems like a running thread in these cases."

"That tends to happen when your past is full of bodies," Xavier calls from the recliner in the living room where he's half buried in a blanket he's been steadily stitching on for days since discovering Sheridan's abandoned stash of yarn and hooks.

"That's very true," Barrett says, pointing his fork at the screen. "People tend to want to keep things like that in the past."

"Well, Fred-Frank is particularly eager to separate himself from everything that happened before he moved back to Missouri. He insists that he's a totally changed man. He underwent intensive therapy. He's cut off all substance use and has no contact with any of the people he used to associate with. He's tried to make restitution in every way he can and says he is so much better now than he has ever been. He says he knows absolutely nothing about the bracelets or why the order form would have his name on it. And he definitely doesn't know anything about any bodies," I say. "The only other connection I can find is that he used to be a member of the church next to the farm, but we already know that church had nothing to do with the case. He offered me a timeline of what he's been doing and his whereabouts prove he couldn't be the killer for at least a few of the women in the Garden of Bodies. He was in in-patient treatment for the months surrounding two of the victims."

"So that's it?" Barrett asks. "We have no idea why his name was on the form other than it was going to a building he used to own?"

"But even then, someone had to put his name on it. Someone had to make that order. And someone had to accept it. According to him, the building was empty at that time. He had already shut down his company and moved all operations out of it, and Windham Debracey hadn't purchased it yet. But somebody got ahold of that delivery because those bracelets ended up on the wrists of murder victims. And I hold very strong doubts the killer just happened on a box sitting in front of an empty building, opened it to discover a collection of custom bracelets with flower charms, and realized they were the perfect addition to the two people they had already murdered," I say.

"That would be far too much of a coincidence," Barrett says.

"No such thing," Xavier says from the living room.

I look over at him. His eyes come up from the blanket, and he shrugs. "Sam isn't here, so I felt I should go ahead and fill in for him."

"Nicely done. The point is, this guy was around all the right places. I'm positive he crossed paths with involved people. But there's nothing to actually link him to it," I say. "But all might not be lost. I did find out something potentially interesting."

"What?"

"The specialty food company Mr. Cary worked for? The one he got promoted through several times and then tried to compete against?"

"Yeah?"

"They didn't just ship food to individual customers or shops. They also have a division as a supplier for companies and events. Including the parent company that runs the types of festivals where Harmony sells her bracelets and the chain of motels that includes Crescent Cove."

"That is interesting," Barrett says.

"Now, he contends he didn't have anything directly to do with employees of those companies other than the management who made the orders. He didn't do deliveries or anything. He just managed the logistics portion. But it's something."

The inside of the Vision of the Future building is considerably warmer the next day when Xavier and I return. Tyler at the desk contacts Jane to let her know we're back, and she sweeps out of the back of the building in a sleeveless top in the familiar shade of light blue. Her hair is swept up off her neck, and when she turns to shut the door, I see the tattoo I'd gotten a hint of at the motel.

"I'm sorry about the temperature in here," she says, fanning herself for effect as she comes over to us. "Somehow the climate control in here went berserk, and we haven't been able to turn down the temperature.

With it so cold outside, we thought it might be nice for a little while, but at this point, I'm feeling like a potted plant."

Another woman dressed very similarly to Jane comes up and shows her a stack of papers. She reads over them quickly and jots a signature at the bottom. As the woman walks away, I notice the edge of a blue tattoo sticking out from under the edge of her shirt's armhole.

"It is a bit oppressive," I say. "Do you know when it's going to get fixed?"

"No idea," she says, sounding exasperated. "Apparently, there is only one heater and air-conditioning repair company in all of Virginia, and they are busy for the next six months." She laughs, and something out of the corner of her eye catches her attention. She turns her head sharply for a beat, then looks back at me. "I'm hoping it's soon. We called this morning." She looks to her side again. "Windham, come here for a minute."

A man coming from the far hallway walks toward us. A woman in a flowing pale-purple dress follows very closely behind.

"Hi, Jane," he says.

"Windham, this is the man I was telling you about. Dean Steele. Dean, this is Windham Debracey," Jane says.

"It's good to meet you, Dean," Windham says, taking my hand in a firm handshake and covering it with his other one for a brief squeeze. "I heard you're a private investigator."

"Yes."

He's far more unassuming than Jane's description of him would have led me to believe. But I suppose when she said he was a lot of man deserving of a lot of name she was referring more to his personality and capabilities than any phenomenal physical size. Windham isn't a small man, but he isn't any taller than me. With round brown eyes and a thick beard, he looks approachable and friendly, someone I can absolutely see being able to start up something like this.

"And the case you're investigating brought you here," he says.

It isn't a question. He's using carefully honed conversation skills to make me feel on his equal plane and that he's interested in what I'm saying. That, in a way, I have the power over the conversation because he's intrigued about what I have to tell him. By doing that though, he's maintaining a hard hold on the control, able to shift and move the conversation as he wants to. It's the kind of interaction and interpersonal skill that most people in this kind of industry—self-help gurus, community directors, motivational speakers—either learn themselves or are taught as they are building their careers. Within this realm trust, connection, and management of other people are paramount.

"I told him what you told me," Jane says.

"She did," Windham confirms. "And I'm afraid I'm not going to be much help to you either." He smiles and leans toward me conspiratorially. "Maybe I shouldn't say that so loud. It might not be great for my business."

I smile. "We can just say we're still on a journey to discovery."

He gives a bold, unencumbered laugh. "I like that." His eyes drift to the side, and he seems to remember the woman standing with him. "Oh, I'm sorry. I didn't introduce you to Linda."

He steps to the side enough for the woman to come closer. She extends her hand, and I shake it.

"It's nice to meet you," she says.

"You too."

Windham runs his hand over Linda's belly, smoothing the thin fabric over a burgeoning swell.

"And this is Roland. My son."

He bends down to press a kiss to her belly, and Linda laughs softly. She looks at me, shaking her head.

"I swear this baby will have been kissed more times before he is born than most babies do in the first year of their lives," she says.

"General consensus among medical practitioners specializing in pediatrics and public health professionals dictates neonates should not be kissed, particularly by those other than their parents and others from their households, for the first several months of life. Especially during the fall and winter seasons due to increased germ activity and a tendency for germs to spread rapidly within contained indoor areas and the hot, humid atmospheres created by climate control systems. It puts them and dramatically heightened risk of contracting potentially devastating illnesses including whooping cough, the flu, the common cold, and chicken pox, which can have lasting effects if the baby survives," Xavier says. He looks around at the widened eyes staring back at him. "I mean… yay, baby!"

I hang my head. I'm not going to try. There's no coming back from that one. We're just going to move forward.

"Well, speaking of hot indoor atmospheres, how are you enjoying my terrarium?" Windham asks, snatching the conversation back into his own control. "I'm thinking about throwing up some flowers and decorations and calling it a luau theme week."

The women laugh, and I manage to crack a smile.

"I heard you were traveling," I say.

"Yes. That's all part of our mission If we are really going to change the world, we have to think bigger. Our community can't just be the people right here around us. It has to be all of humanity. Going out and finding those who need us, in whatever capacity that might be, is an important part of my ministry. I am always inspired by the people I encounter during the trips, and some of my most driven members and devoted staff have come from other places. I believe having space for everyone means we are the right place for anyone.

"How about you? Dean? Xavier? Do you believe there is potential within you that hasn't been tapped? Something that you might be missing and that you hope to find in the course of your life?"

"If there's something in the course of my life, I'm going to end up finding it one way or the other," Xavier says. "It's just sitting there. I'm going to end up stumbling on it."

Windham looks at him for a beat, then bursts into that deep laughter. "I would love to talk to you gentlemen more, but I have meetings I need to tend to. After trips, there are always many people to update and plans to put in place. If you'll stand for a while, I can find time to meet with you later."

"Yes!" Jane says as if answering for us. "That would be perfect. Stay for dinner. You can meet more of the staff and some of the members."

"There's dinner here?" I ask.

She laughs. "There's all meals here. Most of us live here."

"The staff?" I ask.

"Yes. And some members too. It makes it easier to do our work to the fullest. Some of us, like me, have other jobs as well so living here at the center makes it possible for us to devote the most time to our work. If I lived somewhere else, I might not have the energy after working a shift at the motel to go home, get changed, and come here to the center. But since this is home, I can come here, refresh, and have time to connect right up until bed."

While we wait for dinner, Xavier and I roam the center again. We explored most of it the first time we were here, but there are sections we haven't gone into or places we've only seen briefly. As we walk around the large library, technology center, meditation space, and gym—as well as more classrooms and activity spaces—we meet more of the people from the organization, and the disquiet in the back of my mind keeps growing. There's the feeling of being watched without being watched, of having everyone around us monitor what we are doing even as they seem to offer us complete freedom. They are showing us their little self-contained world as if it were fully open for anyone to experience, but we are never alone.

"Do you feel like we're going to see eyeballs moving in portraits at any second?" Xavier whispers to me in a brief second when we don't have someone talking to us.

"Something like that," I reply.

"Are they grooming us? Is that what this is? Are we being groomed, Dean?" he asks.

"I don't think we've gotten quite to the grooming stage, but I definitely feel like something is happening. Everyone here is perfectly nice. It seems like a great group, and they're obviously doing good things for the community..."

Xavier makes a large, sweeping gesture with his arms like he's creating a globe. "Of the world."

"Yes. The community of the world. But some of the staff..."

"They're trying to get to us."

"Hey, guys." I look toward the voice and see Jane smiling at us from the corner. "Time for dinner."

We follow her back through the hallways, and she gestures at a door. "If you want to go in there and wash up, you can."

It's said in the way that an elementary school teacher would say it. She's framing it as an offer that can be taken up or not, but it's not really optional. Xavier and I go into the bathroom and wash our hands. We leave the bathroom and turn down the hall toward the dining room. As we approach, I notice Linda ahead of us. She's carrying a box of something, and I start to offer to help her, but before I can, a door to the side opens, and a man steps out. He immediately notices Linda and rushes to take the box from her. But rather than continuing in the direction she's been walking, they pause briefly and look at each other.

"How are you feeling?" he asks.

"Tired," she says. "And really heavy. It's getting close."

He touches her cheek with the back of his fingers to brush away a piece of hair that has fallen over her face, and I notice her lightly tilt her cheek into the touch. We keep walking toward them, and he suddenly notices we're there. Stepping back from her, they turn and continue the way she was going.

"Are you two joining us?" she asks as if she hadn't been there standing there when the decision was made earlier.

"Yes," I tell her.

"Wonderful. I'll see you in there."

As we're filling our plates from a massive buffet set on a table positioned along one wall of the dining room, I hear rain start to pound down on the roof. Moments later, the lights flicker, and there's a deafening crash of thunder. A few people gasp, and I notice Linda grab at her belly. I take out my phone and flip to the weather.

"There's a massive storm coming down on us," I say. "They're expecting winds at over seventy miles an hour, hail, and possible flooding."

There are a few murmurs throughout the room, but what I notice most is the way they are staring at the phone in my hand. No one else has taken one out, even though I would expect not to be the only one to want to check and see what's going on. Feeling oddly self-conscious about the phone, I slide it back into my pocket. Its disappearance seems to get the group moving again. A few look over at Windham, whose eyes are locked on me.

"Then I insist you stay," he says. "You can go out in a storm like that. It's dangerous. There's plenty of space here. You'll stay and let the weather pass."

Another crash of thunder makes the floor shake. Maybe it's the heat of the building clouding my thoughts. Or maybe it really is the knowledge that I can't drive out even the relatively short distance in winds that aggressive, but I hear myself agreeing that we'll stay.

After dinner, the group dissipates throughout the building. The storm is still raging, and I notice some people seeming to cling to each other and whisper between them until they decide where to go. I have a feeling these after-dinner activities are usually far more individual than they are tonight, but the storm has forced them to stay together.

"What's happening now?" I ask Jane as she starts out of the room.

"Evening reflection," she says. "Some of us go to group sessions. Others do individual work or study. You and Xavier can do as you please for the evening. Windham will have time to meet with you in the library after nine. Then I can show you where you'll sleep."

The meeting with Windham later is no more enlightening than our conversation earlier. He looks at the picture of Sienna for a long time but eventually shakes his head, apologizing and saying he doesn't know her. The door opens, and Linda comes in carrying a tray with a teapot and cups. She has changed into a different dress, but still the same shade of pale blue.

"Thank you," he says tenderly to her. He pats her belly. "Are you going to rest before Misha's arrival later?"

"Yes," Linda says.

"Good. I'll see you in the morning."

She leaves the room library, closing the door behind her, and I look at him with what I hope is obvious curiosity and not prying. I want him to tell me what he is talking about without me having to ask, extending the information as a friendly gesture rather than a response to an investigator's inquiry.

"As I mentioned earlier, certain very trusted people within the organization are selected to join me on my trips. They are valuable for making connections with people and encouraging prospective donors to support our ministry. Sometimes there are further matters that keep them from returning with me," he explains.

"Do you select these people from all members of the group?" I ask.

From the moment we arrived, people have been trying to tell us more about the organization and its programs, obviously trying to draw us in. I ask the question like I'm intrigued and want to know more. The flicker of a wider smile at the corner of his mouth tells me I've succeeded.

"No. The membership of Vision of the Future is more complex than that. Some of our members are just casual participants. They come to take classes or participate in improvement sessions. But it's just a part of their life. For others, it becomes the defining feature of their lives. They take several classes and participate in several sessions or activities each day. They become ambassadors to engage with the wider community. And then for others, it is their lives. This is a very select group formed by invitation only. They are mostly staff, but occasionally, there is a member who has proven themselves valuable enough to be brought in closer for more intensive focus and training. This is the group poised to really make a difference. These are the ones who travel with me, who work with the hardest-to-reach people, who work alongside me as I build a new future for everyone," he says.

The conversation cuts short as the power goes out. Windham mutters something angrily under his breath, and I hear jostling in the pitch darkness. A second later, a flame appears, then another. He holds one of the candles he has lit out to me.

"You should get to bed. It's late. Hopefully, this storm will pass soon."

As if she were waiting outside the entire time, Jane is standing just a few feet from the door to the library holding a flashlight. She gestures for us to follow her, and we make our way deeper into the building. Every step feels heavy. I don't like the sense of Windham being behind me, blackness ahead.

She brings us back to the front of the building and through the glass door behind the desk that leads to the bank of offices. Beams of other flashlights flicker around as people try to navigate the dark space.

I notice some of them seem stationary, as though rather than moving around, the people holding the flashlights are just standing by the doors to the rooms like guards.

I feel extremely visible and singled out with the candle in my hands, like it means something I'm not aware of. We get to the large door I've noticed at the back of the room, and Jane reaches into her pocket to pull out what looks like a large coin. She lifts it toward a small panel at the side of the door, then glances around, as if just remembering there's no power in the building.

She stuffs the coin back in her pocket and opens the door.

"This is the private sleeping quarters," she tells me. "Most of the people who live here sleep in the bunks on the other side of the building."

"Windham mentioned there are different levels within the group," I say. "Are the select few the ones who sleep back here?"

"He told you that?" she asks.

"Yes. Does that surprise you?"

"Oh no. I mean, that is how the organization is structured. I just didn't think he would describe it that way, that's all. Even though there are different levels within the group, he tends to be far more focused on unity. If a member or someone on the staff shows promise that warrants their inclusion, they are approached privately and invited to take the next steps. It's not something that's openly discussed or celebrated, because it's about personal growth and development of our vision for the future as a whole rather than individual successes."

"But I thought that was the point of this group. To further every person as an individual. Isn't it about accomplishment and fulfilling potential?" I ask.

"Of course, but this is only possible as part of a community. It is not for people to get big-headed and arrogant. When you think only of yourself and forget about how others engage, support, challenge, and better you, and in turn, your responsibility to help others who are still struggling, you are still just a shell. Everyone is a part of something bigger. Windham is the perfect example of that." She gestures to a door. "This is you."

"Do I need one of those coin things?" I ask, more to see if she will tell me what it is than out of concern that I actually need one.

Her hand presses against her pocket. "No. That's only to access this main area. Your room locks from the inside with a regular deadbolt. Hopefully, the power will come back soon. There's a flashlight in the top drawer of the dresser just in case. I'll see you in the morning."

I open the door to the room, squinting to see through the dim light of the dying candle. I hold the candle up as high as I can to get as much light as possible and cross to the dresser for the flashlight. Once I have it, Xavier shuts the door, and I hear the lock click into place. I extinguish the candle and put it aside, then sweep the flashlight through the room. Windows on the wall allow in a flash of light each time the lightning slashes across the sky. In an effort to allow in more, I move the curtains out of the way.

"Xavier," I say, stepping back from the window.

The glass is contained within a wrought iron cage.

"To keep people out or in?" he asks.

I shake my head. "This place is messed up. Did you hear Windham mention his 'ministry'? That's not something the head of a community center says."

"But it is what a religious leader would," Xavier says.

I nod. "They talk about him like he's above everyone but that we should be so honored because he doesn't act like is. That he acts like just a normal man and that's so impressive. But isn't he supposed to be just a normal man? He's done great things, yes. I've seen the pictures and heard the stories. I know how many people the group has helped. But does that make him something I'm not seeing?" I ask.

"It's obvious this group is more than what people see on the surface. He admitted as much. But why would they offer us not just to stay here overnight, a place in an otherwise secured area of the building where only that select few he was talking about are usually allowed? He knows I'm a private investigator. He knows I'm investigating murders. If there was something happening under the surface, why would he put us right in the middle of it?"

"To prove there isn't," Xavier says. "The witch invited Hansel and Gretel into the gingerbread house too. It's easy to look through a pane of glass and forget it used to be a sandcastle."

I start to pace, the darkness and the heat closing in around me.

"Are you all right?" Xavier asks.

"I feel like I can't breathe. It's so fucking hot."

"At least the power is off, so the heater isn't still working," Xavier says. "It's getting cooler."

I stop and look at him. "It's getting cooler in here because the heater turned off when the power went out."

He blinks at me. "Yes. That is generally how that works."

"Then why didn't they just turn the heater off?" I ask. "They're boiling in here because the heater supposedly malfunctioned and won't stop pumping out obscenely hot air. Which they all believe because that's what Windham told them. So why didn't someone just go turn the system off?"

"Because he didn't tell them to," Xavier says.

My heart is pounding, my pulse throbbing in my temples. "I need some air. The storm is dying down. I'm going outside. Do you want to come?"

"No. I need to stay here as your beacon in case you can't find your way back."

"There's another flashlight in the drawer. I won't be gone long," I say.

I walk out of the room, and the eerie feeling returns. I don't see any other flashlight beams, but I feel watched. I haven't noticed any cameras anywhere throughout the building, but that doesn't mean anything. Xavier has more than proven to me that camera technology has made it so you can be completely surrounded by surveillance and not have any idea.

Rather than going back through the circular inner lobby and out the front door, I scan the hallway to see if there are any access doors. At the very end of the hall, I see a glass door and the remnants of the storm beyond. As I approach it, I notice a panel to the side much like the one Jane tried to open with the coin. The door must have magnetized locks that release only for authorized people. From how she described the coin, I have a feeling that doesn't mean everyone.

The power is still out, so I pull the door open. It's far heavier than I expected. Looking at the door, I realize it's made of very thick reinforced unbreakable glass. Fresh air from outside washes over me, and I let the feeling pull me out to the balcony. I know we climbed stairs during our exploration of the building and after going through the door with Jane, but I didn't realize we were this high up. The building must have been built in such a way that the back is higher than the front, allowing visitors to enter on an upper floor while feeling like they are entering on the ground.

I draw in breath after breath of the cold November air. It revives me, chilling the sweat on my skin and clearing my mind. I lean against a high railing, and just as I'm closing my eyes to savor the feeling more, I notice headlights in the distance. A car is coming not from the road that I drove down but from the back of the property. Leaning down slightly over the edge, I see flashlight beams spilling across the paved stone parking area seconds before three figures appear. There's enough light around them for me to recognize Linda and Jane, but I don't know the third woman dressed in similar colors.

The car pulls up in front of the women, and a driver gets out. He opens the back door, and another woman, this one dressed in green, climbs out. The women gather around her, and Linda puts her arm around her shoulders. They say a few words to the driver, then usher her toward the door. As they turn, I see the beam of the flashlight reflect off something metallic on the girl's wrist.

CHAPTER TWENTY-NINE

THE POWER COMES BACK ON A COUPLE OF HOURS INTO TRYING to sleep, and as the sun comes up, Xavier and I are ready to leave. It's too early for Jane to be in her office, so we make our way to the dining room. Breakfast is already underway though it is barely dawn. The room is full of chatter and the smell of coffee. I notice the temperature is far cooler than the day before. Jane is filling a bowl with fruit from the buffet, and I cross directly to her.

"Good morning," she says with a bright smile. "I hope you slept well last night. Especially after the power came back on. That's something I've just never understood. We sleep in the dark, and yet somehow it's scarier to sleep when there's no power."

She laughs softly, and Xavier interjects. "The vibrations."

She looks at him and tilts her head in an unspoken question.

"Electricity generates waves. Your body feels them as vibrations, and you can hear them even though it is very unlikely you actually process that there is a sound. It's so ubiquitous that your mind and body are fully accustomed to the feeling and the sound of the electricity flowing through buildings. Even when there are no lights on, there is power flowing through electronics and appliances. When the power goes out, those vibrations stop, which is startling to the body. The darkness seems more frightening because there is a more absolute void when the removal of light also includes the removal of auditory and tactile sensory input. You feel cut off from something you didn't consciously process as even being there."

"Oh. Well, thank you for that," she says. "Sit down. Have some breakfast. We can talk more about the case or about the center if you'd like."

"Actually, we have to get going," I say. "I just wanted to say thank you for your hospitality."

"Really? So early?" she asks.

"There's a lot to be done," I say. "Since the bracelet order being directed here was apparently unintentional and no one here remembers Sienna or any of the other women, I'm going to try to come at this from another angle. It's my responsibility to get answers for the families and justice for the victims. One of the six was killed within the last few months, which means this guy is still active. I don't want to risk him acting again. I appreciate all the help you were able to give. Thank Windham for me when you see him."

Without waiting for a response, we wave and leave the center. Not wanting to show any kind of discomfort, I start the car and drive away immediately. It isn't until we're half a mile away that I pull into a gas station and park to take a breath. Leaning over the steering wheel, I place my forehead on the cold surface and let myself settle.

"Did you really believe what you just said to her?" Xavier asks.

"Of course not," I say. "But like you said, windows and sandcastles. They brought us into the center of their web so we could see there was no danger, and I made sure they knew it worked. I don't want any suspicion until we can find out exactly what's going on." I look through the windshield at the gas station. "It looks like they have a little lunch counter in there. You want to see if they have breakfast?"

I grab my bag and bring it with me inside. The counter already has a couple of customers sitting at it, and when I notice a table off to the side, I gesture at it, and the waiter behind the counter lifts his pot of coffee in acknowledgment. There aren't many options on the menu, so we both choose breakfast sandwiches, hash browns, and coffee when the waiter comes by. When he walks away, I take a handful of papers out of the bag and set them on the table between us.

"The first time I looked at that bulletin board in the hallway, something about it stuck with me, and I couldn't figure out what it was at first. But I looked at it again, and it finally clicked this morning. The apostrophes. Remember the note from Sienna's apartment? You pointed out the transposed apostrophe. It showed up on three different papers on that bulletin board, and then look…"

I pull a brochure out of the stack and show it to him.

"Most of the booklets and things that are around the center were written by other people. Their names are on them with little blurbs about their involvement in the organization and how long they've been around like it gives them credibility. This brochure has a letter at the beginning that's from Windham. Right here." I point at the paper. "Transposed apostrophe. There's another here and then two more. I thought it was just a slip the first time I saw it, but it's not. That's something he does regularly. When he writes with apostrophes, he puts them in the wrong place. And then at the bottom of the board…"

"'Good morning, sunshine,'" Xavier says. "I saw it too."

I nod. "That's nothing significant on the surface. It's obviously a common phrase. But it's written in the same handwriting as the note in Sienna's apartment, and there's so much emphasis on fulfilling your potential but then being a good influence and source of hope in the lives of others."

"Being the sunshine in someone else's storm," Xavier says.

"Exactly. It's a subtle detail, and maybe it wouldn't mean much of anything if that was the only thing I noticed, but that place…" I shake my head. "He told us so openly that there are levels within the group. It almost feels like a challenge. You said it was to show there was no threat, like if he told me a little bit and even let me into the area of the center that's usually only accessible by the closest people to him, then I couldn't possibly suspect anything about him. And I believe that is a part of it. But I think there's more to it. He's obviously used to being revered. Just the way people talk about him is enough to show he's seen as far more than just an inspiring leader of an organization."

"He's a god," Xavier says. "With his own bouquet of women around him."

"Each one of them with the forget-me-not tattoo on her shoulder, just like the ones growing near the graves. It's so blatant. It's right there, and people exist around it without even noticing. He told us about the smaller, select groups within the organization because he wanted to challenge me. He wanted to show that he could put it right in front of my face and I would still not know what I'm looking at.

"I completely believe the self-help group is real. I believe the community outreach efforts are real. I even think there are members of the staff who don't have any idea that anything else is going on. But if you know where to look, there's so much of an undercurrent of servitude among those women. Dressing alike. The same tattoos. Following after him and looking at him like he literally controls the sun. Those are his inner circle. The most trusted members of the group."

"Like Jim Jones," Xavier says. "There was a small number of women he trusted above anyone else in the entirety of the Peoples Temple. They made things happen for him."

"I think these women make things happen for Windham. He told us that girl who was coming back to the center had stayed behind on the outreach trip because she had more pressing matters. You would think he would want to see her and talk to her after something like that, but when I went outside, I saw Jane, Linda, and another woman meet her. She wasn't dressed like them, but I saw something on her wrist. I was on a balcony, and it was dark, but the light shone on it for long enough that I think it was a bracelet."

The waiter comes to the table and sets our food in front of us.

"Anything else?" he asks.

"No, thanks. I think we're fine," I say.

He nods once and takes a step away from the table, then pauses and turns back around.

"I didn't mean to listen to your conversation or anything, but I overheard you. Are you..." he pauses and takes a breath, letting his shoulders drop. "Are you talking about Vision of the Future?"

"Yeah, we are," I say. "Do you know it?"

"I used to be a part of it," he says. "I left about two years ago. That place is messed up."

"Do you have a break coming up soon so you can talk with us?" I ask.

"Yeah. My backup is supposed to be in at seven-thirty."

"We'll be here," I tell him. "Just keep the coffee coming."

"No problem."

While we wait for him to have his break, Xavier and I try to piece together connections to make sense of Tamara Booth's land, Frank Cory's address on the bracelet delivery, and Windham Debracey. I know he's at the heart of this. I just have to find out how.

A girl who looks barely out of her teens arrives a couple of minutes before seven-thirty, and the waiter comes over to the table with a pot of coffee and his own mug. He sits beside me and refills our cups before filling his own.

"I'm Dean," I say. "This is Xavier."

"Abe," he says. "Before I say anything, can I ask you why you're talking about Vision of the Future? It didn't sound like you're interested in joining up."

"You can say that," I tell him. "I'm a private investigator. A case I'm working on led me directly to them. I'm trying to unravel why."

"That doesn't surprise me," he says. "I just can't believe it took this long."

"What do you mean?" I ask.

"Like I said, I used to be in that group. My girlfriend and I joined up a few years ago when we were trying to figure out what we were going to do with our lives. That quarter-life crisis everybody talks about, I guess. Anyway, neither of us had any idea what direction we wanted to go or what we wanted to do, and she came home from the library one day with this brochure. She said she met an amazing woman at the library talking about this group that was really making waves in the world and was going to do all these incredible things that sounded exactly like the type of stuff we wanted to do.

"I never wanted to get some job in some corporate office doing the same thing every day for the rest of my life. I wanted to really be out in the world making a difference. I wanted to interact with people. I saw so much bad going on in the world, and I wanted to be part of making it better. Before then, I hadn't really felt like that was a possibility for me. I had a lot of people telling me I needed to go to college and get a real job, then volunteer when I had time. Or I needed to work for a big nonprofit that was doing things. But that wasn't right for me. When I heard about Vision of the Future, it was everything I'd been trying to find. We went to an open house at the center, and I met Jane, the woman my girlfriend met at the library."

Xavier and I exchange glances, and Abe notices.

"We know Jane," I tell him. "She's the first of the group I met as well."

He gives a slight, knowing bounce of his head. "That sounds about right. She introduced us to Windham, and we listened to him talk about what the group was all about. He talked about the self-improvement courses, the wellness seminars, the mental health small groups. It sounded like we could just go to the center and live there doing yoga, talking about everything that was bothering us, learning, and becoming these elevated versions of ourselves. And on top of that, they were doing amazing things in the community.

"He started telling us about the projects he had in the works that would provide housing and sustainable living resources for the homeless. They'd offer food and necessities to children in low-income neighborhoods, develop free childcare centers for working mothers, and turn abandoned city buildings and empty lots into green spaces and playgrounds. It sounded absolutely incredible. It was everything I'd been wanting to hear. We joined immediately."

"You felt at home there?" I ask.

He nods. "Things were good at first. We participated in the sessions and started volunteering. After a little while we got more involved, and they asked us to move into the center. That sounded like a dream. Then my girlfriend started getting more attention from the core women. She was invited to additional classes and given more responsibilities. She became very close with another girl, but I noticed my girlfriend started wearing those blue-and-purple clothes the other women wore when the other girl wasn't, but she wouldn't tell me anything.

"I started paying more attention and realized how… worshipful the women were about Windham. Some of the ways he talked about himself and the things that he did were starting to sound over the top. It was like he thought he was elevating beyond this earth. One day the girl my girlfriend had gotten close to just wasn't around anymore. I asked about her, and she told me she had progressed through her chosen program and moved on. It didn't make any sense. I tried to find out what happened to her but was shut down by everyone. It started to feel like Windham was turning against me and the ones closest to him were trying to force me to comply with what they were saying.

"My girlfriend was barely speaking to me then. She was gone for days at a time and would never tell me why. I couldn't take it anymore, and I told them I was leaving. They tried to get me to stay, and when I said I wouldn't, they warned me not to tell anyone anything about the group. Every one of us was on a private and sacred journey that could be shared only by those who were committed to their growth and to Windham. I left and never spoke to any of them again.

"But I saw those girls. Our friend wasn't the only one. They would come in all ready to improve their lives and give back to the community, and if one of them caught Windham's eye, they would suddenly disappear behind that glass door. We'd still see them, but they were different. They were being brought out to talk to prospective supporters and encourage new members. I never saw them leave, only heard about it, but I saw them come back a couple of times. They were always wearing green.

"I knew what was happening. I couldn't prove it, and when I tried to talk to the police about it, they acted like I was crazy. But I knew they were trafficking those girls. They were passing them out like candy to the people whose pockets they wanted to pick or names they wanted to leverage. But because it was only a small percentage of the girls who walked through those doors and there were so many others who genuinely didn't know what was happening, it kept happening. And they always came back. All of them came back. Until she didn't."

He takes a long sip of coffee, and I notice his hands shaking slightly. I can feel Xavier's eyes on me. I know he's thinking the same thing I am.

"Abe, what was the name of the girl who disappeared?"

CHAPTER THIRTY

"Courtney Rogers," I say, handing a picture of the girl I remember as the body wearing an iris bracelet to Jane. "What can you tell me about her? Because I know she was here and now she's a corpse."

I wait for her to come up with a story, to try to lie about never knowing her the way she did about Sienna. If she does, I'll just show her the picture I took with Abe and let her read the statement he wrote. It's not enough to get the police involved. Not yet. I need much more than a statement from a scorned boyfriend to convince the detectives something is happening inside that center and that Windham is at its core.

But Jane takes a breath and hands the picture back to me. "Yes, I know her. Well, I knew her. Years ago. She was part of a version of the group years ago."

I frown. "A version of the group?"

I know from what Abe told me that she was at this center, but I want to hear what Jane has to say.

"Yes. Vision of the Future has gone through different stages in its development. It's a massive undertaking and an accomplishment beyond the scope of anything I've ever seen," she says. "Even Windham had to build toward what he has achieved here. After parting ways with a leader he recognized as not being visionary enough for what he has always known could be done, he had to find his way. He had to begin the process of creating something new, something that would change the world. He went through several iterations before this was born."

Jane is beaming with pride as she unknowingly hands me a key detail I hadn't yet been able to piece together. I don't acknowledge it but push ahead.

"What happened to her?" I ask.

A touch of disdain glazes her eyes. "What we want to happen to everyone who joins us, if they aren't destined to commit themselves to our ongoing work. She was very successful with her personal development and growth, was able to free herself of addictions and the destructive behaviors they bring with them, discovered new parts of herself she never knew were there, and she moved on. It's always hard when that happens because we become so close here and never enjoy saying goodbye. At the same time, it's a joyful time, and we're proud to see the program work.

"Courtney was exceptional. She stands out to me. She was beautiful and funny, and when we were finally able to get past the walls she'd put up and discover such an impressive well of untapped potential, she blossomed into something incredible."

The words chill me, and I hope Jane doesn't notice the twitch of the muscle on the side of my jaw.

"No one in Courtney's life had any contact with her after she came here," I say. "I know when she joined and I know when she was last seen here. According to the medical examiner's estimated range for her date of death, Courtney was murdered at the same time."

"Which terrifies me," Jane says.

"Terrifies you?"

"Clearly it means she wasn't as progressed as we believed. She hadn't yet reached the point where she was able to stay at the elevated version of herself. The only explanation I can think of is that she fell back into her old ways almost immediately after leaving. It doesn't surprise me that she wouldn't get in touch with her family. They were the source of so much of her pain and inability to be what she was designed to be. And I'm devastated that something so horrible happened to her.

I was honored to know her. My life was enriched and my own journey heightened for her being a part of it. I will never forget her."

"Jane, can I have a word with you?"

I didn't see Windham come into the room, but now he's standing a few steps into the doorway, his eyes boring into her.

"Of course," she says. "Dean, will you excuse me?"

"It's all right. I was just leaving. I really appreciate your help, again. I know you tried with Courtney. I'm sure it meant a lot to her," I say.

As I head for the door, Windham walks past me toward her. His face stretches into a smile, and he shakes my hand, pounding jovially on my back.

"Good to see you again, Dean. Does this mean you're thinking about taking us up on some of our offerings? I know you'd be a great member."

"We'll see," I tell him.

I step just outside the door and pause to see if I can hear their conversation. Windham is speaking low, but his voice travels out to me.

"Jane, you need to be more careful. You know how we feel about talking about those closest to us. Meditate on your strength, Jane. On the peace and the power you contain within you. You must never forget them."

The mirroring of the words splashes images of blue flowers across my mind. I'm heading back to the front door when I see Linda. She smiles at me and gives me a little wave.

"Hi, Dean," she says, stopping at the head of the hallway she was about to walk down. "How are you today?"

"I'm doing well. How are you? How are you feeling?" I ask.

She runs a hand over her belly and lets out a little sigh along with a chuckle. "Like I've been carrying this baby around for about three years. But I'm so blessed. I really shouldn't complain. My baby boy is a miracle, and I am honored to have been chosen as his mother. I know he's going to do such amazing things."

"Linda?"

The sound of the man's voice comes up the hallway.

"Bill," she says, taking a slight step back.

"I couldn't find you. I brought this for you."

She glances over at me almost nervously as he comes into view. His hands fall to his sides from where they were lifted in the air like he was reaching to embrace her. He's holding a restaurant takeout container in one hand and for a moment tries to conceal it behind his leg. When he realizes I have already seen it and their interaction, he holds it out to her.

"You were saying the other day that you were craving tacos, and my sister very firmly informed me that if a pregnant woman is craving something, she needs to have it," he says. "I know Windham would want to make sure you and the baby are healthy and happy."

That last part sounds forced, like it's been tacked on to what he was saying for my benefit.

"I've got to go," I tell Linda. "It was good to see you."

"You too," she says.

I wave to Bill and head out. The interaction between the two is just as significant as the first I witnessed. It stands in such apparent contrast to the rest of the group. Everyone here is so devoted to Windham, and Linda seems to be his most important companion. The only possible exception might be Jane, but even she has a more distanced, reverent approach to him. Yet Linda has never been described with any kind of affectionate or meaningful label such as partner, girlfriend, or wife. She's also pregnant with his child yet is clearly carrying on a deeply emotional relationship with another man. I'm struggling to understand the dynamic and what it may mean.

I accidentally left my phone out in the car, and when I get to it, I see a missed call and a voicemail.

"Hi, Dean, this is Harmony. I'm sorry to interrupt your investigation, but I really feel like you needed to know this. I haven't been able to stop thinking about my bracelets being used as part of ritualistic murders. I started going through all my old orders starting all the way back to when I started making these bracelets twenty years ago. I need to ask you if any other bodies were found with similar bracelets beyond the ones you already told me about.

I found another instance of someone buying my entire inventory of flower charm bracelets at the same time. It wasn't an order, so there's no form, but it was done in person at another festival. They obviously weren't custom because they were bought right off the display, but they were all of very similar design and appearance, so the person who bought them bought them all. Since it was done in person and in cash without an order form, I don't have any kind of record of who it was or where they live. I hope it's nothing. I hope someone just needed a bunch of bridesmaid's gifts or a party favor or something. Please let me know."

I throw my phone into the passenger seat and slam my foot on the gas, shooting out of the parking area and back toward Sheridan's house where Xavier is waiting. I know there is a possibility someone could simply have bought the bracelets as gifts, or they wanted their own floral collection, but I can't force myself to believe that. The way Harmony said it, it's obviously not common for someone to buy that much jewelry all at once when the pieces are very similar.

Which means there are more victims. The timing she gave me explains the apparent large time gap between Sienna and TD on the farm and the bodies in the garden, which hadn't made sense to me. He didn't just go from two on the arm to a multi-year hiatus to a string of murders. There were others in between. There could be another whole garden waiting to be found.

With this added sense of urgency putting an edge on my confidence that the inner circle of Vision of the Future is behind the horrific murders, I know I have to change my tactics. I need a more aggressive approach, something that will get me the answers I need quickly.

"I can't go in myself," I say to Sheridan and Xavier when I get back to the house. "They've seen me far too many times. The same goes for Xavier. They've talked to us a few times about the possibility of joining, and we've never said we were interested. They would know something was strange with us suddenly wanting to join up and get all the details about the organization. I need someone who can blend in and who they will give the information to without realizing what they're doing."

"I'll go," Sheridan offers. "None of them have ever met me. They would have no idea I had anything to do with you."

"Absolutely not," I say without a second of hesitation.

"Why not? I'm the one who got you involved in this in the first place. And I know Sienna's case better than anybody. I want these answers, and I want to know the person who is responsible for hurting all those women doesn't ever get to do it again," Sheridan says.

"I know. But this isn't just about Sienna. This is about all those women, and possibly more. Which makes it extraordinarily dangerous. You don't have this kind of experience. You aren't in law enforcement."

"Neither are you," she fires back.

"I'm a private investigator. I'm trained to handle these situations. You aren't, and I can't in good conscience put you in that kind of danger. Even if you feel like you can do it, I won't put you at that risk," I say. "I'm going to call Emma."

"Emma is not going to join the cult," Xavier says. "I think this would be her third, and at some point, you have to slow down with the extremist beliefs. Something's going to start sinking in."

"I'm not going to ask Emma to go undercover. But she might have a suggestion," I say.

Reaching out to my cousin proves just as valuable as I hoped. She immediately suggests I get in touch with Kelly Mercer, an FBI special agent she worked with recently on an intense undercover operation. I take her up on the suggestion, and the next day Emma arranges for Zara to transport Kelly here to Virginia.

We waste no time when she arrives. I've already mapped out as much of a plan as I possibly can to help her get accepted into the group and chosen as one of the inner circle. She will then be able to collect specific information for me while I continue to investigate to solidify links, locate the possible other victims, and move to prevent anything else from happening. Now that I know the girls wearing green are the ones at risk of becoming some of Windham's flowers, I can't move quickly enough.

By the next evening, we've finalized a backstory for her, changed her appearance enough to make her fit the story, and put together the belongings she would have with them.

"One more thing," Xavier says as she's looking over everything to ensure she's ready. "I need to fit you for your tracking device."

Kelly's eyes snap over to me. "My what?"

"Your tracking device," I repeat. "Emma, Sam, and I have them already. Xavier designed them for us a few years ago. It will pinpoint exactly where you are and can begin recording voice or video whenever you need it. It's a basic security measure."

"I even improved the technology and added a feature Dean's doesn't have. Yours has an added emergency feature that enables you to instantly contact emergency services and provide your exact location without you having to speak," Xavier says as he shows her the device. "It's designed to fit into the band of your bra."

Kelly tucks her arms into her shirt and jostles around for a second.

"You know, these devices are pretty much like those Life Alert things. We got my great-grandpa one because he liked to wander around in his later years and we kept misplacing him," she says.

Her arms come back out of her sleeves, and she pulls her bra out from her neckline, holding it out to Xavier. He looks at it for an incredulous beat, then takes it using two fingers.

"That's true. Versions of the technology do exist. My designs are just far more streamlined and subtle than a giant plastic speaker around your neck. Though, if you prefer, I will happily craft you one of those," he says.

CHAPTER THIRTY-ONE

Sienna

Eleven years ago

The headlights blinded me, and I felt rooted to the ground, stuck where I was standing. Art had stopped calling my name, but it was like I could still hear it bouncing around in my brain. I couldn't go back toward the gas station. I couldn't get out of the street. I braced myself for the impact.

None came. Tires squealed, and the headlights swept off to the side. I'd turned my head away, and I opened my eyes to see a van stopped just a couple of feet from me. My heart started pounding harder. I didn't want to get into another van. Flashes of the tattered back of Art's van made my knees shake. Now that the headlights weren't bearing down on me, I could move, and I started to run around the van, but the back door opened. I saw light pour out, and the face of three women staring out at me.

"Are you all right?" one of them asked. "What's happening?"

"You're hurt!" one of the others said. "Is that man chasing you?"

"Get her in!" the third said. "She can explain later."

"Come on," the first said. "Come on and get inside. We'll keep you safe and get you away from here."

It was what I needed to hear. It was what I'd needed to hear for months. Sobbing, I scrambled to the open door and let them help me in. They guided me to a clean, plush seat while the door closed and the van started moving again. A blanket came around from somewhere to wrap around me. The light was off now that the door was closed, but we were driving away. Art Bellinger was behind me, and I would never have to go back. I'd actually done it. I'd gotten away.

"What's your name?" one of the women asked, her hand resting with comforting pressure on my shoulder.

"Sienna," I said.

My body was shaking violently from the cold and the adrenaline dump of the danger finally being over, making my voice tremble.

"Hi, Sienna," she said. "I'm Jane. You don't have to be afraid anymore. Your future belongs to you. You can do anything you want with it. Don't worry. The sunshine is coming."

Kelly Mercer

Now

Kelly drove up to the Vision of the Future complex in a car that wasn't hers.

Technically, it was, because she'd bought it for a few hundred dollars down just the day before from a used-car lot. But it wasn't the car she drove every day. The one she recognized from across the parking lot and acted as a little place of solitude when life was stressful. When this was over, she'd turn around and sell this car.

For right then though, it was doing exactly what it was supposed to, along with the suitcase full of clothes she'd gotten from a thrift store just after buying the car. They weren't her style. They didn't feel exactly right when she was wearing them. And that was what she intended. They weren't hers. They belonged to the person she was embodying for her undercover work. She didn't want those pieces of her true self to come along with her and risk breaking her focus.

A different car. Different clothes. They made her a different person. Because she bought used, they came with their own stories as well. People recognized when clothes were brand-new or a car was a rental. They wanted authenticity, so she would give it to them in the form of a slight dent over one tire, broken-in jeans, and well-worn shoes.

Before getting out of the car, she ran her fingertips over her shirt, feeling the band of her bra, to check that the tiny tracking device was still in place. She sent Dean a text from her own phone before tucking that away in the center console and tossing a burner into her purse. A quick glance in the mirror and she was ready.

As she walked toward the glass doors toward the figure of a young man behind a large desk, she went over everything Dean had been able to tell her about the group itself as well as the women who fell prey to it. That was what she needed to know. She wasn't just walking into the building in hopes of being accepted by them. She wanted them to notice her. She wanted to appeal to them so they would want to draw her deeper into their inner circle and show her what was behind the facade. She was playing a delicate game.

Tyler behind the front desk greeted her with a warm smile and asked what he could do for her. Kelly gave a tiny sampling of her cover story, offering just enough to make her seem like someone who would be drawn to the self-help offerings at the center but who was also yearning for something more. He invited her to read through brochures while he went to get someone to talk to her.

Moments later, a beautiful woman in a long, purple dress that skimmed her body and showed off the gentle slope of her neck came toward her. She looked into Kelly's eyes like she'd known her for years.

"Hi," the woman said, reaching her hand toward Kelly. "I'm Jane."

"Hi. I'm Melanie."

"Welcome, Melanie. What brings you to Vision of the Future?" Jane asked.

Kelly forced emotion into her voice and willed tears to pool in her eyes. "I've been going through a really rough time, and I feel lost. I know there has to be something else out there, but I'm afraid everything I've gone through… I'm afraid it's ruined what I could be. I want to make a difference."

Jane nodded and wrapped a comforting arm around Kelly's shoulders. She steered her toward the glass door behind the desk.

"Let's go talk, just the two of us. What I'm hearing you say speaks so much to my heart and my own experience, and I want you to know you don't have to feel that way. You don't have to be afraid anymore. Your future belongs to you. You can do anything you want with it. Don't worry. The sunshine is coming."

CHAPTER THIRTY-TWO

I haven't heard from Agent Mercer in more than a week.

She texted me when she got to the center and then again when she left that night for the hotel. As tempting as it was for her to stay at the Crescent Cove, that would require her to use her true identity to check in, so she chose a different hotel on the other side of town. Our goal was for her to stay there for as short a time as possible. The hope was for her to catch the attention of Jane and Windham so they would choose to move her into the center immediately.

I hope that's what's happening. I don't want to worry about her, but I can't help it. It doesn't matter to me that she's a special agent and extensively trained to handle dangerous situations surrounded by criminals. Not only is she doing this on a consultancy basis rather than in her official capacity as a favor to Emma, but she is also a human being. One I feel responsible for because I brought her into this. That's enough for me.

"She has the device Xavier made for her," Emma reassures me over speakerphone. "If something had gone wrong, she would be able to handle her own, and she would have used that device to call for help if she needed it. You have to trust that she knows what she's doing. She's good, Dean. Let her do what she needs to do, and you'll get the answers you need.

"I wanted to let you know I briefed Eric on the situation. Because all this crossed so many state lines and deals with cult activities and human trafficking on top of serial murder, I have a strong feeling the Bureau is going to get involved. I wanted him to know ahead of time what we're going to be dealing with."

"That was probably a good idea. What did he have to say about it?" I ask.

"He wants to act as soon as possible. He's waiting for enough to go on," she says.

"I'm trying to get it," I say.

"What have you been doing?" she asks.

"I'm trying to track Windham Debracey's movements to see how many versions of this group have existed. I need to be able to prove he was involved in that other group, the Comfort Circle, as he was building up his own group. It looks like the two overlapped for at least a few years. From what Jane said, he split off on his own to something more radical because the group he was with wasn't doing enough.

"I want to find concrete links that put him in the proximity of Tamara Booth and Pastor Laurence, which would give him access to the land. I believe Tamara Booth and Fred Cory crossed paths at some point. He was a part of the church right next to her property, and Howard said sometimes members of the congregation would go over there to try to reach out to Benjamin and Mae. They may well have encountered each other there. He is also linked to Windham and to Harmony Soleil through the festivals the company he worked for supplied with food for their events. It's all starting to knot together. I just have to keep looking," I say.

"Let me know if you need help," she says.

"I will."

As I delve deeper into Windham's past, I find myself leaving the twisted world of contorted religion and misdirected faith he'd built up around himself and stepping into a life that seems utterly normal. Ten years before his first victim, he was in college, doing normal college things. He worked a retail job. He was married.

That revelation stops me. I've never heard mention of his wife. The worst possible scenarios dance through my head as I run a search for Marla Debracey. Relief washes over me when I see she's still alive and apparently thriving. Her social media shows her living in Pennsylvania with teenage children. I've come across Pennsylvania already in this investigation, which could mean nothing, but I think it's far more likely a hint that Windham, consciously or not, has never fully let go of the wife who divorced him when he was still in his twenties.

I send her a message, and she gets back to me immediately. Within the hour, we're on a video call. She looks slightly uncomfortable. Not agitated or afraid, just like she doesn't really want to have this conversation.

"The last thing I would have thought I'd do today is talk about Windham," she says.

"I'm sorry if talking about him is upsetting to you," I say. "I'll make it as fast as I can."

"No," she says, shaking her head and giving me a slight smile like she wants to reassure me. "No, that's not what I meant. Thinking about him doesn't upset me. We had a wonderful marriage. Until we didn't. He's unlike anyone else you'll ever meet, and that was what I loved about him. He could always get me thinking about something in a different way or make me laugh when I was having a hard time. He always made me feel like I could do more, do better, or get out and really make a difference in the world around me," she says. "He never wanted to sleep. He always wanted to be doing something."

I'm hearing the same words come from her that I've heard over and over. Long before any of his wild ambitions came to fruition, Windham Debracey was carrying ideas that could have done nothing but beautiful things but instead turned dark.

"What happened in your marriage?"

"Windham had an exceptional knack for making anyone and everyone feel important. That was a big part of what drew me to him. He could make me feel like I was the only person in the world even if I was in a crowded room. I loved him desperately. And I believe he loved me. I really do. But he was always distracted by his ideas.

"If there's a word I'd use to describe him, it would be fanatical. He was never cruel, never abusive. I don't want you to get that idea. But he was so wrapped up in his view of the world, completely focused on these great accomplishments he would someday achieve. He believed in a very specific idea of what society should be, and he was driven to make that happen. It sounded utopian. I always used to tell him he should have lived in the sixties because he sounded like one of the hippie gurus from that time."

She laughs, but I can't bring myself to find the chilling comparison funny. He is exactly like those men, and like so many of them, he has left a trail of broken lives and broken people in his wake.

"How was he with your children?" I ask.

Marla looks briefly confused, then shakes her head. "Oh no, Macy and Leon aren't Windham's children."

"I'm sorry," I say. "I just assumed when I saw them."

"It's all right. I had them very quickly after the divorce. It was a whirlwind rebound I convinced myself was going to be my brand-new life, and a year later, I had twins and no man. It's been the three of us ever since. And honestly, I love it. We take on the world together, and it's been amazing. When I found out I was pregnant with them, I was so happy. Even though it was incredibly fast, I just knew this was what I was meant for. But it also hurt. I wanted to call Windham because I didn't want him finding out from someone else, but I also couldn't bear to cause him pain again so soon after the divorce.

"From the very beginning of our marriage, we were talking about our children. We could just see it in our hearts. Even though we were really young newlyweds, we couldn't wait to start our family. We'd joke that we'd just bring the baby to class with us and they would be so advanced as toddlers. But it never happened. We wanted them so much and tried so hard, but I never got pregnant."

"Never?" I ask.

"No. My doctor ran tests and said I was very healthy. There was no reason I shouldn't be able to conceive and carry a baby. Windham refused to go to his own doctor. He believed when it was time to happen, it would. That we both just needed to focus more on bettering ourselves and becoming our fully realized selves. Then we'd be truly prepared to be parents and the baby would come. I tried to tell myself that for a long time. It hurt so much less to let myself be deluded into thinking it would happen for us one day than it did to just accept that Windham couldn't have children."

My breath catches painfully in my lungs, but I try not to show my reaction.

"Do the two of you still keep up with each other?" I ask.

Marla shakes her head, a sad expression falling over her face. "No. We lost track of each other after the divorce. I haven't seen or spoken to him since about two months after the papers were signed. Why? What's happening with him?"

~

I'm still reeling from my call with Marla when I finally hear from Kelly. Before she went in, I warned her about how unwelcoming they all are to having cell phones inside, and by her hushed tones, it seems she has recognized the same thing. It sounds like she is tucked away somewhere trying to keep anyone from hearing her. She speaks rapidly like she wants to get all of it out as quickly as possible in case someone does come along, so I listen closely as she updates me on her experience.

I haven't heard from her because she was almost immediately invited to come live at the center and has been fully immersed in the experience since. On top of the classes and wellness sessions she chose for herself, Jane and the other women in the inner circle have been suggesting other classes and activities. She's been paying close attention to the people around her and has no doubt my suspicions of trafficking are right. Already she can feel how the women are treating her differently, something she recognizes as being groomed, and she has a feeling they are readying her for the next stage.

When I ask about Windham, she admits he seems to have developed a particular fondness for her. They spend no time alone together, but he makes it a point to acknowledge her and invite her personally to come to a private session he is running with what he calls his select few. She describes what's called the Temple, a gathering room where he brings everyone together to listen to his impassioned speeches.

"Sometimes they sound like pep rallies from high school," she tells me. "And sometimes they sound closer to sermons. When it's the entire group, including the members I don't think have any idea what is actually going on beneath the surface, he's less intense. He's happier and uses every charming, charismatic trick in the book to keep them enraptured by him. But even then he's starting to talk about things like self-reliance, moving away from the dependencies of society, and thinking about what they are willing to do to really improve the world and make it all they believe it should be.

"It's become so different just in the time I've been here that some people have left and not come back. I'm seeing something even beyond that. Now that I've been invited into a closer level of the group, I'm invited to his private sessions. In those, the energy is almost painful it's so intense. These conversations are far more than just wanting to live on their own or forego consumerism. These have the vibes of Jonestown or Heaven's Gate," Kelly says. "There are moments—brief flickers, really—when he loses all the smile. He becomes dark and obsessive. But then a second later he's smiling again and talking about feeling the power of all of us there with him. Those moments are actually the most frightening."

I know this is exactly what we wanted when I asked Agent Mercer to go undercover in the organization, but it's unnerving to see it unfolding. I know she's walking on a fine edge.

I can't stop thinking about TD, the unidentified victim we believe was Windham's first kill. She was pregnant at the time of her death. Now that I know what I know from my conversation with Marla, I have a strong suspicion about what happened, and it cranks up my urgency and worry to a fevered pitch.

The child Linda is carrying is clearly not fathered by Windham Debracey, and it can't be a coincidence that his first victim was also carrying a child when she was killed. Something very bad is brewing, and I need to stop it.

"Are any of the other women in the inner circle pregnant?" I ask.

"No," she says. "Linda is the only one."

"I need you to pay close attention to her and to her interactions with Bill," I say.

"I haven't seen her in a couple of days."

"What?" I ask, a shock of adrenaline going through me.

"Linda. I haven't seen her in a couple of days."

"Did something happen?"

"I know Windham saw Linda and Bill talking. But it seemed like nothing. He barely even reacted. All he did was call her over, and they went to dinner. But now that I piece them together, that was when things got darker. And leading up to that, she had been talking about how she and Windham decided that they are going to have a home birth rather than going to the hospital."

"We need to get them out of there. We need to find Linda, and we need to get all those women out. I need you to help me get inside without any of them knowing I'm there," I say.

We both know there isn't enough evidence to call the police at this point, let alone the FBI. A wellness check would be futile. They would show up, and any of the people there could simply tell them that everything was fine. They could even give them a tour to show just how wonderful everything was

They would do nothing, and it would waste time we can't afford to waste. It's up to me to make sure everyone is safe, collect the evidence, and then turn the information over to the police when we can lay it all out and have the women as witnesses. If things go wrong when I'm there, I'll call for backup. But I'm hoping I can get in and get the women out with little incident.

"I can meet you at the door and let you in," Kelly says.

"No. I'll be seen." I think for a second. "You know the coin Jane has that lets her through the locked doors?"

"Yes. Only a handful of people have those."

"I know. But I need one. Find a way to get one for me and put it outside behind the back of the center near the balcony."

"I'll see what I can do."

CHAPTER THIRTY-THREE

Shaelyn

Fourteen years ago

I KNEW HE WOULD BE BACK SOON.

I had been pacing around our room on the top floor of the big house, trying to decide how to tell him. He chose this house because it came with two other houses built as guesthouses. They were small, but we needed the space. As soon as Windham offered his most trusted and most devoted members to live with us, we saw what he really meant to them. The house he was living and teaching in was far too small, and we needed to expand.

Now in the evenings, he moved from the big house at the top of which we lived—the select few lived on the floors beneath—to the two houses where the others lived, giving closing comments for the day and saying good night.

That morning I decided it would be that night, when he came back from the rounds, that I would tell him.

I hadn't told anyone else. It wouldn't have been right. He deserved to be the first to know.

I took in a deep breath as I walked by the mirror hanging on the wall and turned to the side. I ran my hand down over my stomach, seeing if the swell was becoming obvious. It was the reason I chose tonight. I didn't want him to guess.

A knock on the door pulled my attention away from the mirror, and I went to open it, expecting one of the women to be standing there. Instead, it was Clay.

"What are you doing here?" I asked in a sharp whisper. "You know you shouldn't be up here."

"He's not here," he said. "I just watched him walk into the back house. I needed to see you."

"Someone else could see you here. You need to go."

"Why are you doing this?" he asked. "Why are you pretending that he's the one you love?"

Tears were stinging at the backs of my eyes now. I never wanted to have this conversation. I just wanted it to all go away. And after tonight, it would. That was why I needed to tell Windham. Once I told him, we would move forward, and there would be no reason to look back.

"I am loyal to Windham. He chose me, and I do love him," I told Clay. "He has given me far more than anyone else ever has in my life."

"Including never once telling anyone else that he loves you? Or calling you his partner? He demands complete devotion from you, expects you to do anything and everything he says, but does nothing for you in return," Clay countered.

"That isn't true. Everyone sees I live up here with him. They see us together. They know the importance of our relationship. It doesn't require words," I said.

"Then why have you been with me?" Clay asked. "On the nights when he doesn't bother to come to bed? During the long days when he's traveling and just doesn't come back even after he's told you that he would?"

"He can't be held to the same standards as everyone else. He isn't like everyone else," I insisted. "He isn't weak like I have been. Now I need you to leave. This is over. We can't ever talk about it again."

I forced Clay out of the room and locked the door. I fought the tears from falling. This was the choice I'd made. Falling into Clay's arms was never something I intended. Windham was an incredible man. He did so much for everyone around him, and he cherished our time together. I know he did. But he was committed to changing the world, to taking care of everyone in it. I couldn't expect to always be the only thing he was thinking about.

Clay left the room that night not knowing I could have been carrying his baby. I couldn't be sure which of the men I loved fathered my child, but I'd quickly made the decision that it didn't actually matter. My plan was to just let everyone assume it was Windham's so everything stayed the way it was supposed to. I knew he would be thrilled.

I heard the doorknob shake, and I whipped around to face it, wiping at my eyes to make sure all signs of tears were gone. I heard the key in the lock and took my place in the center of the room, ready for the reveal. Windham came in and gestured at the door.

"Why was the door locked? Is everything all right?" he asked.

I nodded. "I'm fine. I just didn't want to talk to anybody tonight until I got to talk to you."

"What's going on?"

I couldn't help the smile that stretched across my face as I walked toward him. I slid my arms around his waist and stood on my toes to kiss him. Leaning forward, I rested my forehead against the center of his chest, right above his heart.

"We're going to have a baby," I said softly.

His body went still. He said nothing. I pulled back to look at him, expecting joy. What I saw was rage. Terror rushed through me, and I didn't even have a chance to scream before his hand was around my throat.

Windham Debracey

There was blood on my hands.

I didn't know if I opened my eyes or if they had been open and it was just consciousness that was coming back. But when I looked down, my hands were covered in blood. For a moment I didn't remember anything. I couldn't understand what was happening. Then I saw Shaelyn lying on the ground. Without even touching her, I knew she was dead.

I had to do something. Everyone was going to wonder where she was. Especially those in my inner circle. I had been linked to her and had been promoting her as the most important woman within the group for months. She got all the attention, all the privileges. The other women especially were not going to believe she suddenly turned away or decided to leave.

As I stared down at her, my mind was reeling over her obvious betrayal. It confirmed suspicions I had had about her but didn't want to believe. People had come to me. They had hinted at her behavior. But I refused to accept it. Not her. She wouldn't do that to me.

Even then, I struggled to accept it. There had to be something more. Another explanation. This wasn't real.

But it was.

On the floor below me, I could hear the other women preparing for bed. They'd been so devoted to developing themselves, to becoming the best versions of themselves that could exist. But there were always limitations. Something keeping them back.

I looked down at Shaelyn again. This time when I looked into her face, the blood was gone. Her features weren't swollen and broken. She was beautiful. More beautiful than she ever had been. From the moment I met her, I knew she was special. I knew there was something more to her, and now I understood. She wasn't meant for this earth. She was meant to be sacrificed so everything within her could be offered up to the others. They would be imbued with those qualities, and they would enhance each of them to a new level.

Something sparkled on the floor beside her, and I reached down to scoop it up. The delicate tulip bracelet she was wearing the day Jane met her at the festival was what brought us together. It was always meant to be this way. I understood that now.

Everything I needed to do flowed into my mind fully formed, like the awareness had always been there and it was only now unlocking because I had reached this pinnacle moment. It was my own growth, my own discovery to learn this path.

I knew she must be purified.

I went to the cabinet on the wall and took out a white sheet that matched the nightgown she was wearing. I laid it out on the bed and carefully rested her on it, wrapping it around her so no one could see her face. I could see her for what she truly was, but I didn't know if others would see the same. The damage to her body wasn't what needed to be acknowledged tonight. It was the offering she gave to us.

I gathered the other women to the room and showed them.

"Tonight we have all reached a precious moment in our journeys," I said to them. "I can see the shock on your faces. I know this is frightening. But fear is just a challenge. It means you are ready to push through to your next achievement. Tonight you are all being invited to a new level. Each of you knows how truly precious Shaelyn is to me. Because of that, she is the one who was called to be sacrificed.

"Through that sacrifice, she is passing on to you her beauty, her strength, her wisdom, her love, her power. After tonight's ritual, they will be within you. She is only the beginning. There are others out in the world, chosen women meant to enhance each of you and bring you up to higher levels of existence. We need to find them, cultivate them, purify them, and sacrifice them. We will create beautiful gardens with them where they will be cherished and honored, and we can all be restored."

None of the women tried to leave. They all understood.

We spent a long time preparing scented creams that I allowed them to rub into Shaelyn's hands as I drew them from the sheet and tucked them away without revealing her face, speaking over her and thanking her for her sacrifice, and cleaning up the room before we brought her to the van. I knew of a piece of land that had been shown to Pastor Laurence, the head of the group that once counted me among its most devoted members. They still believed I was. They didn't know I'd already broken away and begun the process of creating what he could never create.

It would be perfect.

We brought her out to the land covered by the protection of night with only the light of my lantern to guide us. I let the land lead me to the right place, a lovely spot next to a run-down structure that would offer protection so she wouldn't be disturbed.

The land was meant to go to Pastor Laurence, but the woman who owned it was facing a series of conflicts that stopped the transfer from going through. What she didn't know, what no one but those closest to Pastor Laurence knew, was that he didn't need this piece of land. He had already found another piece in a different state and was starting to prepare for the purchase. It would likely be a long process, and there was always the chance that something would fall through, so he hadn't said anything to the rest of the group. I knew it would go through. I could feel it. It would go through because this land was meant to be mine.

The farmland was desolate, and the people living on it were old and disconnected from everything else. I hadn't known when I first learned about it, but I could see so clearly now it was the perfect spot to begin my garden. I would find a way to gain true ownership of it later.

For now, what mattered was Shaelyn. We dug a grave for her and rested her inside with branches and fragrant leaves. Her bracelet was broken, but I put it in with her. Come spring, I'd make sure there were tulips planted here with her. Nestling sage on top of her, I burned her as the final step in her purification and offering. I asked the women to go back to the car so I could have a few minutes alone with her. When it was just us, I covered her gently and said goodbye.

Turning off my lantern, I walked back through the woods to the flicker of fireflies.

CHAPTER THIRTY-FOUR

Now

I wait to leave Sheridan's house until I get the message from Kelly that she's managed to get her hands on one of the access coins and has hidden it outside like I've asked. She tells me the energy is tense. Something is happening, but she doesn't know what. There are so many people around, she thinks I need to wait until night to come. It's hard to wait, but I know she's right.

I still haven't seen them or any evidence of them, but I'm sure cameras are covering the road leading up to the center, so I don't go on it. Instead, I go around toward the back where I know there is another access road because I watched the truck drive up it the night Misha was brought back. I park a short distance away and walk through the scraggly woods that lead to the grounds. I know I'll be exposed while I cross the back of the grounds to the building, but if I move quickly enough, I'll go unnoticed.

I get to the back of the center and search where Kelly told me she would hide the access coin. I find it and tuck it into my pocket. Using a wrought iron chair set out on the patio near the parking area for leverage, I run and push myself off it to launch myself up to the edge of the balcony. My hands just wrap around the spindles. I struggle for a moment, but I am finally able to pull myself up enough to use my feet against the brick column to climb the rest of the way.

Coming up and over the railing, I drop to the floor of the balcony and look around to make sure I haven't been heard. When no one comes, I move quickly to the door and use the coin on the panel outside the heavy glass door to release the lock. The click deep within the doorframe makes my heart pound.

Inside, the temperature of the building, which I still remember being blistering, is cold. It feels like the night air, as if there's no heat on at all. It's one of his sick ways of controlling the people within the center and testing their loyalty to him. If he tells them everything is all right, they should believe him, regardless of the conditions.

Kelly is supposed to be waiting for me, but I don't see her. Worry creeps into the back of my mind. There isn't time for the plan to not be followed. She needs to be here so we can get the women out. I head down the next hallway, toward the bedroom where I slept what feels like a lifetime ago.

"Hey! What are you doing back here? You aren't authorized."

I turn toward the deep male voice and see a man in black coming toward me. A band around his arm reads "SECURITY." I didn't see anyone like this in any of the times I've been here. Windham must have added them recently.

"You need to get out of here," the man demands.

"Where is Melanie?".

"That's not something you need to know."

He reaches out to grab me, and I punch him. My fist lands in the center of his face and knocks him back a couple of steps. He comes toward me again, and I spin around, planting my elbow in his neck and then in his face. A final blow to the head drops him to the ground. I don't pause long enough to feel bad. This situation is dire, and I have to move on.

Kelly Mercer

I didn't realize I was unconscious until I started coming to. My head was groggy and heavy. I felt like I had been drugged. I tried to move my arms and realized I was tied to a chair. Squeezing my eyes closed, I waited until some of the dizzy feeling passed and opened them again. Windham's face was hovering in front of mine, just inches away.

He smiled, but there was no warmth in it. My stomach turned. I fought against the ties on my wrists, but they were tight and secure.

"It's all right, darling. I know you must feel so strange. But it will pass. Just relax. I only have you tied here for your own safety. It can be very disorienting returning to this plane of existence after being offered a glimpse into the next realm."

I didn't know what he was talking about, but I suddenly remembered the tea. Jane brought it to my room every night for the last several nights; this time it must have had something in it.

"I hope you understand just how much of an honor it is to be here tonight. Only my favorites are ever allowed to come here."

He stroked the back of his hand down my cheek, and I pulled away from the touch. Anger flickered across his eyes, but he kept the chilling smile.

"That's all right. I know you must have been nervous. So sweet. This is why my flowers have to go through a process. They are prepared and purified in life through their training and offering themselves to others, including me, then they are sacrificed and purified again to offer all within them to the women of my circle. You haven't been introduced yet to the joy and selflessness of giving yourself for the good of the future. I was planning on starting you soon.

"In fact, I had promised you to some very important people. But I can see now how special you really are. You have qualities within you that my women need desperately. They can't wait. You are needed for the garden now. And it's an exciting time. I have had to start a new garden. Mine was desecrated, and the women have been suffering for not being able to visit the flowers and draw in their essence. It's been a painful time coming to terms with that. But now we get to begin again. I'll start a new garden, and I will have the most perfect first flower."

He reached into his pocket and pulled out a bracelet. Forcing it beneath my arm where I was tied to the chair, he secured it around my wrist. I saw a chrysanthemum blossom charm dangling from the chain. Fear was starting to take over. I needed to find a way to get out of this.

I had to stay alive and get out of the room without bringing attention to myself. Windham's security would come, and everything would become all the more dangerous for everyone involved.

"You are so beautiful. I honor you for all you are going to give for the enhancement of the world around you. Your sacrifice will be cherished, and you will never be forgotten."

As he said this, the door to the room opened, and the women of the inner circle came in. I did not see Linda with them. I looked back at Windham and realized Jane had stepped forward to help him undress.

"It's time to start your purification. Your benefactors are here to witness you rising above human to celestial element."

CHAPTER THIRTY-FIVE

THE TENSION RISES INSIDE ME WITH EVERY EMPTY ROOM I encounter. They should be here. The inner circle. Those just outside of the inner circle who have been brought here to be used and traded. They should be here, but I can't find any of them. I'm about to leave this section of the building when I finally find someone.

Misha cowers when I open the bathroom door and find her looking at herself in the mirror. She backs up, her body seeming to close in around itself. She's obviously terrified, but she also looks exhausted and so broken she can barely stand.

"It's all right," I tell her. "It's all right. I'm not going to hurt you. I'm here to help you. Your name is Misha, right?"

She looks slightly startled to hear me say her name, but she nods, "Yes."

"I'm Dean. I'm a private investigator. You can trust me. I'm here to help you get you out of here."

She looks relieved almost to the point of tears for a moment, then shakes her head. Darkness rolls over her face.

"I can't leave. This is where I belong. I was chosen. I was meant to be here always. He said he knew the moment he saw me. I was meant to be one of his. I shouldn't be complaining. It's a dishonor and a disgrace. There are so many who would want to be in my position. I have to find ways to better myself, and then I will rise above my own selfish means. I will be able to see what I can do for others rather than living only in myself."

I can almost hear the words coming out of Windham's mouth rather than hers. She's been so brainwashed that at least a part of her believes what she's been taught. She believes the narrative of the horrific abuse she has been enduring and is poised in front of the possibility of death, but still won't back away.

A deafening alarm suddenly breaks through the silence, making Misha cry out and her knees buckle. I gently take her by the hand and pull her back to her feet. There's even more fear etched on her face now.

"Come on. I'll get you out of here," I say.

"No," she says. "I have to go. You need to be careful. They're always watching. Someone is always watching."

She tries to walk around me, but I stand in her way. "Don't go. I don't know what that alarm is, but don't go to it. I will get you out. You don't have to do what he says anymore. It's far too dangerous for you to stay and do whatever it is he expects you to do right now. Just come with me."

"It will be much worse if I'm not there. That alarm means Windham is calling everyone to the temple. He expects every single person to be there. No exceptions. All of us are expected to report within three minutes of the alarm. Things get much more dangerous if people don't comply."

She's shaking now, and her face has gone sickly pale.

"There's a purification happening tonight. It should have been me. But I didn't prove myself enough. The leader should be there. Windham should be a part of the purification. It's the only reason I've left my room. And if he has gone to the temple and is calling for all of us, something has gone wrong. I have to go. Please, get out of my way."

I step back. "Linda. Do you know where Linda is? Is that what the purification is for?"

"No. Linda doesn't need to be purified. She has already been imbued with the essence of all of the flowers that have been sacrificed. I don't know where she is. She has stepped out of public view to prepare for the birth of her baby. I don't know where the birth room is. I have to go."

I search as fast as I can, running through the building without a second thought of more security or if anyone knew I was there. I realize there are hidden doors and passages concealed in the walls, noticeable only because of the small panels where the coins can be pressed. I'm not paying attention to how I've moved through the building, but it doesn't matter. I'll find my way out one way or another.

I've gone through another concealed entrance when I finally find Linda. She's in a back room, lying on a large cushion on the floor that reminds me of a dog bed. The terror is evident on her face, and I notice sweat beading on her forehead.

"Dean," she says, then cringes, her body tensing.

I realize she's in labor, and I rush over to her.

"Come with me. I'm going to get you out of here."

"You need to get her," Linda says. "Get her out."

"Who?" I ask.

"The woman you sent here. The woman you convinced should be here."

My blood goes cold.

"What do you mean?"

"He doesn't know. But he will. I could tell as soon as I saw her, but there was nothing I could do. She is in extreme danger, Dean. You need to find her. That alarm is gathering everyone. Something very serious is about to happen," she says.

She's wracked with another contraction, and I reach into my pocket for my phone.

"I'm going to get you help," I say.

"No. You have to put that away. You can't call for anyone."

"I'm getting the police and an ambulance for you," I say. "This has to stop."

"No," she says more angrily. "He'll know they're here. If Windham sees any type of emergency services coming toward this building, things will go horribly wrong. He's been preparing the men. He's been training us in the inner circle. He's been riling up the members. If he sees lights, it will be another Waco. I need you to trust me, Dean. The rest of the inner circle and I know far more about what happens in his head and his extreme beliefs than the other people in the group. Particularly those who haven't been brought into the deeper levels. Some will never know what's happening right in front of them. But I know. And I need you to understand that what I'm saying is the truth."

"You can't just stay here. You have to get out and get help for your baby. And I need to find Kelly. That's her name. Kelly Mercer. She isn't a friend I convinced to join. She's an FBI special agent, and she went undercover to help me with my investigation," I say.

The terror surges in her eyes. "She's an agent? Maybe he found out, and that's why the alarm is going off. He favors her. She caught his attention as soon as she came in, and he hasn't been able to stop talking about her. He's become completely wrapped up in her and has been talking about starting his next garden with her. He told me the sacrifice wouldn't be me with the strength I need to get through labor." She gasps and closes her eyes to get through another contraction. When it's over, she looks at me again. "I don't believe he intends me to live once the baby is born."

I shake my head. "I don't either. This baby isn't his, and he knows. It's the same reason the first victim was murdered."

"Shaelyn was pregnant?" she asks in a powdery voice.

It's the first I've heard a name attached to her.

"She was Windham's favorite. Jane and I brought her back from a festival, and he welcomed her like I'd never seen. He adored her. When he told us about the sacrifices, it made sense." She sobbed, closing her eyes and letting her head fall back against the wall behind her. "Dear god, it made sense."

"Come on," I tell her, taking her hand. "I'm not going to let this happen to you."

"No. The only way you're going to have a chance of getting Kelly out safely and protecting the others is to get Windham away from them. If they're all gathered in the temple, they're vulnerable. You won't get them away. But if he's distracted, there's a chance. You need to get a message to him that I've gone into labor. It will get him to come here to me, and you can get the others out," she says.

"No. I'm not doing that. It will put you and your baby in far too much danger."

"You have to do this, Dean. And so do I. I've been a part of the sacrifices. I've not only watched them happen, but I've facilitated them. I participated in the purifications. I was a part of planting the flowers in the gardens. I visited them. I allowed Windham to control me, to convince me he was far more than a man, perhaps even a god. I owe those people my life. Of course, I want my baby to have a chance. But Windham won't hurt him. He cares about him. He's the one who named him Roland. No one else but his true father knows this baby isn't Windham's. He won't hurt him."

She is not looking good, and I am extremely worried, but I know arguing with her is just going to take more time—something none of the vulnerable people in the compound have to spare. Linda won't change her mind, so I agree that I'll get the message to Windham if she tells me where to find Kelly.

CHAPTER THIRTY-SIX

"I'll be back as soon as I can. I promise. You can do this. Think about your baby. Think about what you want to name him. He'll be in your arms soon. I promise."

I brush some of Linda's sweaty hair off of her forehead and run out of the room. I agreed to do as she asked, but I didn't really intend to go through with it. I need to get to Kelly and make sure she's safe. Together we can get everyone out more efficiently than I could on my own.

Linda told me where to find the purification room, and I go straight to it. I use the access coin to get in, realizing now that it must have been Linda's all along. Kelly explained she got it from the shared office, and the only way no one would have noticed it missing is if it belonged to one of the trusted few who possessed it but who was not able to use it.

The room is large and round with mirrored walls and various cushions and raised beds arranged throughout it. As soon as I walk in, Kelly rushes toward me from the opposite side of the room where she's been running her hands along the walls like she is looking for a way out.

"Dean," she says. "You're here."

I see a cut across her face, and her arm is swelling. There's blood all around the room, and it looks like far more than what would have come from those injuries. Around us, there are signs of a ritual just getting started. Candles are lying on their sides, melted wax pooling under them. Jars of creams and various liquids have fallen from a tray knocked from a marble table near the largest of the raised beds. The air is thick with the smell of herbs.

"What happened?" I demand. "You're hurt."

"He drugged me. I woke up tied to a chair, and he told me he was going to make me the first flower in his new garden. He had the women untie me, and he was going to rape me as part of the purification. I attacked him, and we fought. Kaya lashed out at him. He dragged her out of there and brought the others with him. He sealed the locks on the doors and said he was going to leave me in here. That's when the alarm went off," she tells me.

"Where's your firearm?" I ask.

Even undercover, she wasn't going to come into the center without her FBI-issued weapon. I knew it would be a challenge for her to.keep them from finding it, but now we need it.

"It's in my room," Kelly says. "I always keep it hidden while I'm sleeping. Windham has been doing sessions in the middle of the night and keeping us from sleeping much. I knew you were coming, but they would be suspicious if I didn't go to bed with them. Jane brought us tea, but mine was drugged. They took me out of the room so I didn't have a chance to get my gun."

"We need to go. Linda is in labor and doesn't look good. I can't explain it all right now, but if we don't get her out of here fast tomorrow, everyone will find out she died in childbirth whether she gets through it safely or not," I say.

I start for the door and see Kelly touch the front of her shirt. My stomach sinks.

"What did you do?" I ask.

"I activated the emergency button on Xavier's device. I didn't want to do it while I was still trapped in this room because I didn't know if they'd be able to find me. But if Linda needs help..."

"Shit," I say. "I wish you hadn't done that."

I explain to her what Linda told me, and her face goes pale. "Oh god."

"We have to keep going. We can't think about that. We're going to do one thing at a time until those lights start flashing. I'm going to bring you to Linda. You're going to bring her with you to get your gun, then you're getting the hell out of here. Tell me where to find the temple, and I'll go there."

"All right," she says, not willing to argue after realizing the mistake she made.

I can't blame her. That button was put there so she would be able to call for help in an emergency. She had no way of knowing the consequences.

We run back through the building, Kelly using her knowledge of some of the areas I only newly see tonight to help us navigate. When we get back to Linda, we find her lying on the cushion, blood pooled around her.

"She's hemorrhaging," Kelly says, running over to her and dropping to her knees beside her. "The baby is crowning."

There's a sudden wave of shouting and loud sound from deeper in the building.

"How do I get to the temple?" I ask.

Kelly tells me the easiest path but sees me hesitate, looking at Linda.

"Go. I've got this. You need to help the others."

I'm terrified for Linda's safety, but I have to trust Kelly. There are dozens of people in danger right now, and I am their only hope. I run toward the sound, eventually finding myself at the doors of the temple. It's essentially a large assembly hall that Kelly described to me as where Windham does his gatherings and speeches. It's only shown to members, which is why I never saw it.

I try to force the door open, but there's something in front of them. Windham has barricaded them inside, and I can hear screaming. There's a sudden blast of gunshots. In the next moment, I hear the police outside.

CHAPTER THIRTY-SEVEN

WITHIN SECONDS I SMELL SMOKE COMING OUT OF THE ROOM. At this point, they are already here, so I take out my phone and call 911 to tell them to contact the officers responding to the center and let them know what's going on. Unable to get into the temple, I run back to the room where I left Kelly with Linda. Kelly has the baby cradled in her arms, but Linda is fully unconscious now from the blood loss. I relay all this to the police and try to get across to them how crucial it is for them to come in without police to get Linda and the baby. I'm worried she isn't going to survive.

It's immediately obvious they don't want to comply. The police want to speak with Windham and negotiate directly with him.

Frustrated, I go back to the temple. People inside have started clawing at the barricade, and I'm finally able to get the door open. Flames have taken over the space. Tapestries on the walls let the fire crawl up the ceiling while pews burn in front of the platform. Panicked men and women begin to stream out of the room, but I push in further.

Windham is standing at the altar, his head back and his arms stretched out to his sides. He's shouting toward the sky, telling everyone about his sacrifices and all he's done for the world. He is fully immersed now, lost in his own delusions. I can hear it in the tone of his voice that he believes everything he's saying. He truly believes he has discovered the true religion and has full power over all who come to him, that the life force of the women he has killed is within him, making him immortal.

Behind him, a woman in nothing but tattered, bloodied blue rags is hanging from a rafter. I can only assume she is the one who helped Kelly. At Windham's feet lies the body of a dead man. Several feet away, I see Jane holding a gun. She turns to look at me, and I realize she is actually the one who shot the man.

"Put it down," I say.

"I had to. I couldn't let everything get taken away," she replies, a wild look in her eyes, and I already know I need to duck out of the way. There's no talking my way out of this one, not with her.

As she lifts the gun again, a shot rings out from behind me, and the gun falls from Jane's hand. I turned to see Kelly holding her own gun. As I run toward Windham, Kelly helps more of the members get out. I try to get up to the altar, but before I can get there, Windham tosses a bottle of something behind him, and the fire rages. It pushes me back, and I know I won't be able to get to him. We have to get out of the building.

We run out and don't stop until we're behind a barrier of police and rescue vehicles. Almost instantly there's the sound of an explosion from inside, and I know Windham is dead.

I find out Linda and the baby are on their way to the hospital. She is in very serious condition, but the baby is doing well. There's nothing but chaos around us as the police try to sort out the statements being shouted at them by dozens of people. I walk away from it, needing to breathe. I'm suddenly exhausted, and when I look at the center burning to the ground, I feel nothing but devastation.

CHAPTER THIRTY-EIGHT

THE NEXT DAY I'M ABLE TO VISIT LINDA IN THE HOSPITAL. SHE'S weak and will have a long recovery, but she's alive, and she's going to stay that way. Xavier and I walk quietly into the room, and she smiles at us, gesturing for us to come to the side of the bed. A bassinet is up against the side, and lying inside is a tiny swaddled baby boy.

"I want to hold him all the time," she tells me. "But I'm not strong enough yet. That's going to be my motivation to get better."

"It's good motivation," I say, touching his soft little cheek.

"This is for you," Xavier says, holding a white box out to her. It looks like a jewelry box, but when she opens it, I see a crystal flower tucked inside. "To remind you of your own strength and that you can never be cut down and forced to fade away. You should reclaim the beauty that was taken and turn flowers into something more."

Linda blinks away tears, obviously touched by the gesture. "Thank you."

I'm struggling to deal with what happened. Guilt weighs heavily on me.

"I'm so sorry this turned out this way. It wasn't meant to. I should have made different decisions. I should have done something else," I say.

Linda shakes her head. "No. You did exactly what you needed to do." She cups her hand over the top of the baby's head. "If it wasn't for you, this little boy would be named Roland. He would be the next generation being raised by that twisted man. But he's not that. Thanks to you, Daniel Dean gets a chance to live a happy life. I'll make sure he does."

"Oh..." I say, a sudden surge of emotion welling up in me. I'm not really sure what to make of that. "Um. Thank you."

She smiles. "I should be thanking you. You saved him."

"And me."

I turn around and see Kelly standing at the door to the room. She's bandaged, but doing well. She comes in and holds a bouquet of flowers out to Linda, then winces and pulls them back.

"I'm so sorry. I didn't even... It's just what..." she stumbles over her words.

"It's all right," Linda tells her. "They're beautiful. And I think it's time I take back my own control and power."

She glances over at Xavier, who gives her a little nod. We have a few minutes to pass the baby around before the doctor comes in and makes us leave so he can check on Linda. While Xavier wanders off to look at the other babies in the nursery, I walk slowly along the hall with Kelly.

"I feel like I failed," I tell her. "I should have called 911 from the beginning, even with Linda warning me not to. I should have figured it out sooner. I should have done a thousand things, and because I didn't, people are dead."

"Not even close," she assures me. "You took down a monstrous cult leader. You gave two women back their identities and gave their families closure. You gave other families answers. You saved many other lives. You can't be responsible for everyone."

"Thank you for your help," I say.

"Let Emma know she owes me one," Kelly says, winks at me, and leaves with a wave.

Two days later we hold a memorial service for Sienna. There's a new stone on her grave now, this one with her real name and her birthdate. In addition to roses, fresh bouquets of siennas have been laid there. Her family is there, just like I promised. They have decided not to move her from her current grave. It was the original plan, and most people assumed she was going to be reburied closer to her family, but after everything was done, Seth has decided this is where she has been loved and protected for all these years. This is where she has a community. A true community, full of people who actually care for her. Not the lies of any of the abusive men who manipulated, controlled, and ultimately killed her. He appreciates it so much and plans to visit frequently, but she is home here.

Standing with his arm around the cousin he hasn't seen in years but was brought back into his life with this tragedy, he tells me how proud he is of his sister for doing everything she could and never giving up. Because of her, he tells me, this nightmare is brought to an end. It might have taken a long time and there were many lives lost, but she was there to guide them to the truth.

I know this is far from over, but I don't tell him that. There are still bracelets to be found. Another garden to be uncovered. But we will. And when we do, their stories will be told.

Sheridan and the rest of the group come up to me after the service, and she hugs me.

"Thank you, Dean," she says through tears. "Thank you for everything you did for her."

"I couldn't have done it without you," I tell her. "You know, I'm really impressed by your investigative skill. Maybe you should think about getting your PI license."

"Maybe. I'm not quite there yet," she says. "But I think the group and I will continue investigating cold cases rather than just talking about them."

"I wanted you to know an official investigation into Art Bellinger and his company has been opened. I'm going to do everything I can to see him brought up charges for what he did to Sienna and to countless other people."

"Thank you."

She squeezes my hand and leaves the cemetery. Xavier and I have already packed everything from her house into the car and are going to head home. We were planning on stopping by Sherwood, but Emma isn't at home, so we have to settle for a video call over fast-food burgers to salvage some of Thanksgiving week.

As we're arriving in Harlan late that night, I'm surprised by a call from Owen Bardot.

"You need to talk to my grandparents," he says. "You can't tell them that you've seen or heard from me, but you need to confront them about what you know about Dad. They're helping him. They need to know who he really is and make sure my sister is protected."

It's the last thing I want to do after getting through that case, but two days later, I'm back in Georgia.

I never thought I would have to see them again. I never thought I would have to stand in their living room again and listen to them berate and insult me like they did when I was a teenager. But I'm not that kid anymore. I fight back. I make sure they know how incredible their daughter was and how much we loved each other—and exactly what kind of man they've been coddling as her husband for all these years. That's who they chose for her to chase me out of her life. A criminal.

"It's not like we had many choices," Brielle's mother snaps at me. "We needed someone with a decent name willing to marry a woman who didn't love him and pretend he didn't know she was already pregnant."

Lights burst in front of my eyes, and I feel like I've been slammed into the ground.

"Brielle was pregnant when she got married?" I ask.

"You couldn't keep your mouth shut," her father seethes. "We managed to keep that hidden, to push it down where it wouldn't humiliate us, but you are so unable to control your own mouth around this ..."

"Shut up," I say. "Shut the fuck up right now."

"Excuse me?" Mr. Adair says. "Who do you think you're talking to, boy?"

"I am not your boy," I growl at him through clenched teeth.

But now I know that Owen is mine.

AUTHOR'S NOTE

Dear Reader,

Thank you so much for choosing to read *The Garden of Secrets,* the fourth book in the Dean Steele Mystery Thriller series! Now that you've flipped through the last page, I sincerely hope you're left both satisfied and craving more. So let me entice you with a sneak peek of what I have planned in the next installment. Dean finds himself at a Christmas party like no other. With a snowstorm approaching and guests mysteriously vanishing as the night deepens, our favorite PI is caught right in the middle of it. It's a treacherous situation with a rising body count, and Dean's got to navigate it all while the storm rages on.

And hey, if you're up for getting into the holiday spirit ahead of time, I invite you to hang out with Dean's cousin, FBI Agent Emma Griffin. Her upcoming adventure, *The Girl and the Unexpected Gifts,* takes us to the cozy town of Sherwood, all decked out for the holidays. But there's a twist in the air this year. While Emma and her chosen family soak up those special moments, a serial killer's on the loose, leaving eerie, gift-wrapped surprises under the town's twinkling trees. But Emma refuses to let her entire Christmas be stolen. As she attempts to unravel tangles that are more complicated than any Christmas light strands, she gets a reminder of Feather Nest and the most surprising package of all.

As an indie author, your reviews and support are vital in keeping this series going. If you could please take a moment to leave a review for The Garden of Secrets, I would be enormously grateful. I can't wait to hear your thoughts and for you to join Dean on his next adventure!

Thank you for your support and for joining me on this journey, and I can't wait to see where our adventures take us next!

Yours,
A.J. Rivers

P.S. If for some reason you didn't like this book or found typos or other errors, please let me know personally. I do my best to read and respond to every email at aj@riversthrillers.com

P.P.S. If you would like to stay up-to-date with me and my latest releases I invite you to visit my Linktree page at *www.linktr.ee/a.j.rivers* to subscribe to my newsletter and receive a free copy of my book, Edge of the Woods. You can also follow me on my social media accounts for behind-the-scenes glimpses and sneak peeks of my upcoming projects, or even sign up for text notifications. I can't wait to connect with you!

ALSO BY

A.J. RIVERS

Emma Griffin FBI Mysteries

Season One

*Book One—The Girl in Cabin 13**
*Book Two—The Girl Who Vanished**
*Book Three—The Girl in the Manor**
*Book Four—The Girl Next Door**
*Book Five—The Girl and the Deadly Express**
*Book Six—The Girl and the Hunt**
*Book Seven—The Girl and the Deadly End**

Season Two

*Book Eight—The Girl in Dangerous Waters**
*Book Nine—The Girl and Secret Society**
*Book Ten—The Girl and the Field of Bones**
*Book Eleven—The Girl and the Black Christmas**
*Book Twelve—The Girl and the Cursed Lake**
*Book Thirteen—The Girl and The Unlucky 13**
*Book Fourteen—The Girl and the Dragon's Island**

Season Three

*Book Fifteen—The Girl in the Woods**
*Book Sixteen —The Girl and the Midnight Murder**
*Book Seventeen— The Girl and the Silent Night**
*Book Eighteen — The Girl and the Last Sleepover**
*Book Nineteen — The Girl and the 7 Deadly Sins**
*Book Twenty — The Girl in Apartment 9**
*Book Twenty-One — The Girl and the Twisted End**

Emma Griffin FBI Mysteries Retro - Limited Series

(Read as standalone or before Emma Griffin book 22)

*Book One— The Girl in the Mist**

*Book Two— The Girl on Hallow's Eve**

*Book Three— The Girl and the Christmas Past**

*Book Four— The Girl and the Winter Bones**

*Book Five— The Girl on the Retreat**

Season Four

*Book Twenty-Two — The Girl and the Deadly Secrets**

*Book Twenty-Three — The Girl on the Road**

Book Twenty-Four — The Girl and the Unexpected Gifts

Ava James FBI Mysteries

*Book One—The Woman at the Masked Gala**

*Book Two—Ava James and the Forgotten Bones**

*Book Three —The Couple Next Door**

*Book Four — The Cabin on Willow Lake**

*Book Five — The Lake House**

*Book Six — The Ghost of Christmas**

*Book Seven — The Rescue**

*Book Eight — Murder in the Moonlight**

Book Nine — Behind the Mask

Dean Steele FBI Mysteries

*Book One—The Woman in the Woods**

Book Two — The Last Survivors

Book Three — No Escape

Book Four — The Garden of Secrets

ALSO BY

A.J. RIVERS & THOMAS YORK

Bella Walker FBI Mystery Series

*Book One—The Girl in Paradise**

*Book Two—Murder on the Sea**

Other Standalone Novels

Gone Woman

** Also available in audio*

Made in the USA
Monee, IL
06 November 2023